Abigail

Shannon Keys

To My Mom
Thank you for choosing the hard road so we could be restored.
Love you.

AUTHOR ACKNOWLEDGEMENTS

It takes a village to raise children and to write books. I am so grateful for my village. Abigail would not be who she is without the help of these people.

Jana - Thank you for your encouragement from day one. You read every scene, even the ones that aren't in this book today, and you always gave me honest, hopeful feedback. You helped me stay grounded and courageous when I might have backed away. You are my forever writing partner and kindred spirit. Thank you, friend.

Lisa - Thank you so much for your detailed eye for editing. You made Abigail shine in ways I would never have been able to do on my own. And you loved her with me. Thank you, friend, for your sacrifice of time and skills to polish Abigail's story so it would be the best it could be.

Josh – Thank you for reading Abigail's story and speaking prophetically of how she would one day be a beacon of hope that would bring others to Jesus. Your words infused me with belief that Jesus would do just what He said He would do.

Suzee - I knew if you loved Abigail, then she must be special because you are one of the most creative people I know! Thank you for reading her story and loving her with so much passion. You helped me keep believing when it would have been easy to give up.

All my early readers - Thank you so much for the gift of your time in reading Abigail's story. Whether you read the whole book or a few chapters, you truly were like iron sharpening iron, helping refine and smooth out the rough edges. With all my heart, thank you!

Allen - Oh, what to say about you, my perfect puzzle piece! Abigail could never have come to be if you did not love me so well. You are always a reflection of the Father's heart for me, and I learn daily how to love and be loved just by watching you. You are a gift Jesus brought me when I didn't even know I needed you. We're in it together, to the very end. I love you.

My Savior - Where would I be without the depths of your grace and mercy flowing through my life? Thank you Jesus for saving me and restoring my soul. You have made beauty from my ashes, and turned the ruins into a glorious display of your power and might. I love you Lord, and I'll always say yes to your whisper. Always.

A note about the prologue...

The prologue of this story could be a trigger for anyone who is still in the early stages of healing from sexual trauma. I have been gentle with the descriptions of the scene, but it still lends itself to memories for anyone struggling with the same type of pain. I considered leaving the prologue out of the story for fear that it would be too much for some, but the Holy Spirit led me to include it and so I have been obedient. I believe the reason it is included is because our Lord wants us to know that nothing is hidden from His view, and He doesn't turn away from our pain. There is no story that is beyond His power to redeem.

If you feel you are not ready to read a scene that might trigger unwanted memories, then I would encourage you to skip the prologue and begin in chapter one. You won't miss out, I assure you! If you choose to begin with the prologue, I encourage you to do so with a sense of hope that you are going to find Jesus in these pages. May He visit you as you read this story and fill you with the same depth of grace and love that He filled me with as I wrote it. You are His beloved, His dearest, His chosen one.

With Hope,

Shannon

PROLOGUE
1752, a village in Massachusetts

Abigail cried against her raised knees, her small body trembling with pain. She did not want to watch him get dressed.

"Why do you cry, child?" He asked. "You have nothing to cry about." He pulled his shirt over his head.

"Look at me," he demanded, towering over her with hands to his hips.

She didn't want to look at him, but didn't dare disobey, so she raised her tear-streaked face. He reminded her of something that hides in the darkness with his black hair hanging around his shoulders and eyes the color of coal.

"Now, what is the most important rule?" he asked.

"D-don't ever t-tell anyone our s-secret," Abigail said through her tears.

"Very good, child." He tucked his shirt into his breeches. "And why do we not tell?" He sat down and put his boots on.

"Because t-they won't believe m-me and they will p-punish me and m-my family."

He nodded his approval. "Now, you best run along home. Your father will be wanting his dinner soon, and your mother will need help." He walked over to the bed and reached out to stroke her cheek. She flinched but didn't pull away. She had pulled away once before and had been punished for it. The memory filled her with terror.

He picked her dress up from the floor and dropped it on the bed beside her. "Get dressed."

Abigail wanted him to leave, but he stood there, arms folded across his chest, waiting. She knew what to do. He wanted her to stand up so he could watch her get dressed. That was one of his rules, and she knew better than to break his rules. She stood up, wiped away her tears and picked up her dress. She hated standing naked in front of him. She used to vomit when he finished, but he had trained her not to do that anymore. Her stomach still clenched and convulsed every time, but she didn't let anything come up. She didn't dare do anything he didn't like. He told her once before, in the midst of hurting her, that if she ever told, no one in the village would believe her and they would punish her for lying. She knew what he meant. The purging post stood in the middle of the village, stained with the blood of those who had been punished. Every time Abigail saw it, terror filled her and reminded her why she could never tell anyone their secret.

She put on her dress as quickly as he would allow, then walked to the edge of the bed and slid down. Without a word she put on her stockings and shoes then tied her coif around her hair, securing it under her neck. She stood up straight, waiting for his approval.

"Very good," he said with a nod.

He rubbed a hand over her head like a father might do. She wanted to step away from his touch but didn't. He stepped aside and she made her way to the door, careful not to run. Running was against the rules. She left his small cabin behind the schoolhouse and walked along the edge of the village to her home. It hurt to walk, but she did her best to walk normally. She didn't want anyone to suspect something or ask her questions. She might accidentally tell the truth if anyone asked her. She didn't want to talk about what he did to her. He said she was too pretty, her hair too soft, her lips too perfectly shaped, and her eyes too beautiful. If she didn't look the way she did, he wouldn't do the things he did. It was her fault.

Abigail opened the door and saw Mama bent over the cook pot, stirring the stew that would be dinner. Her swollen belly got in the way of her work and she winced as she stood up, placing a hand on her belly. She took a deep breath then smiled when she saw Abigail.

"Ah, good, you're home. You can set the table for dinner."

Abigail nodded and went to the one door cabinet Father had built for Mama. She pulled out three bowls.

"How was your lesson, today?" Mama asked.

Abigail kept her eyes on the table as she spoke. "Fine."

"That's good. We're so blessed that Master Hammond allows you help him with chores as payment for tutoring you in reading." Most girls learned to read at home while the boys went to school, but when Mr. Hammond had offered to tutor Abigail, her Father had agreed.

Abigail glanced up. *No! No! He is not kind! He is mean, he likes to hurt me!* She nodded with a small smile.

"You must remember to thank him often," Mama said then cried out, leaning forward with a hand to her belly.

Abigail rushed to her side. "Mama! What's wrong?"

She gripped the table and hunched over, her breathing strained. "G-go for your father, Abigail. Now!"

Abigail's feet took flight, all her earlier terror forgotten. She ran behind their cabin where Father chopped wood.

"Father! Mother needs you. Something is wrong!"

Her father sunk the axe into the chopping block and followed Abigail back to the cabin. They came in and found Mama lying on the ground, writhing in pain. Father came over and scooped her up, hurried to the bed in the corner, and laid her there.

"What is it, Martha?" Father asked, leaning close to her face. "Is it time?" He stroked the hair back from her face. Abigail came and stood at the foot of the bed watching with panic filled eyes. Father's thin face paled with worry.

"The baby..." She clutched his arm, crying out in pain. Abigail's eyes widened in fear.

"Go for the doctor, Abigail. Go, now!" Father commanded with more urgency than she had ever heard in his voice.

Abigail ran for the doctor. He lived on the other side of the village and she had to run fast, even though it hurt to run. She didn't care that it hurt. mama needed help. She found the doctor, and he grabbed his small brown satchel, then rushed out the door with her. They walked in to the sound of Mama's screams.

The doctor turned to Abigail. "Go to Mary's house, Abigail. Tell them the baby is coming, and you are to stay with them for now."

Abigail was scared. She didn't want to leave mama but she didn't dare disobey.

"Yes, sir." She went next door to her friend Mary's house. They took her in, and she stayed for what seemed like hours, sitting with Mary by the fire. Two hours later a knock at the door startled everyone in the room. Mary's father answered, spoke to the doctor in murmurs Abigail couldn't understand, then turned to her. "Come, child."

She left without a word and followed the doctor back to her house. When she walked in she froze, eyes wide at the scene before her. Mama laid on the bed and there was blood everywhere. Her eyes were closed and she didn't move. Father held something in his arms, and he didn't look happy. Abigail walked over to him, clutching her black skirt in her hands. "Father?"

He looked at her, then back at the bed.

"Is Mother okay," she asked in a timid whisper. Father stared at mama on the bed, but he didn't speak. She saw the bundle in Father's arms move. Her eyes widened. He held a baby!

"Your mother had the baby, Abigail," the doctor said. He placed a hand on her shoulder and turned her to look at him. "She did not survive, though. Only the baby survived." He said it so matter-of-fact as if it were a minor detail.

Abigail took a step back, turning abruptly to Mama. "No! She is only asleep!" She ran over to the bed. "Mama! Wake up, please, wake up! You had the baby!" She shook mama's arm, trying to wake her. "Mama! Wake up!" Tears filled her eyes. The baby started to whimper.

"Abigail," Father said with a hand to her arm. He turned her to look at him.

The doctor came and took the baby from Father's arms. "I will take him to the Bailey's. Sarah will feed him. T'is God's will that's been done this day." Father stared at the doctor, then released the baby into his arms.

A boy. A baby boy. Abigail turned back to her mother's lifeless form. "The baby is a boy, Mama! You wanted a boy! Wake up, please wake up!"

"Enough, Abigail!" Father pulled her into his arms, roughly. "She isn't going to wake up." Abigail began to cry. Father pulled her onto his lap and held her against his chest. She shook with sobs but Father didn't cry. He just sat there holding her, staring at the bed.

"You mustn't cry, Abigail." Father didn't sound sad or angry. "This is God's will."

Abigail clutched his shirt, crying harder. *God did this? Why would God take my mama?*

Father moved her from his lap, stood and left the house without a backward glance. Abigail sat in the chair, holding Mama's hand, crying. The house grew dark and the fire in the hearth burned low, but Abigail didn't move. She hoped it was all a mistake, that any minute her mama would wake up.

After a long while, the door opened. Father came in along with Master Hammond and two village elders. Abigail jumped up, eyes wide. Master Hammond didn't look at her or speak to her. Neither did Father or the elders. They just began wrapping mama up in the bloody sheets. Abigail backed away, not wanting to stand close to Master Hammond.

"We must prepare her body and then you must repent of the sin that has brought this death to your house," one of the elders said to Father. Abigail stayed in the corner, not saying a word.

Father nodded. "I-I will repent." His voice cracked, but he didn't cry. They wrapped Mama up, then Father hoisted her limp body in his arms.

"Stay here, Abigail," Father said. "Master Hammond will stay with you until I return." Terror filled Abigail. She didn't want to stay with him. She wanted to go with Father. Where was he taking Mama?

"Father, please, can I come with you? Where are you taking Mother?" She had never questioned before, never. All eyes in the room bored into her.

"Don't question me, child! Do as you're told!" His harsh response brought tears to her eyes. The elders walked out behind Father, leaving Abigail alone with Master Hammond. His footsteps came close to her and fear momentarily paralyzed her. He had never been in her house before.

"Come here, child." She didn't want to obey. She backed away from him and ran to a corner, crouching low, covering her head to try and block him out.

"You run from me?" He asked, with a menacing smile. "What have I told you before about running from me?" He came towards her, slowly. "I will have to remind you of the rules, won't I?" He crouched in front of her, trapping her in the corner. He forced her face up with his hand. "I'm not going to hurt you, child. I'm your friend. I am going to make you feel better." He stood and backed up, staring down at her. Fear glued her there, with her eyes on his. "Remember, your father said to do as you're told. Obedience is most important." He reached out to her. "Take my hand, child."

She shook her head, clutching her hair with her hands. He grabbed her by her hair, pulling her up to her feet. She cried out and stumbled forward.

"You will obey!" He dragged her over to a chair and sat down in it. He turned her to face him, keeping his hands on her shoulders. She couldn't control the flood of tears. She wanted Father to come back. She wanted mama to wake up. She wanted him to leave her alone.

"Now, come up here on my lap." He pulled her up on his lap, and she stiffened. He took his hat off and laid it on the table beside them. "You are sad that your mother is gone, aren't you?" Abigail gave a silent nod, staring into her lap.

"Let's see if we can play a game that will make you feel better." Abigail knew his games well, and she didn't like any of them. She wanted to jump down and run away, to find Father, to see mama. Fear kept her there on his lap, though. He made her play one of his games, making her do things she didn't understand and didn't want to do. He told her it would make her feel better. She cried the whole time. She just wanted her mama.

When he finished with her, he moved her from his lap and stood. "Now, go lie by the fire and sleep. Your father will return soon."

She obeyed, going over and lying down on the cold floor by the fire, shaking all over from what he had done. He moved the chair close to the fire and sat. Abigail was too afraid to sleep with him sitting there watching her. She pretended, though, so he would not touch her again.

After a long while, she heard the door open. Master Hammond had fallen asleep, but he woke at the sound and went to the door. Abigail heard Father speaking quietly, then the door shut again, and all became silent. She turned over slowly and saw Father move over to the bed and fall onto it. He didn't even notice her on the floor. She wanted to go to him, but didn't. Where had he taken mama?

Father begin to weep, and Abigail laid there the rest of the night staring into the fire, listening to him cry into the darkness.

Neither of them remembered the baby boy until the next day.

ONE
1762, Massachusetts

Abigail heaved, lurching forward as she gripped the rutted tree trunk next to her. Gasping, she gulped down icy air once the heaving stopped. She leaned back against the tree, the condensation of her own breath coming out in tiny puffs. Her coif slipped from her head and she pulled it off, throwing it to the ground in a rare show of frustration. She shivered, despite the pounding of her heart and clamminess of her skin. There was nothing in her stomach to come up, but this had been the routine for four mornings now. Each morning, she snuck out of the village and into the woods just before her stomach started to turn. The reality of what it meant weighed down on her, and she leaned her head against the massive tree trunk.

I'm with child...his child. She felt the invisible noose tighten around her neck. *They will purge me.* It was only a matter of time - she wouldn't be able to keep this secret as she had the others. *Why, now, after all these years?* In all these years, she had never once carried a child...until now.

When her father found out he would lead the whole village in punishing her as was the law. Father always led the villagers in restitution. If they didn't die, they wore the scars of retribution on their bodies. Would he purge his own daughter?

Fear gnawed at Abigail's belly and she brought a hand to it. What would she do? She didn't see any hope, any way out. She couldn't let anyone know she carried a baby - his baby.

No one will believe me.

Everyone would blame her and believe she had seduced him into her bed. It wouldn't matter if she told them all the horrible things he did to her. It wouldn't matter if she told the whole village that he had been using her as far back as she could remember. It wouldn't matter if she told them that as a child she kept silent out of fear, then later out of shame. None of it would matter. The horrendous things he did to her stayed locked away, deep inside her mind, where they had been safe…until now.

He always said no one would believe her if she told, and she believed him. Women always paid the price for these kinds of things. Men were never called into account. She was trapped.

Maybe dying is the best option. She tried to shove that thought away. *Maybe God will take this child from me.* What kind of life could she give a child, anyway? She would be labeled as the worst of sinners, and her child would always be an outcast. Panic bubbled up and tumbled out as a cry. She brought a hand to her mouth in a feeble attempt to stifle her sobs.

"Oh, God," she said through shaking fingers. *What am I going to do?*

She didn't expect him to answer. He didn't help her, never had. Her entire life had been one tragedy after another. She had not earned God's favor, and he didn't like her. He didn't really like anyone. Sinking down to her knees, she felt the snow seep through her dress onto her skin like thousands of tiny needles. With one hand on her stomach and the other covering her face, she let her anguish come forth in gut-wrenching sobs.

~~~

Nathan moved along at a slow pace giving Duke a chance to catch his breath. The morning air was crisp. He pushed his tricorn hat down further on his head and pulled his collar up around his ears for warmth.

His trip to Boston had been successful. He had a contract with Boston's largest shipbuilder that would create solid revenue for Bradford Mills. The mill stood on the edge of the river and it had thrived ever since Nathan's grandfather built it years ago.

Nathan decided to guide Duke down to the river for a drink. He climbed down and gave the horse a gentle rub behind his chocolate-colored ears. "Thanks, boy, for all your hard work."

Duke snorted in response, his breath coming out in large, visible puffs. Nathan grabbed the reins, walking off the road into the woods, watching his boots leave marks in the untouched snow. He looked up through the tree branches, relishing the sun's warmth. There was something profound about walking through a forest untouched by man. The pine trees towered above like giant guards of the forest, their branches dusted with hints of the latest snowfall. Nathan's eye caught a small red bird perched high in a tree, a stark contrast to the white snow covering the branches. Winter would let up in a month or so and the forest would come alive again.

As the river came into view, Nathan brought Duke close and loosened the reins so he could drink. He removed his gloves to take a drink when a noise made him pause. He straightened slightly and looked around. He heard the noise again and quickly shoved his gloves in the saddlebag strapped to Duke's back. He wrapped the reins around a tree, then stopped again to listen. It sounded like a person, crying!

"Hold steady, boy. I'll be back." He walked hurriedly in the direction of the sound and came upon a person hunched over near a tree. He realized it was a woman, and she was weeping. The crunch of snow under his boots indicated his approach and she sat up quickly, looking around.

"Ma'am?" Nathan asked cautiously, not wanting to frighten her. Her sobs had sounded so desperate. "Can I help you?"

She stumbled to stand, her movements sharp and guarded. She grabbed her coif from the ground and put it on her head, tying it under her chin. Her chest rose and fell with the quick intake of breath that comes from that kind of weeping.

"N-no. I was just heading h-home."

Nathan stepped towards her. "Is everything okay?" She wore all black and her blond hair coiled into a bun at the nape of her neck. He recognized her attire as that of the village close by. All the men and women wore black.

"I'm fine," she said it on an inhale, then curtsied. She turned and hurried off.

"Wait!" Nathan called after her but didn't chase her. She stopped and turned towards him. He reached down and grabbed her pail. "You forgot this." He jogged to where she stood, handing it to her.

The woman still refused to look at him. "I-I need to fill this. I had forgotten." She looked off towards the river.

"If you'll allow me, I'll fill it for you." Nathan hoped she would say yes. He wanted to help her, even in this small way.

She looked up at him, and his breath stalled in his lungs. Her eyes shimmered like sapphires against her creamy complexion and a faint dusting of freckles covered her nose. Even with her eyes swollen and nose red from crying, her beauty was evident. It was not her beauty, however, that gripped Nathan's heart but the sadness on her face. There was no light in her eyes, no joy. He saw such raw pain that, on impulse, he reached out a hand to the handle of the pail, where she held it. He didn't touch her but took one step closer.

"I don't mind filling that for you, if you'd like." He said with a warm smile.

Her eyes were wide and fear filled. She gave a careful nod and released the pail into his hand. Nathan turned and ran to the river bank, filled the pail, and walked back to where she stood. He took care not to spill the water she needed. He smiled again and she dropped her eyes as she reached for the pail.

"Thank you."

"Is there anything else I can do for you?" He took one small step towards her. He didn't want her to walk away. "Can I take you somewhere? I have my horse tied up by the river."

She looked up into his eyes searching them, looking for what, he didn't know. She shook her head, backing up a step as she did so. "No, I can walk. My village is not far. Thank you for your help."

Her voice cracked, and he thought she might start weeping again at any moment. She set off at a hurried but awkward walk, trying not to spill her pail of water. Nathan ran after her. He caught up to her and walked beside her.

"Will you at least tell me your name?"

She didn't look at him. "I-I have to hurry." She picked up her pace.

"I'm sorry…for whatever has happened to cause you such pain." He said keeping pace with her.

She came to a sudden halt and looked sharply at Nathan. The sound of water sloshing on the ground beside her filled the silence. She stared at him as though she didn't understand.

"I have to go," she said barely above a whisper.

She walked off in a hurry, and Nathan stood, staring after her. He felt a weight settle over his heart as he watched her walk away. She was desperate and, he sensed, alone in her struggle. He knew stories of what went on in that village. They isolated themselves from society and clung to an absurd set of rules. They believed their separation from society would purify them, that God demanded it of them. How could people be so misguided in their views of the Almighty? They made God out to be angry, always looking to punish his children. They suffered in silence, being taught that they must work hard to earn His favor. Shame fueled their doctrine. Nathan could only imagine what burdens this woman might carry.

He jogged back to where Duke stood, trying to snuff out something to munch in the snow and grabbed the reins. "Come on, boy. Let's make sure she gets home safely."

He pulled Duke along, following far enough away that she didn't notice him. She weaved in and out of the trees until she came to the clearing by the road. He stopped when she crossed the road to her village. She didn't go in through the tall wooden gate but slipped around the side out of view.

Who is she, Nathan wondered, frustrated that he hadn't even learned her name. He had seen so much fear, so much sorrow in her eyes. What could he do, though? She lived in that place, where outsiders weren't allowed. Hesitantly, he hoisted himself up on Duke and set off towards home.

TWO

"What took you so long?" Abigail's father demanded as she came into the house.

"I'm sorry, Father. I wasn't feeling well this morning." She kept her eyes down, not wanting him to see her worry or fear - not that he would notice or even care. Her father was a tall, thin man with dark eyes and a long, graying beard. No one would know by looking at him that he wielded such power in the village. He sat in the chair by the fire, his big black Bible open in his lap. Father became a different man when mama died. He had never been overly kind, but he had been somewhat kind before mama died. She thought, as far as she could remember, he had truly loved mama. When she died, he lost some part of himself. Abigail could barely remember the times when he held her as a little girl, reading the scriptures to her, while mama sat near them knitting. After mama died, he stopped holding her, making her sit on the ground when he read the scripture. He never once had held Samuel. He put as much distance between himself and others as possible, especially his own children. He became consumed with God's judgment on sin and making sure the village complied with the law. Then, he became an elder in the village, which only fueled his drive for perfection.

"Be quick about breakfast. I need to be off." He didn't look at her as he spoke.

"Yes, Father." Abigail put the pail of water aside, to be boiled for use later. She hurried to take off her cloak and set about dishing up the porridge. When she set the last bowl on the table, Samuel walked in, milk pail in hand. He hung his hat by the door and set the milk pail near the cupboard. He glanced up and gave Abigail a small smile. He didn't look at Father who stood and put the Bible on the mantle over the fire.

Abigail hated to sit and listen to Father read the scriptures. It only reminded her of what she had lost. She never said that out loud, though, for she knew the punishment would be harsh if she did. She kept silent for Samuel's sake. Her actions or words would affect him in the end.

She brought the small bowl of hard boiled eggs over to the table, setting it in the middle. She then poured three cups of cider for them and set the pitcher on the table. Father walked to his place at the head of the table. Abigail and Samuel took their places on either side of him, standing with heads bowed, hands clasped in front them.

They stood in silence, waiting for Father to say the prayer that would give them permission to sit and eat. He never said the prayer aloud, always silently, as if they weren't allowed to join. That suited Abigail just fine. She didn't have anything to say to God.

Father looked up from his prayer and nodded, the signal that they could sit. They both did so, and quietly began eating their breakfast. Abigail wanted to ask Samuel how he felt this morning after going to bed with the sniffles. She would wait, though because father demanded they eat in silence at every meal. All three of them ate, heads down, eyes focused on their bowls. If they were not done eating when Father finished, they simply did not get to finish eating. He said it showed a lack of respect to be eating after he finished. So, no one spoke. They simply ate as quickly as possible.

Samuel finished first and sat with his head down, waiting on Father. Abigail finished her porridge - thought it didn't settle well in her stomach - and did the same. Father finished and stood without a word, going for his hat by the door. Abigail and Samuel both stood up.

"Come, Samuel, we have much work to do, today." Father settled his hat on his head as he spoke. Samuel went quickly to the door and grabbed his hat. Abigail stood, head down, and waited for them to leave. As they were leaving, Mary came up to the door.

"Sir," Mary curtsied to Father, as he came outside with Samuel on his trail. She kept her head down as she spoke. "I've come to share some of our bounty with Abigail." Mary's family had successfully grown tomatoes this year.

Mary was Abigail's only real friend in the village. They were opposites in every way. Mary had dark hair, with warm hazel eyes to match and stood a little taller than Abigail. She always had something to say and found reason to smile. Though women in the village were expected to keep quiet – and did – Abigail had been alone with Mary enough to know who she really was.

Abigail walked towards the door. Father gave a silent nod as he passed through. Samuel looked up at Mary, and she gave him a little wink. He grinned and hurried after Father.

"Come in," Abigail said, hearing the shaky quality in her voice. She tried to steel herself against sounding fragile or worried. She couldn't even let her best friend know about her problem. If she did, and the elders found out that

Mary had kept Abigail's secret, they would punish her for deceit.

Mary walked in carrying a basket of tomatoes. "I have quite a collection for you, tod-" she stopped, eyes roving over Abigail's face. "Abigail. What's wrong?"

Oh, Mary...if you only knew. "Nothing, I'm just tired today." She gave Mary her best smile.

Mary peered at her with skepticism. "I don't believe you. You're pale and your eyes are obviously puffy from crying." She waited for an answer.

"I'm fine, Mary. Just missing mama and not feeling too good today." She said the only thing she could think of. It was true, too. She missed her mama as much today as she did when she died ten years ago.

Mary studied her, then sighed. "Very well. If you won't tell me what's really wrong, then we'll just pretend, like everyone does, that all is well." She wasn't angry, Abigail knew. She was just being Mary; speaking the truth that no one else would.

She set the basket on the table and opened it up. She began pulling rather large tomatoes from the basket and Abigail retrieved a bowl from the cupboard.

"These do look good!" Abigail said, sounding a bit more cheerful.

"I'm so proud of my efforts!" Mary said. "But don't tell anyone. Pride is a sin, you know." She gave Abigail a smirk. Mary always questioned the rules. Abigail thought she was very brave, and secretly wished she could be like her friend. Maybe she wouldn't be in this mess if she were more like Mary. They both sat at the table.

"I think James is going to ask for my hand," Mary said quietly, looking down at the table. She looked up at Abigail, hope in her eyes.

"Oh, Mary! That is wonderful!"

Mary grinned. "Yes. I'll be thankful to get out from under my father's rule and have my own home." Her brows knit together when she mentioned her father. Abigail knew Mary had suffered under his hand. He was harsh, like her own father, but he used more physical means to impose his expectations. Just another "thing" that went on in this village that everyone ignored. Why did they ignore some things but not others? It made no sense. She grabbed her friend's hands, squeezing them. A look passed between them that required no words. Even though Mary had no idea the things Abigail had suffered, they both knew how trapped they were inside the walls of this village. Mary looked past Abigail's shoulders, gazing at nothing.

"James says he will be kind to me, that he won't treat me the way my father has treated me." She looked at Abigail. "He says I am the most beautiful woman in the world." She sniffled as tears came to her eyes. "I think he means it, Abby." She whispered.

"Of course, he does. You are beautiful."

Mary laughed, softly. "He says we might leave the village. He says he wants to make a life for us away from this place."

Abigail stared, surprised by the admission. "Y-you will leave?"

Mary looked down at her hands, then nodded. "Yes." She looked up into Abigail's eyes. "I don't want to raise children in this place, Abby." A tear fell down her cheek. "I want more for them…better." She took a deep breath. "I hate the thought of leaving my brothers and sisters, but what can I do for them here?" Her voice wavered. Abigail knew Mary loved her siblings. She was like a second mother to them. Leaving them would be hard. "I don't want to leave you, either," Mary whispered as another tear fell.

Abigail felt the lump form in her throat. She would miss her friend, but she wouldn't try to convince her to stay, not when she also wanted to escape this place. The changes that were coming so rapidly to the colonies were having a ripple effect, even here. Where previous generations never talked about or longed for a life outside the village, that wasn't the case anymore. The boys who went to Boston for work would come back with a different look in their eyes, with a sense of longing for something else. It would seem that no matter how hard the elders tried to keep the outside world away, it found its way inside the walls of the village. So far no one had left, but Abigail wondered now if Mary and James would be the first. Her own heart began to pound at the idea of escaping this place.

"Do it, Mary," she whispered. "Get away from here." She said with fervency.

Mary's eye widened through her tears. "Why… Abigail… that's the most rebellious thing I've ever heard you say." They stared at each other, then both smiled. Mary stood, wiping her eyes and nose on her apron. She picked up her basket. "I need to get back. Mother will need help with the children while she gardens today." Mary's family was one of the larger in the community with eight children, Mary being the oldest.

Abigail stood and followed her friend to the door.

"Thank you for the tomatoes." They stopped at the door, Mary's hand on the latch.

"Did you know, in Boston, they use spices and make food we've never even heard of?." Mary asked. The food they ate here in the village was plain and unseasoned. God's law demanded that they eat simple, unflavored foods so they would not stumble into the temptations of earthly pleasure. So, they ate a lot of unseasoned stew and porridge.

"I know…" Abigail said.

Mary hugged her, then left without another word. Abigail closed the door and leaned her head against it. The tears came then, and she let them. She was thankful Mary had found a way out of this place, but what about her?

She turned, slid down to the floor, and laid her head on her raised knees. She saw the face of the stranger she had met in the woods. She remembered his eyes being as green as emeralds and so clear. He was tall - taller than any man she had seen - and powerfully built. Who was he and where had he come from? He had caught her off guard with his apology, especially when he looked so overpowering. No one ever apologized to her for any reason, much less showed concern for her. Something in his eyes had made her want to tell him…everything. She couldn't though, because he was a man. She couldn't trust anyone. She only had Samuel in this world and she had to watch over him, and now this life growing inside of her. What was she going to do? Hopelessness gripped her like a weed strangling a vine, and she felt life slowly begin to leak out of her soul through the tears that poured down her cheeks.

THREE

Nathan saw a stream of smoke billowing from the cabin as it came into view. He smiled, thinking about helping Papa build it years ago. It had been just him and his papa for as long as he could remember. His mother died from a fever when he was only two years old. He didn't remember her, but Papa talked about her often. He never talked about marrying again after she died. He was content with the way his life had turned out.

Nathan steered Duke around the cabin to the barn. He dismounted and led Duke inside. Once he finished brushing the horse down and giving him a bucket of oats for all his hard work, he made his way to the cabin. He thought again of the girl he had met in the woods and paused, looking through the trees at the sun playing hide and seek. He couldn't get her out of his mind. He had spent the rest of the trip home thinking about her, even seriously considered going back to the village to find her. He knew better, though. Those people kept diligent watch over their village, and they did not let outsiders in. Still, he had considered it. Something about the girl had pulled on his heart. The sorrow so evident in her eyes unsettled him, even now.

He made his way to the cabin to see Papa and share the news of his trip. He went up the steps and inside the cabin only to find it empty. *Papa must be down at the mill.* He shed his coat and hat, then his gloves. The day had warmed some since early morning, reminding him that spring was coming. The scent of onions drew him to the pot hanging over the banked fire. He dipped a spoon in to taste and grinned when the warmth and flavor of potato soup touched his tongue. He scooped some into a bowl, and moved to the table. He sat down to eat and as soon as the first bite hit his tongue, he realized how hungry he was. He polished off one bowl and went back for a second. He was finishing that one off when he heard footsteps on the porch. Papa walked in, his big frame filling the doorway. He saw Nathan and his green eyes lit with a smile.

"You're back!" He came over to Nathan and squeezed his shoulder, then took a seat at the table. "I was down at the mill most of the day. Wanted to be there when the boys came in with their wagon loads of logs."

Nathan and Papa shared the same green eyes and dark hair. Papa was just a tad taller, and both had the strong build of timber men. The difference in them was that Papa wore a short, dark beard, while Nathan's jaw was smooth. Papa also had laugh lines around his eyes that Nathan hadn't lived long enough yet to earn.

"Did we get a good supply?" Nathan asked, standing and taking his bowl to the wash bucket they kept on the small work table by the cupboard.

"We did, and there were no injuries, which I'm grateful for." Felling trees was dangerous work. "I see you found the stew. I woke up this morning, and decided stew sounded good. The garden looks good this year, even the potatoes look good. I think we'll have a good harvest of corn, squash, and beans." His eyes twinkled. "I put extra potatoes in the stew. I knew you would appreciate that."

Nathan loved potatoes, which Papa often joked was in his blood. They were, after all, of Scottish and Irish descent.

"Aye, 'tis a good stew, Da," Nathan said, slipping into the brogue he knew well as he sat down again.

Papa laughed. Nathan didn't speak with an accent due to being raised in Massachusetts, but Papa still had the sound of their ancestors in his voice. So many different languages were represented in this land that most people found their accents changing quickly when they settled here. English was the language of the land, but even it sounded very different, depending on where you were in the colonies.

"So, what's the news?" Papa asked. "Did you come up with a contract?" He grabbed an apple from the bowl on the table, rubbed it on his sleeve then bit into it. Apples were Papa's favorite. They had their own small orchard on the edge of their land that Nathan had helped nurture since he was a boy.

"Yes, with a couple stipulations."

"Always," Papa said, chuckling and taking another bite.

"Basically, they need more wood, and faster. The demand from the Crown to build vessels is high. We can meet the demand, I think, but we will have to work harder, maybe bring on more men to send out and cut timber." Nathan finished his explanation and decided the apples looked good, so grabbed one for himself.

"Winter is on us and farmers are looking for work. I just saw James Martin in town two days ago. He asked if we would be hiring any this winter," Papa said. "I'll tell him we have a job for him next time I see him." His smile was lopsided, apple filling his cheek.

"They want twice the amount, but in the same time frame. I don't think we have to double the hands in the mills. It's getting the wood to the mills that takes the most time. If we double the men going out and cutting, we can get it done," Nathan said, absently rubbing his stubbled cheek. He hadn't shaved since leaving for Boston. He also needed a bath. Were the weather nicer, he would just bathe in the river. The thought of jumping in the water that was most certainly frigid made him shudder. He would drag the wash tub inside and heat water, later.

"We can pay the men well, too, since they were willing to pay the price up front," Papa said as he stood and went to the cabin door. He opened it and went out on the porch. Nathan got up and followed him, taking a couple last bites of his apple. They both went down the steps and tossed their apple cores into the woods nearby. The birds would enjoy them.

Papa came to Nathan and cupped the back of his neck with his big hand. "Well done, son." He gave him a good shake.

"Thanks, Papa." Even though he had grown to nearly match his father in size, Nathan would always feel like a boy next to him.

"Any other news from Boston?" Papa asked as they went back up on the porch and sat in their two chairs. Nathan thought about Papa coming out to the porch every morning to read his Bible while the sun rose. When it was too cold to sit outside, he would sit by the hearth and read. Nathan smiled, thinking about it. Papa was a creature of habit - of good habits - which Nathan was grateful for.

"The war will end soon. It must. The French are losing, miserably. Somehow, this war is bringing the people in this land closer together. As if the common enemy has given the people of this land common ground. I heard it in every conversation I passed, at every tavern I visited. The people have found something to unite them."

"Doesn't bode well for the Crown," Papa said.

"How so?" Nathan asked. He rested his head against his chair and closed his eyes, the weariness of the trip settling in his bones. It took one day's ride on horseback, to reach Boston. His trip had been a three-day trip, total. He always enjoyed visiting the city and even enjoyed the journey there and back, but it always left his body weary.

"The colonies haven't joined together over anything, until now. Our people have been a force to be reckoned with, and now they know it." Papa set his chair in motion. "The Crown doesn't know that, though. He will continue to try and hold our people under his thumb and they will not tolerate it as they have before. It won't take long for the colonies to find another common enemy."

"The Crown," Nathan said, realizing what Papa said was true. The people in this land were stirring for a cause that would be dangerous to Britain: the cause of freedom.

"I fear the cost will be great when the colonies choose the Crown for an enemy," Papa said, stopping the motion of his chair, and staring out into the woods beyond their cabin.

Neither said anything else for a time. Then, Nathan remembered the woman.

"I had a disturbing encounter today, with a young woman." He stood and went to the porch rail, leaning against it. Just the mention of her made him restless. He went into the story, telling Papa about the woman, about the sorrow he heard in her cries and saw on her face.

"She was from the village. I wanted to follow her in, even thought about turning around and going back, but I knew it would do no good. They don't let strangers in." He stood and turned, looking off in the distance. Her eyes haunted him, even now. "She was alone, Papa. I heard it in her voice and saw it in her eyes...she had no hope."

"Did she give you her name?" Papa asked.

Nathan shook his head. "I asked, but she wouldn't tell me." He crossed his arms over his chest. "I said I was sorry for whatever caused her pain." He stared at nothing, remembering. "She looked at me with such surprise that I'm convinced no one has ever apologized to her, for anything...or been kind to her."

Papa stood and came over next to Nathan. He leaned his hands against the porch railing, and looked out into the woods. His brow furrowed as he spoke. "If she is from that village, she has suffered. The women, especially, suffer there."

Nathan leaned against the porch post. "I know. I wish I could have helped her. I wanted to help her." He kicked at a rock and it bounced off the porch. He had wrestled with that all the way home. Did he fail by not going after her? She had radiated with fear. He was fairly certain she would have resisted any effort on his part to help. Still, he wondered. What if he never saw her again? What if he had missed an opportunity to do what was right? He didn't recall ever having seen a woman from the village. Only the men came and went, and they kept to themselves. He doubted he would ever see her again.

"I'm going to work on the hen house, while the weather is decent," Papa said. "Those crazy birds have pecked holes in the side walls and now the cold air comes right in on them." He walked down the porch steps then turned to Nathan. "Rest, some." He put his hands on his hips. "And take a bath. You need it." He smirked at Nathan, who grinned back.

Nathan's grin slowly ebbed away as Papa disappeared behind the cabin and his thoughts turned back to the woman. He stayed there a while, thinking about her and wondering what he could have done to help her.

FOUR

Abigail woke with a start, at the sound of beating on the door. "John! Open up!" Someone was shouting for Father. She rose quickly, donning her robe, and hurried from her room to the door right as father came out of his bedroom. She pulled up the latch and opened the door bringing a rush of cold, wet air inside. Father stepped up in front of her and she stepped back, out of his way. It was raining steadily and the night air was crisp.

"John! The elders are meeting, now. We have a situation…" Abigail recognized the voices as Mr. Smithson and Mr. Williams. They were village elders, like Father. He stepped out and pulled the door closed. Abigail listened from where she stood, knowing better than to move forward and be caught eavesdropping when Father came back in the house. Their voices were muffled, and the rain made it hard to hear, but she understood enough.

"We've discovered something about Mary Collins and James Wellington." Mr. Smithson spoke, insistent.

Abigail's eyes widened. *Mary! Oh, God! No!*

"What is it, then?" Father asked.

"Her father discovered her trying to leave the village…with the boy." The sounds of the rain increased and Abigail took a step closer, desperate to hear.

"She said she was going to marry the boy, and he was going to take her away from here," Mr. Williams said.

Abigail's eyes widened, and panic filled her. *Mary!* She closed her eyes, thinking of the consequence her friend was about to face. She had thought Mary would be more careful, that she would find a way to leave unnoticed. Anyone who was caught trying to run away from here was severely purged. It was the worst sin a person could commit according to their law. No one ran away from the village, ever. She brought a hand to her mouth. *Oh God! Mary!*

"Indeed. They must be purged," she heard Father say. "I'll meet you at the church." He came back into the house, heading straight for his room, stopping when he saw Abigail standing there.

"Father?" Was there anything she could say to sway him? She held her robe tight at her neck, wrapping her other arm around her middle.

"The elders have been summoned. I'm needed at the church." He went into his room. Abigail was frantic inside. Her friend was going to suffer! *God, what can I do?* She knew there was nothing to be done to stop it. Still, Mary was her friend, her one friend in this village. Father came out of his room, wearing his boots and breeches.

"There is no need for you to stay up. Go back to bed." He only ever spoke in commands.

"Father, is-is everything alright?" Abigail dared to ask.

He grabbed his coat from the peg on the wall and walked over to her. He looked at her intently as he put on his coat and buttoned it up. "Your friend Mary has been caught trying to leave the village. She must be purged."

"Please, Father. Please...no." She took a tentative step towards him. She wanted to plead with him without invoking his wrath.

"You question my authority?" He spoke in a dangerously low voice, void of emotion.

Her eyes went to the floor. "N-no, Father." She did question him, she questioned everything…but she knew she could do nothing for her friend. "I-I just wonder if there is another way…" she dared to say.

He grabbed her chin with his hand, yanking her head up. "Another way? Why would we want another way? This is God's way. He requires righteous living and payment for sins." His eyes bored into hers, his face set in stone.

Abigail couldn't stop the tears as she searched her father's eyes. He was so callous, so angry. Was it because mama had died? Was that why he had turned into a man consumed with laws and judgment? The elders, at the time, had given father an explanation for mama's death. They told him God took loved ones to remind people of their sinful nature, so they would continue to pursue holy living. When he found out the truth about her, what would he do? She didn't say anything, and he released her, stepping back.

"God requires repentance." His voice was cold.

Samuel came into the room, eyes foggy with sleep. "Father? Abigail?" He rubbed his face with both hands.

"Back to bed, Samuel. This doesn't concern you," Father said.

Abigail moved to go to him. Father grabbed her arm, squeezing tight. "Watch yourself, daughter, and keep your place." He said it like it was a threat. Abigail kept her eyes down until he released her. He left the cabin without a word.

"Father was called to an elder's meeting." She used the moment without Father's presence to wrap an arm around Samuel's shoulder and rub a hand through his blond hair.

He was almost ten and was growing so fast. His head came just above her middle.

"Why is Father angry, Abby?" She smiled at his use of the name he had given her as a toddler when he couldn't say her full name. He didn't use it around Father, only when they were alone. Mary was the only other person who used it. She leaned her head against his, thinking of her friend and the sorrow she would face. Her whole being ached at the thought.

"Why is the whole village angry?" His question came from an innocence not yet stolen. If he asked Father, he would receive retribution, but not from Abigail. She had the same questions.

"I don't know, Sam. It's just how things have always been."

He looked up at her, eyes a mirror of her own. "Why do things have to be this way?"

Abigail swallowed the lump in her throat. Why did things have to be this way? All the rules did not stop people in the village from sinning. The rules only made people afraid. So much went on in secret that was against their law. None of it was stopped by all the punishment given, either. It was only covered up.

"Enough questions for the middle of the night." She tweaked his nose. "To bed."

He wrapped his arms around her, squeezing tightly, and she wanted to weep. How would she protect him from her retribution when it came? She kissed the top of his head, and he padded back to his room. Father would not tolerate such show of affection.

Abigail went back to her own bed, the chill of the night

causing her to shiver. *Oh, Mary. What is going to happen to you?* The elders would not require the villagers' attendance for this purging. Sometimes, they did. It was always up to the elders how a purging was handled. In her mind, she saw Mary's hazel eyes, filled with hope when she spoke of James' promise to take her away from here. Now, what would happen?

Emotion knotted in Abigail's chest, mixed with fear crawling up through her belly. She curled on her side, buried her face in her pillow, and wept. She wept for all that was being lost, and all that would be lost after this night. And, while her tears were mostly for her friend, a lot of them were for her own sorrow. Her secret would reveal itself in time, with or without her permission. What would happen, then? She thought of Hammond, and bile rose in her throat. He wouldn't care what he had done to her. He had never cared about her, only what she could do for him, how she could satisfy his needs. She laid there and wept until exhaustion claimed her for a restless night of sleep.

FIVE

Abigail walked through the village gates, heading in the direction of the river, wash bucket, lye soap, and the laundry to be washed in hand. Even though the washing was back- breaking work, she enjoyed the opportunity to get away from the village. She had a little spot that she always went too, set far enough from the road to be secluded. The river always brought her a small measure of peace. Something about the sound of the water always seemed to settle her, at least for those few moments she visited with it. Normally, Mary came with her and they washed together. Her heart ached at the thought of her friend. She had not seen her since the day she brought the basket of tomatoes. It had been four days. What had they done? How was she? Abigail wanted to go to her, but that wasn't allowed. When a person was purged, they weren't allowed any interaction with other villagers until their time of purifying had been completed. The time was completed with the person publicly renouncing their sin.

Her thoughts turned towards her own situation and the grip on her heart tightened. She had no idea what she was going to do. She knew she had at least two months before anyone would start to notice or question her appearance. If she were very careful, maybe three months. In the still of the night, when the deafening silence screamed at her, she tried to think of any solution. She could run away. She knew that was desperation talking. What if she were caught, like Mary? They would hurt not only her but her baby. She couldn't - wouldn't - go without Samuel. Who

would look after him? *Could* she take him and run away?
Boston wasn't that far, but far enough and big enough that
they could easily blend in. Weldon was closer, but she
worried it was too close. She could be found there.

The man she met last week came to mind again. She
hadn't really met him. She didn't even know his name,
hadn't told him hers. She paused at the tree where they had
met and laid her hand against the massive trunk. The
memory of his voice and eyes came back to her with a great
force. She had not forgotten him since that day. In odd
moments, his face would fill her mind, especially in the
silence of the night. The compassion she had glimpsed in
his face haunted her, even now. Would he really have
helped her? She couldn't let herself believe that. Why
would he want to help her?

She made her way to the river, thankful that the snow
had been melting down over the past week. The last snow
had been ankle deep, but now it only brushed the tops of
her boots. She stopped, at the bank of the river, set her
supplies down on the ground, and pulled her cloak closer to
ward off the chill from the river. The water was still icy and
would be hard on her hands when she did the washing. She
closed her eyes and took a deep breath. She felt a shiver run
up her spine, and her eyes flew open when she heard the
crunch of boots.

"Well, come to meet me here, have you?" His voice
filled her with dread and knotted her stomach.

Abigail whirled around. "What are you doing here?"

He stood there, tall and overbearing, a sensuous grin on
his face. Many of the single women in the village looked at
him with desire in their eyes and it made Abigail sick to

think about it. They had no idea who this man was and what he was capable of. He played the part of serious school teacher for the village. He wooed the ladies with his charm, but never crossed the lines of propriety. He deceived everyone.

She couldn't fight his size and strength. She had tried, over the years, and paid for it, dearly. He was clever. He knew how to hurt her so that no one saw the marks. He stepped forward and yanked her close with a hand to her waist. He stared at her, and she saw the familiar, dark look in his eyes. She kept her hands at her side, refusing to touch him.

"Feeling a bit feisty today, are we?" He laughed his low, menacing laugh that made her skin crawl. She had believed once that she loved him, and that he loved her. Now, the thought made her want to vomit.

"You're willing to risk being seen with me?" She asked through gritted teeth.

He reached up and trailed her cheek with his cold finger. "No one will see us here, no one else comes here. This is your spot, is it not?" He smiled and moved his mouth to her neck. She closed her eyes and mouth and in a rare show of rebellion, pushed him away. Maybe the image of her friend Mary, shamed and alone was fueling her anger. She saw the surprise on his face, but only briefly, before his cocky smile was back in place.

"Don't touch me! You have no idea what you've done to me!" She backed up a step towards the tree behind her, fear gnawing at her belly because she was standing up to him.

With one step he was in front of her and pinned her

arms to the tree trunk with both of his large hands. "Ah, and what is that, my dearest? I've made you crave my touch, crave me?" He laughed again, his breath puffing out in her face, before he kissed her mouth, hard.
She didn't respond to his kiss, and he squeezed her arms, until she winced.

"Kiss me back." He said, against her mouth. She tried to turn away, and he gripped her chin with one hand. "I said, kiss me back."

"I am with child." She said it flatly, looking straight into his eyes, hoping it would shock him. It did. He said nothing for a moment, just stared back at her.

There were moments in years past that she had glimpsed his fears. Sometimes, when he finished using her, he would hold her and weep, like a child, as if he suddenly realized who and what he was, and he hated it, hated himself. He would tell her in those moments that he loved her, that he wanted to marry her. Then, just as quickly, his heart would harden again, and she would be his puppet, his object of lust. She had learned over the years how to keep her emotions tucked deep inside, where he couldn't see them, where he couldn't see her.

"And you think I'm the father?" he said, arrogance coating his words. He stepped away from her, as if she had just confessed to carrying a disease.

She stared at him, incredulous. "Yes. You are the father. Who else do you think it would be?" She took advantage of his shock and stepped further away from him, beside the tree.

He grabbed her arm suddenly, pulling her up to his chest. "Who else have you been with? Tell me!" He shook her, his anger building.

She stared at him, lost for words. This was his reaction? Assuming there was someone else? She had been prepared that he would not believe her, or that he would laugh at her, or even say he didn't care...but this?

"You are the father. There is no one else." She leaned in for emphasis, staring him down. "There has *never* been anyone else."

"We both know I'm not. We both know you keep secrets from me." He pushed her away, causing her to stumble. "You'll not put this," he looked at her stomach, then back up at her, "*thing* on me."

She stared, dumbfounded. Fury, like a blazing fire, rose up from her middle. She clenched her hands at her sides. There was a warning bell that went off in her mind, but she didn't heed it.

"You are an evil, sick man! You have used me for all these years, never thinking of the consequences! Did you think you were above this? Did you think this couldn't happen to you? Well, it did! I carry *your* child, no one else's!" She pointed at him as she spoke, shaking with rage.

She knew when it happened, knew when the dangerous anger moved behind his eyes. He went still and stared at her a moment before he spoke.

"You will pay for this, Abigail. I will make sure of it." He never used her name, except when he was angry with her. He had all these pet names for her, but when he was angry, really angry with her, he used her real name.

"I'm already *paying* for it, *Thomas*." She never used his name, never called him anything, except when he forced her to say his name when he was using her. Why hadn't she just told him no and taken the consequences of his threat?

Samuel.

He was the reason she had kept quiet all these years; to protect him. The dread washed over her, snuffing out her fury like water on a fire.

Thomas stepped up in front of her and, with a calmness that made the hair on her neck stand up, said, "I will find him, whoever it is you have been with…I will make him pay." He brought a hand to her neck and squeezed it, forcing her to look up at his eyes. They were as dark and void as ever. "And I think it's time you paid for your sins, Abigail. Time to be purified." He pulled her close with his hand still on her neck. "Time to be purged."

He kissed her hard, painfully. Then, he pushed her back against the tree and walked off towards the village.

Abigail stood frozen against the tree trunk, watching him walk away. Her heart fell into her stomach, as reality replaced her rage. He was going to plot an evil plan. He was going to make her pay for his sins. He was going to demand a purging.

SIX

Nathan saw the girl cowering in the corner, heard her mournful cries, and all he could think of was getting to her. She was barely visible through the surrounding darkness. He rushed forward and as he reached out to touch her, a strong hand gripped his wrist and flung him back across the room. His back slammed against a wall and he fell to the ground. He moaned with pain. He couldn't see who had grabbed him, but he could see the outline of a cloaked figure. He stumbled forward again, trying to get to the girl when he was suddenly attacked by dozens of small creatures with long limbs and fangs. He couldn't see the creatures in the darkness. He pressed forward even as he was being attacked. The girl's cries were becoming more desperate and he knew he was running out of time. Then, the creatures began to bite him and let out ear piercing screams that disorientated him. He fell to the ground.

Nathan woke with a start, heart pounding, sweat rolling down his bare chest. He had been dreaming of her, again. He threw the sheet off and sat up on the edge of the bed. He rubbed his hands over his face, then leaned his eyes against his palms. He took deep breaths, waiting for his heart to slow down. Really, it wasn't a dream but a nightmare. He still felt the presence of evil around him even though he was awake. He absently rubbed his arm where the creatures had bitten him in the nightmare. It was clear to him that the girl was in danger. Was God warning him? This was the third time he had awakened in the night because of nightmares involving her. Each time, the nightmare seemed to get darker and cause him more pain. He got up and went to the main room, over to the hearth. He stoked the banked fire a bit and added a log. There was a chill in the air to match the darkness. He went back to his room, grabbed his shirt, and slipped his arms into it. He went back to the hearth and sat in his chair. With elbows propped on his knees, he leaned his face into his hands. He began praying for the woman, the only thing he knew to do. He prayed against the evil presence around her. He prayed for provision, courage, everything he could think of. Each time he had these nightmares, he woke with a knot in his gut and a sense of urgency. He stood up again, restless. This dream had been the first one where the dark figures attacked him. He absently rubbed his arm where they had been biting at him in the dream, then looked down at it. What did all of it mean? He had never dreamed things like this before. *Why allow these dreams when I can't do anything about it?* He wondered, with frustration.

Papa came into the room and sat in his chair, rubbing a hand over his face. "Dreaming again, son?" He asked, his voice foggy with sleep.

"Yes." Nathan said. "She is in danger, Papa. I feel it. Should I go there, try to find her?" He felt helpless.

"I don't know, son, but God knows what she needs, and if you have a role in helping her, he will show you. We don't need to know to fight. Remember, we fight with weapons, not of this world."

Nathan sighed, "I know." He knew what God's word said. "We fight not against flesh and blood but against the powers of darkness." He whispered the words Papa had taught him as a boy. He felt strength and a small measure of peace come into his heart as he spoke the truth, but it didn't satisfy his need to do something. He was a man accustomed to doing whatever was necessary to get the job done. He leaned both hands against the mantle, staring down into the flames. His muscles strained against his shirt, shoulders taut with tension. He breathed deep, trying to relax and let go of the worry.

"God knows. If I'm meant to help her," he looked at Papa, "he will show me." He was saying it to remind himself of what he knew, rather than focusing on what he felt.

Papa nodded his agreement. "Now," he stood and laid a hand on Nathan's shoulder, "Rest. Tomorrow will be here soon enough."

With that, they both returned to bed.

~~~

Ian stared at the dark ceiling, thinking of how tense and frustrated his son had looked tonight. He had been fighting, there was no doubt about that, and he looked battle weary. Ian had always been amazed at Nathan's heart of compassion. Even as a boy, Nathan had noticed other people's pain. He would often ask Ian, "Why, Papa, why do people suffer? Why are people mean to each other?" Ian had always felt his heart twist at the innocence in his son's questions. He had done his best to protect Nathan, as a boy, from the darkness of this world. He had done his best to raise him into a wise man with a keen eye, while still encouraging his compassionate heart that always noticed the helpless and the hopeless. How could he not? Compassion was exactly what this world lacked. Listening to his son pray for the woman he had met with such concern and care…well, it made him proud of his boy. He knew, though, that Nathan's compassionate heart would also cause him a lot of pain. Caring for the weak and helpless would always be met with opposition, always. He didn't know how, but he knew resistance would come, and Nathan would need strength to endure. *Be his strength, Father…be his strength.* He prayed for his boy, for strength to endure whatever battles lie ahead.

SEVEN

Abigail's stomach seized at the sight of Mary walking from the back of the meetinghouse to the front. Her heart pounded in her chest, and she desperately wanted to go to her friend. Mary came to the front and turned to face the gathering. She stood, flanked on both sides by the elders. Her head hung low, and her dress was dirty and torn. *What did they do to you, Mary? What did they do?* Her heart was racing with panic. She couldn't make out any cuts or bruises…and then Mary looked up, and their eyes connected.

Abigail's eyes widened. She brought a hand to her mouth, muffling the cry that tried to slip out. Mary's left eye was swollen shut, and her cheek was bruised all shades of purple and blue. Her matted, tangled hair framed her pale face and dirt smeared her other cheek. She stared at her friend, so desperate to run to her aid, and save her from this public shaming.

Mary! Her mind screamed as she sat, frozen, eyes glued to her friend. She saw no sign of the spunk that characterized Mary. She saw only a girl, beaten into submission, punished for her supposed sin.

"Mary Collins has been purged of her transgressions and is here before you all to denounce her sin so that God will once again look on her, and the elect, with favor."

Abigail closed her eyes at the sound of her father's voice, booming off the rafters of the meetinghouse. She felt such a mix of emotions: anger, despair, fear. All of them warred within her. She ached for her friend, punished so severely. Her hand unconsciously went to her belly. She looked up, scanning the crowd, looking for Hammond. He sat a couple benches in front of her. Her eyes narrowed. *I hate him.* He should be there, in Mary's place, suffering for his sins. He paid no price for his actions, yet her friend suffered and was being publicly shamed. Were it not for Samuel, Abigail would have confessed a long time ago. He threatened her, though. He threatened to make Samuel pay if she ever revealed the truth. As a child, she had complied out of sheer terror. Now, she complied because she knew he meant what he said. She had seen the evil in him, had experienced it repeatedly over the years. If she told anyone, Samuel would pay, and no one would ever know. She looked over at her little brother sitting beside her. His eyes were wide, and his face was pale. Abigail closed her eyes. *No child should have to witness this!*

"Mary Collins, do you before this gathering and before God, renounce your flesh and commit to repentance and holiness?" Abigail's father spoke with no emotion as if this were a simple matter to be handled. How could he be so callous?

She watched her friend, intently. Mary was a strong girl. She had always been fearless, willing to test the limits. She had never done something so obvious, though. She had never been purged. The gathering was silent, waiting for Mary's response. She knew what to say, everyone knew what to say when they were brought before the gathering.

"Yes. I renounce my flesh and commit to repentance." Mary looked up as she spoke, and her eyes found Abigail's, again. Abigail saw the tear drop from her swollen, discolored eye and a lump formed in her own throat.

Mary's face was etched with defeat, and Abigail felt as if she were looking in a mirror. They had broken Mary, deep inside, where Abigail was sure healing could never come. She knew because she felt the same way. She just hadn't been purged…yet.

Abigail looked towards Mary's parents, Esther and William. Esther kept her head down, hands clenched together in her lap while William stared straight ahead. Their other children sat, heads down, a few of them crying softly. *This is madness!* Abigail scanned the crowd, seeing nothing but stoic faces. Most of the women had their heads down. The men just stared. How she hated this place! She wanted to run away, and were it not for Samuel, she would have a long time ago. She couldn't leave him here, though, and she couldn't leave with him. She was trapped, just like Mary.

"Then, as a people set apart, holy before God, we commit to keeping you on the paths of righteousness, and holiness." Her father's voice rose with authority.

"So be it." The congregation responded, as was customary.

Two of the elders then took their places on the bench, facing the gathering. Father stayed where he was, hands resting on the wood podium. Mary was ushered down the center aisle, an elder leading in front of her and one following behind her. She didn't look up, just kept her head down, and shuffled out of the building. They would escort her home, and she would be required to stay there until her time of separation was complete.

"James Wellington is no longer with us," father announced. "He left us last night to go work on one of His

Majesty's vessels."

Abigail stared, horrified. They had not only purged Mary but permanently separated her from James! Father gave the sign of dismissal and everyone began filing quietly out of the meetinghouse. Samuel scooted closer to Abigail and slipped a hand into hers. It was almost her undoing. She squeezed her eyes shut and held his hand tight. This place…she felt like she was sinking in an ocean…and she didn't know how much longer she could tread water.

EIGHT

Abigail was nervous. It had been a month since her encounter with Hammond and almost the same since Mary's purging. She hadn't been alone with him since the day she told him she carried his child. She hadn't been summoned to one of his secret places. He ignored her in public, didn't acknowledge her in the gatherings. He had never gone this long without demanding her presence. She felt a deep down premonition that something was coming. Exhaustion weighed on her, both from physically carrying this child and from the emotional burden of all the secrecy. Fear of what was to come loomed over her like a dark cloud. She knew she was about three months along, and the little bump under her dress was becoming more obvious by the day, to her at least. She was careful to wear enough layers to cover it so no one would notice.

She had tried to visit Mary a week ago when she was finally allowed to associate with others again. Abigail had gone to her house with a loaf of fresh bread. Mary had taken it, but she said she was too tired to visit. She had thinned considerably since her purging and her hair still hung in matted strands around her gaunt face. She did not look like the Mary Abigail had always known.

Abigail paused as she was about to cut into a squash, thinking of the emptiness she saw in Mary's eyes. It was as if her friend no longer existed; as if the real Mary had been extracted and replaced with a shy, fearful girl. Abigail didn't know what to say to her. She could hardly offer comfort to her friend when her own life was falling apart at the seams. She scooped a handful of squash and was dumping it in the pot when she heard the meetinghouse bell. Her heart stuttered at the sound and she froze. The bell was only rung in emergencies, and on Sundays for the gathering. This couldn't be good. She wiped her hands quickly on her apron. Samuel was in the barn working on horseshoes for Father. Just as she was tying her cloak on, the cabin door opened, and Samuel walked in.

"Everyone is making their way to the meeting house. What's happened, Abby?" Concern creased his brow.

She rubbed a hand over his soft blond hair. "I don't know, but let's get there as quick as we can." She smiled at him, "And don't worry. I'm sure it's nothing."

She knew something was very wrong, but she wanted to ease his worry. She donned her cloak and stepped out of the cabin ahead of Samuel. The winter air was slowly thinning into a spring breeze but today, the air was crisp. She pulled the hood of her cloak up over her head and put an arm around Samuel. "Come," she whispered, and they made their way, with the rest of the village, towards the meeting house.

"What is happening, Mother?" A little boy asked his mother as they walked.

"Quiet! Don't ask questions." His mother responded, sharply, hand around his shoulder.

Abigail knew she was probably afraid and spoke harshly because of it. Everyone in this place just followed the rules, without asking questions. Abigail was no exception. She did exactly what she was told, always. They came to the meetinghouse and everyone filed in quietly and orderly. Abigail saw Mary sitting with her family towards the back and led Samuel over to them. No one else would sit by them. She sat beside Mary, Samuel following close. Mary glanced at her and Abigail smiled, hoping to see the light in her friend's eyes. She didn't. Mary only looked at her, then back down at her own hands.

Oh, Mary...

The five elders sat at the elder's bench. Father was there, and as he stood to address everyone, he showed no sign of concern. That wasn't unusual, though. He was very skilled at showing no emotion, except anger. Anger seemed to be the one emotion no one could hide here.

"Brethren, we are called here today to address a most grievous sin." The crowd was silent, holding its breath in nervous anticipation. Fear was heavy in the room.

Father pulled something from under the elder's bench, some sort of paper. He began to unfold it, and a couple soft gasps went up. Abigail's eyes widened, as he unfolded what was clearly a newspaper. He held it up before them all as if it were some kind of dirty rag.

"This was found behind the school house last evening." Abigail squinted, trying to make out what the paper said. She couldn't read any of it from her place at the back of the crowd.

"What is that, mama?" she heard little Sarah whisper in front of her.

"Shh!" Sarah lowered her head at the harsh reprimand from her mother. Children were not to speak in the meeting house. It was a rule.

"Someone among us has broken the law and we must deal swiftly with the transgression." Father's voice boomed.

The crowd rustled a bit, everyone looking around, wondering who the sinner could be. The only reading aloud in the village was the Scriptures and material written by their own people. Bringing any books, newspapers or any type of writing from the outside was strictly forbidden. The punishment would be severe for whoever did this. There wouldn't be a purging but there would be public humiliation, then isolation for a time.

What is going on around here?

First Mary, now this. Things like this just didn't happen in the village. Fear had ruled this place for all of Abigail's life. Fear of God's wrath, fear of punishment, fear of being shunned. She glanced at Mary. She didn't look less afraid now, after her purging. She only looked broken. Emotion clogged her throat as she thought of the vibrant, laughing Mary…the Mary that had disappeared. That's what happened in this village. Personalities were twisted and punished until they conformed to the way God wanted.

"Who among us has defiled our village in such a way?" Complete silence reigned. "Who risks our good standing with God by bringing such corruption into our midst?" His voice grew with fervor. He slowly scanned the crowd. Everyone bowed their heads as he looked their way, afraid of hearing their own names being called out.

"No one will confess?" Some sniffled, a child coughed, but no one spoke up.

Abigail glanced at Samuel who sat completely still, eyes wide, glued to Father. She reached over and grabbed his hand, giving it a small squeeze. He looked at her, and she gave him a tiny smile. He didn't smile back. He just whispered so low, only Abigail could hear him. "What's going to happen, Abby?"

She wanted to tell him it would all be fine, but she was old enough to know that wasn't true. It would not all be fine. Someone would pay, even if the person who brought the paper to the village never came clean. Someone always paid for breaking the rules.

"Then we will begin questioning until we find the one among us who has strayed from the truth," Father said. He was good at making people afraid with only the sound of his voice.

All the elders rose signaling the end of the gathering. The people stood and began shuffling out of the meeting house without a word. Elizabeth Thames came out of her pew across the aisle with her baby girl on her hip. Abigail exited right behind her. Abigail smiled at baby Eloise who kicked her feet as babies always do when they are excited. They came out of the meetinghouse and squinted in the bright sunshine. Abigail and Samuel stopped beside Elizabeth once they were away from the crowd.

"Head on home, Samuel. I'll be right behind you." He nodded then set off at a quick pace. Normally, he would ask to visit with his friends, but not today. The fear was palpable and made everyone on edge. She saw the crowd quickly thin as everyone made their way home, not stopping to make small talk. No one wanted to be caught saying something that might incriminate them. The best course of action in these situations was just to keep to one's self until the elders completed their inquisitions. It all made Abigail sick to think about.

"How are you, and baby Eloise, Elizabeth?" She turned her attention to them both, doing her best to sound at ease. Elizabeth was a recent widow, having lost her husband in a horrible boating accident.

"We are managing," Elizabeth said softly.

Abigail saw Mrs. Biggs approaching them and her muscles tensed. She nodded to both Abigail and Elizabeth as she came close.

"Abigail. Elizabeth." She looked at baby Eloise and sniffed, looking as if she was pondering whether or not to smile. She didn't.

"Well, a fine mess this is." She folded her hands in front of her and lifted her chin a notch. "Whoever did this will be punished for their rebellion. They must be. We cannot tolerate deception in our midst."

Mr. Biggs was a village elder, and because he was older than Abigail's father, he was the final authority in all matters.

"We will see God's judgment in this matter." Mrs. Biggs said, as if to warn them. Abigail nodded as did Elizabeth. Mrs. Biggs gave them a curt nod and, without another word, turned and left them to stare after her.

Abigail let out a breath she didn't realize she was holding.

"What is going on in this village, Abigail?" Elizabeth asked, absently rubbing Eloise's back. Abigail turned and looked at the crowd again, as it continued to thin.

"I don't know, Elizabeth. I think some are becoming bolder in their desire to question the way things are." She gave Elizabeth a sad smile. "Perhaps the growth of our colonies and the talk of freedom is stirring in our people, too."

News reached them in the village, even without the benefit of the newspaper. News would always travel, no matter what laws were in place to try and prevent it. Abigail reached up and rubbed the top of baby Eloise's head and at that same moment, felt something inside her stomach flutter. Her eyes widened and she put a hand to her middle. Elizabeth looked at her.

"Abigail?" Elizabeth touched Abigail's arm.

Abigail quickly recovered. "I am fine. Just an upset stomach."

The baby moved! That thought caused a whole range of emotions. The baby suddenly became just that: a real, growing life inside of her.

"I think I'll head home and make myself some tea. Please let me know if there is any work you need Samuel's help with. He is happy to come over anytime."

She knew her voice wavered, but she smiled at Elizabeth, gently squeezed little Eloise's hand then turned and hurried off.

Oh, God! This baby was real and growing inside of her. She carried *his* child! She hated the thought, but she couldn't hate the baby. How could she hate the life that was part of her, too? How could she want something and not want it at the same time? A knot formed in her chest, as she made her way home. She had to figure out something, some kind of plan. Time was running out.

NINE

Nathan hammered the last nail into the wheel, securing the new paddle in place. He climbed up onto the stone walkway parallel to the wheel. "Give it a crank, Will!"

He squatted down, watching the paddle with a critical eye, making sure it could handle the pressure of slicing through the water as it flowed in and out of the stream. He was satisfied when he saw the wheel spin effortlessly, causing the chain reaction of moving the belt with logs on it. He walked down the stone steps of the walkway, stopping on the bridge directly in front of the water wheel. The wheel picked up speed as the water began to flow more forcefully over the top of it. He watched the sash saw begin to move slowly through the log it had been working on before the wheel stopped. He turned to Will, who manned the wheel crank, and gave him a nod of approval then crossed the bridge and walked down the walkway that ran along the log belt. He dropped his hammer in the box they kept close by with tools they needed, regularly.

Ben Weems manned the saws as they cut through the logs, scaling them down to size so they could be sent through the shaft into the river below. The men would then load them onto rafts that took the logs down river where they were tied to the mill's small boats. From there they would be towed to Boston's docks.

Nathan slapped Ben on the shoulder as he passed by. "She should be good to go, now." He shouted to be heard over the movement of the saw cutting through the log. Ben nodded with a smile but kept his eyes on the log being sliced. Nathan went down the steps and out of the mill house where Matthew Steele, the mill's foreman, stood with ledger and pencil in hand.

"Looks good, sir," Matthew said as Nathan walked up to him.

"My father is the "Sir," Matthew. I'm just Nathan." He gave a crooked grin as he stuck his hand out to the man he considered a friend. Matthew took the offered hand with a grin of his own.

"That paddle was just worn out," Nathan said. "I put in a new one. Should be good to go now."

Matthew nodded as he scribbled something on his ledger. He had the strong accent of an Englishman. He was the first generation of his family to come to this land, bringing his wife and two daughters with him. He and his family had sailed into Boston harbor and he had quickly set out to find work. Nathan had been in Boston only days after Matthew had arrived, and they had met in a tavern. Nathan had recognized a hard, honest worker and offered Matthew work in the mills that very day. Matthew and his family had been here in Weldon for five years. Ian had given Nathan permission to offer Matthew the foreman job, about a year ago. The pay raise came in handy, as his oldest daughter had a medical condition that was a financial burden on their family, though Matthew had never mentioned it.

Matthew looked up from his ledger. "We will be behind today, but I think we can make up what was lost without overworking the men too much."

"Not one bit worried, Matthew. I know you'll make it up, somehow." With a slap to his friends back, Nathan turned to go. "I'm off to load the wagons for my trip to

Boston."

"What for this time, sir?" Nathan ignored his use of the "sir". Some things were just habit. He turned around and kept walking backward as he responded. "Orders to deliver. Custom made dresser and table with chairs."

"Ah. Safe travels, then. And when you return, you and your father are both invited for a meal. Millie's orders." Matthew said with a grin.

Millie was a gracious hostess and a great cook. "Tell her I'll look forward to the food and the company, as will Papa."

Matthew gave a nod, and Nathan turned and set off down the dirt road that connected his cabin to the mill. He thought about the trip to Boston, one he was familiar with after all these years. This time, though, his thoughts were filled with her, and the fact that he would be passing her village, again. Was she okay? Did she still need help? After two months, she still came to his mind often. He hadn't had another nightmare since the one where he had been attacked, but the memory of those nightmares was vivid. Many prayers had passed his lips for her. Would he see her again on the road? He was so tempted to visit her village, just to see her, to make sure she was well. He breathed another prayer and set out to prepare for his trip.

TEN

Abigail and Samuel were at the table, working on his sums when Father came through the door. Both looked up at him but said nothing.

"Samuel. You'll pack your bag tonight." Father said, tone clipped.

Abigail sat up straighter, surprised. "Why, Father?"

"He leaves tomorrow for Boston." He responded, matter of fact.

Abigail looked at Samuel, who wore a stunned expression. "What for?" She asked, rising up from the table as she spoke.

"He has the opportunity to apprentice with an established blacksmith in Boston."

Abigail's heart began to pound. "But, who will go with him, Father? Are you going?"

He looked at her, lips thin, eyes void of emotion. "No. He goes alone."

Abigail's eyes widened. She moved around the table to stand in front of him. He meant to send Samuel away!

"Father. He is just a boy. He can't go alone." She was never bold with her father, but she had to try and reason with him.

He took a step forward, eyes narrowing. "You dare to question me?" He said it low, dangerously low. "It's time the boy learned a trade."

Panic rose in her, clouding all reasoning. "He's barely ten, Father! You can't send him away!"

She didn't see it coming, but in a fraction of the next

second, she felt his hand come against her cheek with such force, that she stumbled back, crying out. The metallic taste of blood oozed into her mouth, and she clutched her jaw. She didn't cry, she was too shocked to cry. Had he really just hit her? Samuel began to cry behind her.

"I am the head of this house, *daughter*." He said daughter as if it were a foul word. "You will submit to my authority!" He looked at Samuel. "You will leave at sun up with Mr. Biggs." With that, he turned and left.

Abigail went to Samuel and knelt beside him. He fell into her arms and clung to her as he wept. She cried with him, holding him as close as she could. "A-abby. I don't w-want to leave! I want t-to stay with you!"

"I know, I want you to stay, too." *He is a boy, father! A boy!* She knew there was no changing her father's mind. She gently pulled his head away from her shoulder and clutched his face in her hands, his tears streaming through her fingers. She brought his face closer. "You are going to be okay. I will come for you. I won't leave you there, alone."

"B-but, A-abby. You've n-never left the village."

"It doesn't matter. I will come for you." She pulled a rag from the table and wiped his tears.

"You go where he sends you, and stay there. I will come for you." She put her hand on his cheek again. "I promise." He nodded and then burrowed his face into her neck.

"I-I'm scared." His voice was muffled against her.

She closed her eyes, anger and hate for her father stirring in her chest along with the panic she didn't want Samuel to see. Boston was overrun with people and not safe for a child, alone.

"I know. But you are strong and smart, and you'll be okay. Just stay in the shop where father sends you, and do what you are told. I will come for you, soon." She wrapped her arms as tight as she could around him. "I love you, Samuel." Her voice wavered.

"I love you too, Abby."

She would find a way to go to him. Somehow, she would find a way, and once she left this place, she was never coming back.

ELEVEN

Abigail stood outside the cabin with Samuel beside her, his bag clutched in his hand. Her stomach was tight with dread, and her heart pounded out the seconds she had left with him. She was determined to stay strong for him, to send him off with a smile and assurance that everything would be alright.

Everything will not be alright! How can this be happening? She felt the tears well up and she forced them down. Father had said nothing to either of them at breakfast. She had never allowed hatred for her father to consume her, until now. What he was doing was unforgivable. He had never treated Samuel like a son, and she had done her best all these years to make up for it. Now, he was ripping Samuel from her side.

Mr. Biggs made the trip to Boston once every season to trade for the village. Most things the villagers grew or made on their own, but there were certain commodities they couldn't provide for themselves. She heard his wagon coming down the center of the village. She turned to Samuel, adjusted his coat and hat, then fisted her trembling hand at her side. At least the weather had warmed, and she wouldn't worry about him freezing. She closed her eyes trying to steady herself for Samuel's sake.

"Okay. Remember what I said." She smiled down at him, wanting so much to take away the fear in his eyes.

"I remember," he said, voice shaky.

She pulled him close, not caring one bit that this public display of affection might be frowned upon. His arms came around her waist. She squeezed him tight and knelt down in front of him.

"Be brave." She said. He took a deep breath and nodded, though his eyes were glazed with tears. Abigail kissed his forehead, then rose. She turned as Mr. Biggs pulled the wagon to a stop in front of them.

He nodded at her. "Abigail."

"Good morning Mr. Biggs." He wasn't a man given to smiling. His balding head was covered in the required black hat. He had a long pointy nose, and his eyes were small and dark. His graying beard hung down to his chest. Abigail hated sending Samuel with him.

"We need to be on our way." Mr. Biggs said.

Where is Father? Why wasn't he here to send off his own son? Abigail took Samuel's bag and put it in the back of the wagon and turned to him. She grabbed his hand, gave it one last squeeze, then stepped aside so he could climb up into the bed of the wagon. He didn't even ask about Father.

Abigail stepped away from the wagon, and just as she did, Father came around the side of the house, wiping his hands on a rag. What could he be doing that was more important than saying goodbye to his son? The son he was sending away.

Mr. Biggs nodded in his direction. "John."

Father nodded. "Thank you for taking the boy."

The boy? He is your son! Abigail fisted her dress at her sides. She kept her eyes on Samuel, and swallowed hard. She was determined to be strong. She gave him a shaky smile, but he didn't smile back. And he didn't look at Father.

"I'll take him there, first, before I take care of my business."

"Very good." Father reached up and shook Mr. Bigg's hand. Then he stepped up to the wagon and looked at Samuel who leaned back a bit as if scared of him. "You do what you're told, and learn all you can."

"Yes, Father."

With that, Mr. Biggs flicked the reins and set the horses off towards the village gates. Abigail crossed her arms over her chest and stepped forward, away from Father. She couldn't stop the tears, now. She raised a hand to Samuel, and he raised one in response.

She followed the wagon to the gate of the village, and stood there, watching until it was nothing more than a dot off in the distance. Her heart had been trampled when mama had died. Today, it was being ripped from her chest. She had to keep a clear head and think of a plan…quickly. She had to figure out which blacksmith's shop Samuel was being sent too. Father hadn't told her and she couldn't ask. She knew Samuel would do what he was told and work hard. He always did. Time wasn't on her side, though. It wouldn't be long before her secret became obvious and she was trapped with the consequences.

Her eyes stung as she turned and made her way home. Who would watch out for Samuel, keep him safe in such a big place? She glanced around and saw that Father had walked away at some point. She didn't care. She didn't want to look at him or speak to him. She felt the flutter of baby movements and stopped. She closed her eyes and took a shaky breath. The ocean was overtaking her, she was sinking fast, and there was no land in sight.

TWELVE

Abigail was kneading bread at the table, thinking of Samuel as she did every moment since he had left yesterday, when the door to the cabin burst open. Her father filled the doorway, hands clenched at his sides, eyes boring into her. She stood up straight, pushing a wisp of hair from her face with the back of her hand.

"Father?" She questioned, hesitantly.

He walked in and came to where she stood. She looked up into his eyes and dread filled her entire being. *He knows.* She stood there, waiting, heart pounding. He didn't speak but reached over and jerked her skirt tight around her stomach. He looked at her, eyes narrowed.

"It's true, then," He stated, with icy eyes and a cold voice.

Abigail looked down at the small mound of her belly and barely whispered the words.

"Yes. It's true." There was no sense in denying what her body proved. The small mound under her skirt was obvious if one was looking for it.

He stepped back as if she had thrown boiling water on him. "How dare you!" He hissed, hands fisted at his side.

She felt the anger rising around him like heat from a fire. It was written in his stance and his face. Nothing but anger. *These foolish people act like hiding their emotions will make them go away!* She wanted to scream, to cry, to run.

"You have shamed me and this village." He spoke with a calm that did not match the moment. He grabbed her arm and began pulling her towards the door.

"Father! Please! What are you doing?"

"The village is being summoned, now." He continued pulling her towards the door.

Abigail panicked. She tried to pull away, to break free. "Father! No! Please let me explain!"

He jerked her to his chest so hard she gasped. "There is nothing to explain! You've brought corruption to our people! You must be punished before God!"

Abigail began to cry. She dropped her head and put a hand on her belly, no longer having to hide it. "Please, Father. You must believe me. I did not want this." She looked into his eyes, desperate for him to believe her, desperate for him to want to help her. "I was forced to give myself...have been since I was a little girl."

"Don't lie to me! Master Hammond told me your story of seduction and secrecy. You are the one who brought that paper to our village, from your lover outside these walls!"

Thomas did this? Her tears ceased as reality crashed over her like a cold bucket of water. Of course. It made sense. He had probably been planning this all along. He planted the newspaper to stir the people up, make them afraid and suspicious. He was an expert at manipulating people. He had told her she would pay for this, and he had planned it out. He had pitted the entire village against her. There would be no use in telling her father that Thomas was the one who did this to her. He wouldn't believe her, no one would - just as Thomas always told her. Everything was happening exactly as Thomas had said it would.

Her father pulled her towards the door. She heard the meetinghouse bell, which meant all the people would be coming to see her punishment. *Oh God! What am I going to do?*

She wasn't worried for herself. She was worried about her baby. They were going to purge her. She knew it. This was a sin that required purging.

"Father. Please! Think of the baby."

He stopped, abruptly. "The baby? You think I care about a baby born out of fornication and lust?" He leaned in close.

She was rendered speechless by his callous words. How could he be so cold and hard hearted? Then, something inside of her snapped and all rational thinking left, replaced by the deepest and most rooted type of anger a person can ever feel.

"You are the vilest of sinners!" She screamed at him. "There is no love in you! You only know how to punish and hate!" She twisted to try and get free but he kept a hard grip on her arm. She would just run if she could get away. She would run out of the village and keep running until she was far away. Surely, it was safer outside these walls.

Father grabbed her hair, and she cried out as he yanked her head backward. "You will submit to authority!"

"I don't care about your authority! I don't care about you or anybody else here!" She screamed, kicking at him and twisting to try and break free.

He slapped her, stunning her into silence. He grabbed her hair again and pulled her face close. "You will be purged for your sin. Then, you will leave the village until this," he looked down at her stomach, then back again, "*thing*, is done."

The disdain in his eyes drained the last bit of hope and fight out of her. *Let them purge me. Maybe I'll die and my baby won't have to enter this wretched world!*

Father began pulling her along again, and she didn't fight him. She let him drag her out of the cabin, where the sunlight pierced her eyes and she stumbled from momentary blindness. As her eyes adjusted, she saw the people hurriedly moving towards the meetinghouse. No one knew she was the reason they came, but they would know soon enough. Father kept a tight grip on her arm and pulled her along. She saw Elizabeth just ahead, with baby Eloise. She saw Mary, walking with her head down, behind her mother and father. She was going to be exposed before all of them - men, women, and children. They were going to watch her suffer today, watch her own father purge her. She knew she could not escape, not this time. She had no reason to fight now, either. No one here cared what happened to her. They only cared about following the law.

Father pulled her through the village, to the square. He pushed her down beside the whipping post and turned towards the gathering crowd.

"Brethren! A grievous sin has been brought to our attention! We must deal with it swiftly!"

Abigail looked up and saw Mary, standing off to the side, behind her mother. She stared at Abigail, eyes wide in her pale, thin face. Abigail's began to cry and dropped her head. Father grabbed her hands and began wrapping them in rope, then tied them to the post.

"My own daughter has been caught in the act of lust!" There was a pause, and the crowd was silent. "She is with child." Gasps went up and some visibly stepped back, as if she were contaminated.

Abigail closed her eyes, feeling shame like dung being smeared on her head.

"She must be purged," Father said, voice booming with authority.

Any hope she had felt before now, left. Any light that flickered inside of her died in this moment. She had been holding on to the hope that she would somehow escape this place and go to Samuel. She realized now that she had been clinging to dust. She would never be free of this place. She had nothing and no one, and the burden of living in this world became too much. If God held any mercy for her, he would end her life today...and then she could be free.

THIRTEEN

Pulling the wagon to an abrupt halt, Nathan leaned forward, eyes narrowing as he listened, intently. Was someone shouting? The noise was coming from the direction of the village. The scent of burnt wood drifted on the wind, and smoke was billowing up from behind the wooden walls of the village. A sense of danger prickled over his skin. He pulled the wagon off the road a bit and set the brake. Jumping down, he ran towards the village, heart pounding as his sense of danger grew. He thought of the girl he had met and ran faster.

The gates were wide open, which Nathan had never seen before. There was a crowd, gathered in the small village square. Something must be wrong. He went inside the gates and moved towards the crowd. Some were yelling. What were they yelling about?

"She is a sinner!" Someone yelled. "Purge her!" Another shouted.

Nathan moved hurriedly at the sound of those words, coming closer to the back of the crowd. His eyes widened and he came to a sudden halt. There, tied to a whipping post, was a woman. Squinting, he tried to get a better look.

Oh, God! It was her! It was the woman who had filled his dreams, had been in his prayers these past two months. The very woman he had met on the road that day. She didn't struggle, just sat there, head down, shoulders slumped. The man standing beside her took a handful of her blond hair, yanking her head up as he did, causing her to cry out in pain.

"She has committed a vile sin, and she must be purged!" The man beside her yelled.

The woman kept her eyes closed tight and didn't speak. Nathan saw tears trailing her cheeks and the urge to go to her was so overwhelming, he unconsciously took a step forward.

"Give her the whip!" Someone near him shouted.

Whip her? What has she done to deserve that? Nathan's mind was frantic. He knew these people had some distorted views about salvation and they lived by a strict set of rules, but what could merit this? He looked out over the crowd seeing no one who seemed concerned for the girl. Everyone just stared, wide-eyed, as if they were puppets on a string. No one noticed his presence, they were so consumed with the scene before them. He looked back at the girl and his heart broke open in a way it never had before.

"She earned it!" Someone else shouted.

The crowd began moving forward, around the whipping post, blocking his view of her. What should he do? *Lord, what should I do?* His mind and heart were racing.

Save her.

The words were clear, and they echoed deep down in his soul. He had to rescue her. The man standing at the whipping post bent over the woman. He heard the ripping of her gown down the back and saw the man bring the whip up above his head. *NO!* The people shouted in exultation. How could these people think this was right? He felt the presence of evil hovering close, breathing cold on his neck. Then, on its heels, he felt as if the very hand of God gripped his shoulder and whispered in his ear...

Go!

That put his feet in motion. Shoving his way through the crowd, he shouted for them to stop. "No!" Nathan shouted. "Stop!" He shoved his way forward and just as he broke through, he heard the whip crack against her flesh, and she cried out. The sound of her cry pierced him to his core and unfurled a fury he had never experienced. He ran towards her - seeing only her - and just as the whip was coming down again, he threw himself between her and the man, covering her with his own body. He felt the whip crack against his back, but he didn't flinch. He covered her trembling body with his, arms protectively around her.

The crowd gasped, went silent.

The man with the whip stepped back, shocked. "Who are you?" He demanded, voice booming. Nathan stood slowly and turned to face him.

"What do you think you are doing?" Nathan demanded, fiercely.

The man pointed at the girl, with the whip in his hand. "She must be punished. She has broken God's law." He stepped close to Nathan. "Who do you think you are to stop God's work?" The man's eyes were empty, cold.

"What has she done to deserve this?" Nathan asked, not backing away. He thought, briefly, that if the crowd became a mob they could take him out, but he also didn't see anyone with courage in their face. Everyone looked afraid. He knew this was not God's work. This was the work of evil and God had sent him here to rescue this girl. *Help me, Jesus.*

"She is a fornicator, the vilest of sinners!" The man looked over at the girl, and spit at the ground close to her.

"She is with child, and she is unwed!" He glared at Nathan. "Now, move aside." The man had a calm about him that did not match the intensity of the moment.

Nathan could hardly believe his ears. This man, this village full of people, was willing to beat a girl carrying a child? He would not allow it. He knew how society in the colonies treated unwed mothers. The fathers were never called into account; it was the women who suffered. He had seen women in other places humiliated, but this...this was the worst he had ever seen. *What do I do, Lord? How do I stop this?*

Take her with you.

He had to take her with him. That was the only way to save her. "No! I will take her with me!"

Gasps went up from the crowd.

"Impossible!" The man sneered. "She is one of us. You are not." He tried to step around Nathan, to get to the girl, but Nathan grabbed the man's thin arm.

"No," Nathan said, firmly. He was not going to let this man touch her again.

The man looked down where Nathan's hand clutched his arm. Nathan could take down this man with no trouble...it was the crowd he worried about. Then he had a thought. He turned to the crowd, and let go of the man. The crowd could easily be swayed. He saw it in their faces.

"If you find her so repulsive, so sinful, then let me take her from here. Let me take her out of your village! I will not bring her back, I promise! Her life and the life of her child will become my responsibility." He heard the authority in his own voice and knew God was speaking through him.

The crowd began to murmur, some leaning in to whisper to each other. The man with the whip stepped up beside Nathan.

"We cannot send her with him. He is not one of us! It is our responsibility to guide our own. We must guide her to repentance, back to God! She will leave us for a time, then come back, holy before God!" Some in the crowd agreed, loudly.

What absurd logic. Where would they send her? *Jesus, help me convince them.*

"And when she comes back with her child? Who will help her and provide for her?" He asked.

He looked around and saw some eyes widen in fear, while other heads went down. No one wanted to help her. He noticed one man off to the side who stood stoic, arms folded, eyes focused on the girl. He saw darkness in the man's face. Nathan watched him lean in and whisper in a woman's ear, then the woman yelled, "Maybe he is the father!"

More gasps. Nathan didn't respond. If they thought he was the father, maybe they would let him take her. He didn't care what they thought of him. He just wanted to save this woman's life.

"Give her to him!" Someone in the back of the crowd shouted. "She is unclean!" Another yelled.

Nathan stood his ground, ignoring the lies, but praying they would agree to give her to him. The crowd grew louder, and the consensus became the same. They thought he was the father. They didn't want her to stay here in the village.

Nathan looked at the man with the whip. "Untie her.

She is coming with me."

The man's thin face was set in stone, but Nathan saw in his dark eyes that he knew to go along with the crowd.

"Are you the father?" He hissed.

Nathan said nothing, but stared at the man, jaw clenched. There was no movement, no words for a moment.

"You are a fool!" The man said through clenched teeth.

Nathan did not respond, nor did his eyes waver. The man went over to the girl who sat on her knees, silent and still, eyes glued to Nathan. He saw that her face was smeared with ash, her hair dirty and matted with mud. Her belly was only slightly swollen indicating the life of her child. She looked so afraid. Nathan didn't blame her. She had just been beaten by her own people, and now she was being cast out with a complete stranger. The man pulled his knife from his side, and slit the ropes tying her hands to the post. He looked at her lowered head intently for a moment, then turned and walked away, not looking back.

Nathan hurried over and helped her stand. She stumbled as she stood. She was probably weak and shaken from fear and shock. Nathan put an arm around her shoulder and spoke softly in her ear.

"I'm going to carry you out of this place. Will you trust me?"

She looked at him, eyes clouded with doubt and fear, but also desperation. She gave a barely perceptible nod and Nathan immediately lifted her in his arms. She was just a slip of a girl, even with the small swell of her belly. She kept her head down, against Nathan's shoulder.

The crowd parted as he walked towards the gate, leaving the village. No one said a word to them as they left.

Everyone just stared, wide-eyed, shocked. Nathan knew no one had ever come into their village and done such a thing. He walked through the gates and did not stop until he came to his wagon.

"Can you stand?" He asked.

She nodded, and he lowered her down, gently, keeping a hold of her in case she needed help. She was trembling. She looked up into his eyes but said nothing. His heart hurt for the tragedy she carried that was etched on her face.

"I promise not to hurt you." He hoped she saw the sincerity in his eyes. He gave a slight nod and gentle smile.

She looked away, then back up at him. He did not see trust in her eyes, but defeat. She looked as if her very soul had been beaten down.

"What is your name?" He asked, stepping back a bit to give her space if she wanted it.

"Abigail." She said in a small, raspy voice, still staring at the ground.

"My name is Nathan, Abigail." She looked up at him. "We've met before," he said, wondering if she remembered. He saw in her eyes that she did.

"Thank you, Nathan." He saw a sheen of moisture in her eyes. "You saved my life." She looked back towards the village, the gates now shutting her out. "My father would have beat me to death," she whispered, brokenly.

He was her father? The shock of that revelation left him speechless. How could a father do this to his own child? He wanted to take her in his arms, to comfort her, but he sensed that was not the best thing to do right now. He determined right then that he would not touch her without permission, ever. He stepped slightly away from her. Somehow, he knew without asking that she had never been asked what she wanted, never been given a choice about her life.

"Will you let me take a look at your back?" He asked, gently, hoping she would trust him at least a little. She gave a small shrug and turned slightly. Her gown was ripped down to her waist, and there was one wound that ran across the middle of her back. The bleeding had stopped, but it needed cleaning. Nathan went around to the back of the wagon and pulled out a jug of ale. He came back to where she stood. "I'm going to use this to clean your wound a bit." He showed her the jug.

She nodded, and put her hands on the wagon, leaning against it. Nathan pulled out his handkerchief and drenched it in the ale.

"I know this is going to hurt, and I'm sorry." He said, pain evident in his voice.

She gave a slight nod. Laying the cloth across the wound and pressing into it, he cringed when she gasped in pain. Her clenched fists turned white, her eyes squeezed shut. He felt the anger rise up in him. Those people had done this to her! They had hurt her, a defenseless girl! The need to protect her came again, and he determined that he would keep her safe, no matter what. No one would ever do this to her, again. He pulled the cloth off, gently rubbing at the edges of the wound, cleaning the dried blood off.

"All done," he said, stepping around her so she could see him. He saw the beads of sweat on her brow. She was a brave girl. Nathan would tell her that one day when the time was right. For now, he said nothing but offered to help her into the wagon.

"Would you rather sit in the back?" he asked, wanting to give her a choice, knowing even this small decision would be a first. She looked at him a moment then answered softly, "I'll sit with you."

That surprised him, but he was glad she would be next to him. He wanted her close, so he could watch over her. He helped her into the wagon, then grabbed the coat he had discarded earlier because of the warmth of the day. "Here, this will protect your back."

"Thank you." She let him drape the coat around her shoulders. Nathan walked quickly around the wagon and climbed up on the seat. He grabbed the reins and set the horses in motion at a gentle pace.

FOURTEEN

Abigail gripped her hands together in her lap trying to control their trembling. Fear and shock had depleted her of all strength. Her back was on fire with the lash. It took every bit of her willpower not to slump over on the seat – not to pass out. It all felt like a horrible nightmare. Had it really happened? Had her own father whipped her? She felt numb even though she shook. Her heart still pounded out her earlier terror, but she didn't feel anything else; no sorrow, no hate…just numb shock. She glanced at Nathan. His brow was furrowed as he kept his eyes on the road. She saw his shirt was torn, from his shoulder to his back, where he had taken the whip that was intended for her. Who was this man that had swooped in and saved her? He was strong, she could see that in the muscles straining his shirt and determined set of his jaw. She saw the sun catching the auburn hues in his dark hair. He didn't look like any of the men in her village who wore long beards. Nathan's jaw was smooth, and his skin glowed with the bronze hue of someone who spent a lot of time outdoors. Desperation had made her say yes to him, back there. What was her other option? She had resigned herself to dying. Then, this stranger had come in and asked permission to carry her out of the village, and she found herself completely at his mercy. Was this a cruel twist of fate that he came along to keep her alive? He had been kind in rescuing her, but what would he expect in return? She knew all about men and their expectations. She carried proof of that in her belly. She put a hand over her baby. She sat in this wagon, with a man she didn't know, going where she didn't know. She thought of Samuel and emotion overwhelmed her. She pulled Nathan's coat close and lowered her head, trying to hide the tears that threatened to spill down her cheeks.

What about Thomas? Had he watched all of it happen? She knew he had watched her father beat her, watched him humiliate her. He had watched and not cared. Thomas had never cared about her. He only cared about what she was; an object of his lust. She tried to discreetly wipe the tears from her face. She wanted to lay down and sleep, she was so overcome with exhaustion. It was only through sheer will that she stayed upright next to Nathan. What fate awaited her? Would he turn her into a servant to do his bidding? Would he demand that she fulfill his desires as Thomas had done? She glanced at him again and was suddenly aware of how small she was next to him. He could hurt her if he wanted too, and she couldn't stop him. He had to be the strongest man she had ever seen. She wanted to climb down from the wagon and run away, but where would she go? She had spent her whole life trapped by men. This didn't look to be any different. She was trapped, but this time by a complete stranger.

Will I ever be free to make my own choices? Her mind screamed.

She knew the answer, even as she thought the question. No, she would never be free to make her own choices. Her own body wasn't even hers anymore and never had been. She knew the truth. She was just an object - a *thing* - created for the pleasure of men.

~~~

Nathan glanced over and saw the tears trailing Abigail's cheeks. She was trying to hide her pain, and it grieved him deeply. So much tragedy had befallen her, even before today. He wanted to help but wasn't sure where to even begin. He slowly pulled back on the reins, steering the team off the road. He brought the wagon to a halt. They were far enough away from the village now that he felt comfortable stopping for a moment.

"We can walk down to the river and wash that wound a little better if you feel up to it." He didn't touch her, didn't even let go of the reins. He wanted her to make the decision.

She nodded.

Nathan tied the reins to the brake handle and jumped down. He came around to her side and helped her down. He marveled again at how tiny she was. He wanted to ask her how far along she was. He wanted to ask her so many questions, but he didn't want to cause her more pain. Less than an hour ago, he had been headed home from Boston, alone, and now he was responsible for the well-being of not just her, but her unborn child. *What am I going to do for her, Lord? I don't' know what to do.*

Take care of my lamb.

His breath hitched as the answer breezed through his soul. She looked up at him and the hesitation was apparent in her beautiful blue eyes.

"Can you walk?" He would carry her if she needed him too. He would carry her all the way home if she needed it. The need to protect her was so powerful inside of him.

"Yes," was her timid reply.

He grabbed the rags he kept in the back of the wagon,

and they set off for the river, not too far from the road. They came to the bank and Abigail sank to her knees as if she couldn't take another step. Nathan noticed but didn't say anything.

"I'll just soak these rags, make sure they are clean, and then we can tend to that wound a little better." He knelt down beside her, and dipped the rags in the water, bringing them up multiple times and squeezing them out. He watched her pull his coat off and turn her back to him. The wound was swollen red and the blood had already begun to dry over it.

"I'll be as gentle as I can," he said. Inflicting pain on her was the last thing he wanted to do. She lowered her head and said nothing as he set to work cleaning the wound. A minute later, he saw her shoulders begin to shake and realized she was crying, silently. He dropped the rag and moved around in front of her. He wanted to hold her, let her cry on his shoulder, but she barely knew him. There was no way she would trust him right now. He had to earn her trust.

"I'm sorry, Abigail." He whispered, hoarsely.

She made no noise as the tears dripped off her chin, and her body shook with sobs.

"I'm so sorry." He whispered, again. He sat beside her, arms draped over his raised knees while she cried. He didn't ask questions or try to stop her weeping.

Slowly, her sobs subsided until finally, she sat in silence, looking out over the river, eyes, and nose swollen from all the tears she had shed.

"Thank you," she whispered, voice raspy with emotion.

Nathan saw such sadness in her face. Had she never

seen kindness in anyone? He should tell her about himself. Maybe that would set her at ease a little bit.

"I live just outside of Weldon. My papa and I run our family timber business."

Her eyes reflected recognition. "Bradford Mills?" she asked.

"Yes! You've heard of us?" He was surprised that she knew of them.

"Yes. Your work is known by everyone between here and Boston." She gave him a small smile, and it made his heart soar. "I've heard of your business in my village. Some of our people have purchased timber from you for their homes."

"Ah. Well, I'm glad to know it." He responded.

"Do you live with your family?" She asked.

He hesitated, unsure of how she would respond when he told her it was just him and Papa. Would it make her afraid to know he was taking her to a house where only two men lived?

"My mama died when I was just a small lad." He said. He would tell her the truth, always.

"Oh. I'm sorry." She looked down at her hands, then back up at him. "I lost my mama too when I was a girl." She looked out at the river. "She died giving birth to my brother."

She has a brother! Nathan had not even thought to ask about her family when he had carried her out of the village. He had only been thinking of saving her.

"What is your brother's name?" He asked.

"His name is, S-Samuel." She faltered, obviously pained at the mention of him. "He was not there, today. My father sent him away to Boston yesterday." A tear slipped out as she spoke. "H-he sent him to Boston to l-learn a trade." She clutched her skirt in her hands as she spoke.

"I didn't know he w-was going, Father never told either of us. He just came in two d-days ago and told Samuel to pack his bag, because he was leaving the next day." She gasped as another sob escaped. "Samuel didn't want to go. He was scared." She put her hands to her face and wept.

"I'm so sorry, Abigail." He was at a loss for words, but he thought maybe what she needed right now was just a safe place to cry, to let her hurt come tumbling out. He would just sit here with her, let her cry as long as she needed. He sensed that no one had ever been there for her before, that she had been shouldering many, many burdens alone for many, many years.

FIFTEEN

Nathan looked down at Abigail, her blond head resting against his shoulder. She had fallen asleep sitting up. When she had started leaning over, he had carefully put an arm around her and pulled her close, so she could rest against him. His cabin was not too far from her village, only about an hour's ride. She nestled into him, and something warm unfurled in his middle; a need to protect her, yes, but something else Nathan couldn't name just yet. He knew she was exhausted from all that had transpired today. Carrying a child was enough to make a woman tired. Add to that, she had experienced more trauma in one day than some would see in their whole life, and he wasn't surprised she had fallen asleep sitting up. The cabin came into view, and while he hated to wake her, he wanted her to give her time to take it in as they arrived. He slowly brought the horses to a halt and the change in motion caused her to stir. She sat up slowly, looking a bit disorientated. She turned to Nathan, and he saw in her eyes when she realized she had been asleep on him.

"I'm sorry. Did I fall asleep sitting up?"

Nathan smiled. "You did, and with good reason." He pointed towards the cabin. "There's home."

She looked off in the distance and absently put a hand on her belly. He had seen other women do that before as if it was just second nature to constantly put a hand to their bellies, to check on the little life growing. She tried to put the other hand on her side but flinched and pulled it away quickly due to the pain it caused in her back. Nathan's eyes narrowed as he thought of those people again and what they had done to her. He would need to do some praying tonight. At the moment, all he felt was anger and the desire to make them all pay for what they had done to her.

"Papa might not be home right now. He is expecting me back, but sometimes he gets called to the mill unexpectedly." She nodded her response. Nathan set the horses in motion, again.

"It is a nice cabin," she said, softly.

"It is. Has plenty of room, too." He wanted to make her feel at ease, for her to hear him say that they had room for her, that she was welcome here, and that she would be safe. He wanted her to feel safe with him.

~~~

Abigail took in the scene as they came close to Nathan's cabin. Inviting, was the word that came to her mind. The cabin sat in a wide clearing and the forest formed a natural boundary around the area. She noticed wildflowers blooming along the edge of the cabin, where grass grew. The cabin was bigger than any home in her village, but it was simple. There was a wide porch stretching across the front with two rocking chairs in one corner. There was a large door in its center and a large window on each side. None of the homes in the village had windows. She expected something more elaborate for the owners of such a large mill company.

Nathan kept the horses going and went down the dirt road that circled around the house, to the barn. She took in the large building also made of wood, with two wide doors in the center. The barn was significantly larger than the house, but that was common. There were more animals to house in the cold winters than people. Nathan steered the wagon off the road beside the barn and brought the horses to a gentle halt. He looped the reins around the brake handle, then hopped down and came to Abigail's side. She let him help her out of the wagon, and stood with her head down, hands clasped. She didn't know what to do or say. She was in this new place with a man she didn't know. She didn't know what was expected of her and it made her nervous.

"If you'll wait here, I'll get the horses settled, then take you to the cabin, where you can rest. I didn't see Papa, so he must be down at the mill."

She looked up at him, and he smiled. She noticed his green eyes again. They were the greenest she had ever seen, reminding her of the grass that grew by the river in the spring. She saw kindness in them, something she never saw in people. She remembered seeing the same kindness that morning in the woods when he had offered to help her. Everyone in her life had always been angry or afraid. What she saw in his eyes captivated and confused her at the same time. How strange that it was him who came to her rescue today.

She nodded her response, and he set off to do as he said. She turned and looked out over the area. She knew the river was through the forest, to the right of the cabin. The town of Weldon was to the left, but she wasn't sure how far away it was. She had never been there. She had never been anywhere away from the village. She had watched her whole life as men left the village to work or to learn a trade, as Samuel had been sent away to do. Thoughts of him twisted her heart again. Was he okay? Was anyone looking

out for him? She wanted to go to him, but she had no way
to get there, especially now. Tears came at the thought of
her brother, alone, in Boston. She had promised she would
go to him, and somehow, she would keep that
promise…somehow she would get to him. She quickly
dried her eyes, not wanting to appear weak and weepy to
Nathan. She needed to be strong, to show him she could
take care of herself and her baby. She didn't want to
depend on anyone, anymore. Nathan had rescued her, and
she had nothing or nowhere to go, but she wouldn't let the
panic show. She must hide her fear. She had no choice but
to stay here for the time being. It angered her that she found
herself again at the mercy of men. She wanted to be rid of
men.

Nathan came from the barn after he finished with the
horses and led her around the front of the cabin. They
climbed the two small steps onto the front porch, and
Nathan pushed the door open, allowing her to enter first.
She took in the surroundings and wasn't surprised to find
the place practical and simply furnished. There was a table
and four chairs in the center of the main room, and a large
hearth lining the wall. She saw two large, cushioned chairs
near the fireplace. There was a hutch near the hearth and a
shelf that held two, cast iron cook pots. To the right of the
main room were two doors. Both led to a room, each with a
bed in the middle. She assumed Nathan and his father had
made all the furnishings in the cabin by hand.

"This will be your room," Nathan gestured to the room
farthest from the door and walked over to it.

Abigail hesitated. Which one of them used that room?
"I won't take one of your rooms. I'll sleep by the fire. I've

done it many times in my life." She didn't want any handouts! She didn't want to owe this man more than she already did. She wanted to earn her way, to prove she could take care of herself. Maybe she could earn enough money to go to Boston and find Samuel. A little leery, she watched as Nathan walked towards her. He still had that warm expression, as he approached her. Was it an act? Thomas was always good at pretending to be kind, but he wasn't kind when she was alone with him. Nathan stopped in front of her.

"Abigail. I want you to have my room while you are here with us. I know all of this is overwhelming, and you don't know me, but I want you to know you are safe here."

His emerald eyes warmed as he looked at her. "You are safe here."

She was not convinced, but she didn't have another choice. At least if she took the room she might have some privacy. Maybe.

"Very well." She said. "But I want to earn my way as long as I'm here. I don't want anything for free. I can take care of a garden. I can help in the barn, too." She wanted to prove herself. She needed to prove herself. She hated having to rely on this man for her well-being. She kept her eyes on Nathan's, waiting for his response.

"Well, can you cook?" He gave her a crooked grin that let her know he was teasing her. He confused her.

"Yes. I can cook." Her chin raised a notch. She didn't know if he would like anything she cooked, but she wouldn't tell him that.

"Good. Papa will be glad to have some help, seeing as I'm no good at it."

He moved to the hearth to get a fire started and exhaustion weighed on her so much that she gripped the chair at the table, feeling dizzy. Her back throbbed from the wound, and her body was tired from carrying this child. She was so tired - a tired that seemed to go so deep down in her bones that she didn't think she could ever sleep enough. She closed her eyes a moment, hoping the dizziness would pass.

~~~

Nathan noticed Abigail leaning on the chair at the table. She needed rest. She probably needed to go to bed and sleep until sometime tomorrow. He rose from the hearth and turned towards her.

"Would you like to rest, Abigail?" He hoped she would say yes. She was so tired. He saw it in the slump of her shoulders, the dark circles under her eyes. She needed to be taken care of, for once in her life. She raised her head up and looked at him.

"Perhaps, for a short while."

He was surprised she didn't say no and offer to work instead. She must be exhausted if she was willing to rest. He smiled at her and made his way to his room to collect the things he needed. He would sleep by the fire. He grabbed his work clothes that hung on a peg by his door and his Bible that was beside his bed. He went to the chest of drawers Papa had made him when he was a boy, and pulled out his nightshirt, along with extra stockings. He came out of the bedroom and stopped with surprise when he saw Abigail, sitting in the chair, head resting on her arms on the table, fast asleep. The sight of her there moved him with so much compassion that tears welled in his eyes.

He walked over and laid his things on the table, quietly. He went to her, and gently put an arm under her legs, and around her waist, then lifted her slowly, careful of her back. He didn't want to wake her. He wanted to tuck her in bed and let her sleep as long as she wanted. She stirred when he lifted her, but she didn't wake. He pulled her close and her head fell on his shoulder. He took her to his bedroom and gently laid her on top of the quilt the ladies in Weldon had made for him. The ladies of Weldon were always making things for him and Papa. Sometimes they brought pies, sometimes quilts. Nathan loved all of it and all of them. They were sweet ladies. Abigail stirred again when he laid her down but didn't awaken. She snuggled down into the pillow and curled her hands by her cheek. He stared at her, completely captivated. She looked like an angel right now. Her features were soft with the look of peaceful sleep rather than the sorrow and burdens she carried. She was beautiful, no doubt about it. She was strong, too. She had to be strong to survive all she had endured. He would need to ask about her child, about her life, but…for now…she would rest. He pulled the smaller quilt at the foot of the bed up over her and left the room, closing the door behind him.

SIXTEEN

Papa came into the cabin just as Nathan closed the door to his room. "Papa!" He whispered. Papa gave him a funny look when he whispered.

"We have a guest," Nathan said, moving towards the door where they could talk on the porch without disturbing her. Papa followed him outside and closed the door quietly behind him.

"Who?" He asked, moving towards his chair.

"It's her, Papa. The girl I met on the road that we've been praying for."

Papa paused before sitting down. "The same girl?" he asked, incredulous.

"The same," Nathan said. He moved over to the porch railing and leaned against it.

"Tell me the story," Papa said.

"I was passing the village today, on my way home, when I heard shouting coming from inside. I could tell from the noise that something was wrong. So, I tied the wagon down and went inside. I found a gathering in the center of the village, and discovered her there, in the middle of the gathering." He paused, seeing the scene again in his mind and feeling the same rage and pain he had felt at that moment. "She was tied to a whipping post in the middle of the village." He looked at Papa, who stopped rocking abruptly, concern creasing his brow. "They were going to beat her, Papa…and she is with child." Nathan's voice wavered as he spoke.

"Jesus, have mercy," Papa whispered.

"No one seemed to care about her well-being." He looked out at the woods. "I felt the evil in that place..." He looked back, tears forming at the memory that was still so fresh. "I *felt* it."

"I don't doubt it, son. Those people live under a cloud of darkness." He leaned forward, clasping his hands between his knees. "The devil rules it himself."

Nathan nodded. "Her own father was going to beat her. How could a father do such a thing?"

Papa didn't answer this time, just waited for Nathan to continue. Sometimes, Nathan just needed to voice the questions, even though he knew the answer. The answer was simple: Humanity was capable of wickedness when they gave darkness permission to reign in their hearts.

He sighed a heavy sigh. "They accused me of being the father. I let them think it. No one wanted the responsibility of taking care of her and her baby. Not even her own father. They acted as if she carried a disease they could catch." He struggled with the picture of her own father walking away from her. He had been so disgusted with her, so hard-hearted.

"The crowd finally gave in, and her father went along with them. He called me a fool, then walked away, without a second look." He looked back at Papa.

"What is her name, son?"

Nathan breathed deeply. "Abigail. Her name is Abigail." Saying her name stirred something in him, as if he had uncovered a hidden treasure by saying it. "I've seen already that she is strong and brave...and she is beautiful, Papa. She just doesn't know it, yet."

Nathan stared at nothing, seeing a pair of blue eyes

clouded with sorrow. She was quickly taking up residence in his mind, and his heart. He was surprised by how much. "She is sleeping, now. Her father managed to whip her once before I stopped him, and she has a wound across her back from the lash. It is clean, but I'm sure it hurts. She was so tired she fell asleep at the table. I had just carried her to bed when you came in."

"How far along is she?" Papa asked.

"I'm not sure. I didn't want to ask her questions just yet. She might sleep until tomorrow, which I hope she does." He stood up straight and Papa stood with him. "I don't care what the story is, Papa. There is no excuse for what was happening today when I found her. I have a feeling she hasn't had much choice about anything in her life."

Papa looked out at the woods a moment, gave a deep sigh, then turned back to Nathan, putting a hand on his son's shoulder.

"You did right today, son. You saved her, as I would've done had I passed by and heard the noise coming from that place. Now, we watch over her and care for her the best we can...and we pray for her."

Nathan nodded, knowing what Papa would do next. He moved his arm around Nathan's shoulder, and leaning in close, he began to pray for Abigail.

SEVENTEEN

Abigail opened her eyes to sunlight streaming in the window. She rolled over, and as the fog of sleep lifted, she sat up quickly, surprised by her surroundings. In an instant, it all came back to her. She was in a cabin and had been saved by Nathan from a purging. She moved to throw back the quilt and pain like fire seared her back. She breathed through gritted teeth and sat still, as the memory came rushing in. Nathan. Her father. The village. Samuel. The baby. She put a hand on her belly and her stomach growled. What time was it? How long had she slept? She didn't even remember going to sleep or how she had gotten to Nathan's bed. She slid out from under the quilt, moving a little slower this time. Her back felt tight where the wound was. She wanted to take her dress off, but she didn't have anything else to wear. Nathan had brought her from the village with nothing but the clothes on her back. She saw his coat at the foot of the bed, and when she reached for it she winced in pain. She heard movement in the cabin, and, once she had the coat on, walked to the door. She hesitated before opening it. Her hair had fallen out of its pins and hung around her shoulders. She needed to pin it back up, but she couldn't lift her arms without searing pain. She would just leave it, for now, and hope it wouldn't offend Nathan. She slowly lifted the latch and opened the door. She saw a man she didn't know, bent over something he was carving, by the fire. *Nathan's father.*

She was immediately apprehensive. She moved out of the bedroom cautiously, wishing she looked more presentable. Her father would never tolerate the way she looked right now, her hair down and her dress dirty and torn. Her gaze darted around the room. She didn't see Nathan, and that made her even more nervous. She didn't trust him either, but at least she knew him. This man was a complete stranger. When he saw her, he stood, and put whatever he was working on aside. He didn't move from his spot but smiled at her.

"Hello, Abigail. I'm Ian, Nathan's father."

He was an older version of Nathan. He was tall, and she could tell by his stance and his build that he was strong. He had dark hair with streaks of silver and a dark beard, trimmed close to his face. His eyes lit up with his smile. Nathan had obviously inherited his piercing green eyes from his father.

"H-hello." She said.

Ian moved to the table and pulled a chair out for her and gestured for her to sit. "Do you feel like eating something? You've been asleep long enough to work up an appetite." She saw the hint of tease in his expression.

"How long did I sleep?"

"Well, you were asleep when I came home yesterday, and Nathan had his breakfast a couple hours ago."

Abigail's eyes widened. Had she slept since yesterday? She was shocked. In all her life she had never slept so long. "I-I'm sorry. I've never slept that long before. You could have woken me."

Ian still stood by the chair he had pulled out. "You had good reason to sleep, so I'm glad you did. Are you hungry?"

She eyed him with a hint of suspicion, not sure what to

think of him. He had been kind, already. Her father would be outraged at her sleeping so long. She didn't know what to make of these two men. "Yes. I am a bit hungry."

"Good! Well, I have fried apples and potatoes leftover from breakfast." He went over to the small hutch and grabbed a tin plate with a towel over it. "Let me heat this a bit over the fire for you."

"I don't mind it cold. I've eaten many meals cold." She recalled memories of Father making her sit at the table and watch him eat his whole meal before letting her eat hers. He called it a lesson in patience. She had learned to eat her food cold. She looked down at the table, not wanting to give any indications of the memories that surfaced.

"It will only take a moment, since the fire is still going, strong."

She watched Ian set the tin plate on the small rack that hung over the fire. She walked over and sat down in the chair he had offered. She kept her hands in her lap, and her head bowed. She didn't know what would be expected of her at this table. She didn't want to break their rules. It already confused her that Ian would be heating up food for her. No one ever served her anything.

She took the moment while Ian warmed her meal to take in her surroundings again. She had seen it all yesterday, but everything about yesterday seemed like a dream - or a nightmare - and was a bit fuzzy.

She realized she needed to relieve herself. The bigger this baby got, the more often she had to visit the necessary. She didn't want to ask. Maybe they didn't have one since it was just the two of them. She rose slowly. "Is there a…necessary I can visit?"

Ian kept an eye on her plate, stirring the apples and potatoes so they didn't stick. "Ah! Yes. Behind the barn, on the edge of the woods."

Her shoulders dropped in relief. "Thank you. I'll be back shortly and will serve myself."

He nodded his acknowledgment, and she hurried out of the house. The sun was making its ascent, shimmering through the trees, and she paused a moment to take in the scene. This was a lovely piece of land. She saw the gardens off to the left, and going down the porch steps, she headed in the direction of the barn, remembering it was behind the house. She noticed a row of apple trees off to the side of the barn. A murmuring sound coming from the barn made her curious. She peeked around the corner of the door, not wanting to make herself known. Nathan was in there, his back to her, rubbing down one of his horses.

"You're a good friend, Duke. You've run hard lately." She couldn't make out everything he said, but he continued to talk quietly to his horse as he groomed him. She watched his movements and noticed that even with his horse, he was gentle and kind. Not wanting to be noticed, she hurried past the barn and was relieved to find a decent structure that was clean on the inside.

Feeling better once she finished, she made her way back towards the cabin. As she was passing the barn, Nathan came out. When he saw her, his face lit up.

"You're awake!" He walked over to her. "How are you, today?" He searched her eyes. He seemed concerned.

"I feel much better. A little sore." Her stomach rumbled, and she gave him a small smile. "And hungry. I met your father. He put food over the fire for me."

"I'll walk with you, then." He moved forward, and she followed beside him. "How's your back today?"

She didn't want to come across as needy. "Sore, but better today." She didn't want him to treat her like she was sick, or helpless. If she told him the truth, that she could barely move without pain, he would insist she rest some more. She didn't, though, because she didn't want to owe him more than she already did and if she let him take care of her, he might expect payment. The sooner she could start taking care of herself, the better.

~~~

Nathan noticed as they walked that Abigail was careful with her movements. He suspected that she was still in a lot of pain but didn't want him to know. The wound would be painful if it had already started scabbing over, which he guessed it had. She was very independent for someone who had grown up under such strict rules and with such a cruel father. He had been caught off guard when he came from the cabin and saw her standing there, her hair all mussed from sleep and flowing freely around her shoulder. She reminded him of a warrior princess, fresh form battle. He let her precede him up the porch steps, and noticed that she faltered a bit with the movement. His heart ached for her and what she had suffered. He hurried up the steps and opened the door for her.

"I have something for you." He said as she passed by him.

She stopped, looking at him with surprise and the smallest hint of curiosity behind her eyes. He smiled and ushered her in the cabin where her meal sat on the table, with a steaming cup of coffee beside it. He saw that Papa had added a small vase with wildflowers from the side of the cabin. He smiled at Papa's thoughtfulness. Abigail stopped, abruptly, staring at the table a moment, her brows knitting together as if she were confused. She looked at Ian, who sat by the fire, working with his wood, then at Nathan.

Nathan wasn't sure what was wrong, but he could tell something bothered her.

"Abigail?" he stepped up beside her.

"I…" She didn't finish, just stared at the table.

"Abigail, what's wrong?" Nathan asked. Papa stopped his carving and looked at her, brows furrowed with concern.

"You set the table for me?" she whispered the question, incredulous, then looked at Papa.

Papa set his work aside and stood slowly. He moved towards the table.

"I did." He looked directly into her eyes. Nathan watched the exchange, still unsure of what was wrong..

"W-why would you do that?" She asked in a broken whisper, staring at the table. When she finally looked up at him, he answered.

"It was my joy to set the table for you, Abigail." He spoke in the gentle, calm voice Nathan knew so well.

"Come and sit, Abigail," Nathan whispered close to her. "Sit and eat."

She moved quickly to the chair and sat, keeping her head bowed and her hands clutched in her lap. Why would the simple act of Papa setting the table cause her such distress? Nathan looked at Papa who gave him a small nod. Nathan knelt down beside her chair, careful not to touch her when he put an arm around the back of her chair.

"Abigail." He waited for her to look at him.

She did finally, and her eyes glistened with tears.

"You are safe here. Everything is different from what you are used to, but I promise you are safe here." He watched as one tear fell and he ached to pull her close. She was so lost, so wounded. What had she experienced in that village? What had they done to her? She didn't respond, but quietly picked up the fork, and began to eat. Nathan rose and looked at Papa over her head. Neither said anything, but Nathan saw in Papa's eyes that he understood, and agreed. The girl sitting between them was in desperate need of rescuing in more than one way, and Jesus had sent her right to their table.

EIGHTEEN

Abigail ate quietly, overwhelmed. She could not remember one time in her life when anyone had served her a meal and never at such a lovely table. Flowers? For her? The baby kicked, and she put a hand on her belly. She didn't know how to feel about this baby she carried. How would she feel when the baby came? What would she do? Where would she go? What if the baby looked like Thomas? What about these two men who were being so kind to her? What would they want in return? All the questions made her want to scream. She didn't, though. She ate, calm and quiet, just as she had done her whole life. Nathan sat down at the table beside her just as Ian slipped out of the cabin.

"This is for you." He was holding a large package, wrapped in brown paper and tied with red yarn. She looked at him, hand frozen on her fork. A gift? For her?

"Please, take it," he said.

She put her fork down and turned towards him a bit, taking the package. "What is it?"

"A gift," Nathan replied.

She looked up at him. "Why?" She searched his eyes, trying to find the reason for this. She saw only kindness but doubted that was his motivation. Never, in all her life, had she received a gift of any kind, much less from a man. Mary had shared food from her garden and Abigail would give other villager's loaves of bread, but those were all necessities, things they did to help each other survive.

"Open it," he said, soflty.

She untied the yarn and opened the package. Her eyes widened. It was a new dress. She looked up at Nathan, brows furrowed. "What is this for?"

He had a somber expression, but his voice was filled with compassion. "I know you only have the dress you are wearing." He gave her a warm smile. "You need another."

"When did you buy this?" She asked, voice shaky.

The dress was a deep blue that reminded her of the river. She ran her hand over the linen. She had never worn a color other than black. Could she? Should she? She did need another dress. She also needed something with more room in it for the baby who was growing quickly.

"I rode over to a friend's house, early this morning. She is a seamstress, and I thought she might have something. She had this in her own wardrobe and was happy to give it to you." He pulled it out of the package and pointed at the pleats in the waist.

"This one has pleats sewn in that can be let out when needed."

Had he really thought to get her a dress with room for her baby? She looked at him, speechless.

"I hope you like the color. I know you are used to wearing black, so I tried to get something close to it."

She hated the black dress she wore, but she wouldn't tell him. "Thank you. It is lovely." She would be glad to get out of this ripped, dirty dress. She didn't want a gift, though. She wanted to pay for it. She would pay for it when she earned enough.

"Will you let me check your back?" He asked.

"Yes." She needed him too since she couldn't do it herself. She should be mortified at the thought of a man looking at her back, but she wasn't. She was, after all, carrying a man's child. There was no such thing as privacy for her.

Nathan stood and went to a small hutch between his room and Ian's. He pulled out a tin and some rags, then grabbed a water jug. He came back to where she sat.

"Papa won't be back for a while. He went to the mill this morning to check some inventory." He smiled. "We can stay here if you don't mind turning around."

She stood, removed his coat, and sat down with her back to him. She pulled her hair over her shoulder and waited for the pain that was sure to come. She gripped the side of the chair and gritted her teeth when he pressed the wet rag to the wound. She knew he was being gentle, but it still felt like he was slicing through the wound with a knife. Tears rose, unbidden. The cold, hard reality of what her father had done overwhelmed her. She really had no one in this world except the baby growing inside of her and Samuel, if she could find a way to him.

She was just waiting for Nathan to demand payment for all he had done for her so far. He kept helping her, and the debt kept growing. She should run away before he demanded more than she wanted to give.

~~~

Nathan saw the wound and was relieved. It was scabbing over, but it didn't look infected. There were no streaks going out from the wound, and the inflammation had gone down.

"It looks a lot better than it feels," he told her. "I'm going to rub some of this ointment on it. The women in Weldon swear by it, and I have used it myself. It quickens the healing time and lessens the scarring."

"How far is Weldon from here?" she asked, as he carefully cleaned her wound.

"About an hour's ride from here."

He tried not to think about the fact that he was rubbing her bare back with his hand. He'd never touched a woman in any way, other than a kiss on the cheek for the widows at church. He pushed all wandering thoughts aside. He wanted Abigail to know she was safe here, that he would always treat her with respect, and never take advantage of her. He would admit, though, that this woman was beautiful and stirred him in a way no other woman ever had. There were girls in Weldon, close to his age, that would love for him to come call, but it had never felt right, so he had not pursued any of them. In a matter of twenty-four hours, this woman had come along and captured him like no other. It was his desire to protect her that surprised him. He always had been protective by nature. Papa told him his compassion for others was a gift and that he noticed what others didn't. Still, he had never felt such an overwhelming desire to protect a woman, until Abigail. He knew she wasn't weak. He had seen in the short time he knew her that she was the strongest woman he had ever met. She had endured more in just one day than some would their whole lives...plus what she had endured before yesterday. No, his need to protect her wasn't because he saw her as weak. It was because he wanted her to be free and to know she wasn't alone.

"All done." He rose from his chair and she stood with him.

"I think I'll go change into this new dress." She looked up at him and he saw the sadness had returned to her eyes.

He wanted to look in her eyes one day and see joy. "Then, you can show me what I need to do."

She was desperate to work, to earn her way. He understood her desire for independence, but he also wished she would let him take care of her, that she would allow herself to rest for a time. He would give her simple tasks today, and stay close by. Papa was down at the mill, so they wouldn't need him, today. Then, an idea occurred to him.

"If you are up for it, you can ride with me to Weldon. One thing Papa and I don't do is make our own candles and soap." He gave her a crooked grin. "You will need some soap for yourself and for cleaning. We are almost out. We also need to stock up on candles." He waited, praying she would say yes. At least this way he could keep her from working for now. They would go on horseback, which would be less tiresome than being jostled around in the wagon. "We buy from Widow Hatchet. She has been making soaps and candles for years. Best soap in New England, if you ask me. Don't know how she makes it so smooth, but she does."

"When will we leave?" She asked. He was relieved she was agreed, although she seemed to agree out of resignation, not necessarily a desire to go. He suspected she had learned in her life to say what she thought others wanted to hear.

"I just need to saddle Duke. Take as long as you need to change. There's a basin and pitcher in my room. Feel free to use it. There's a kettle on the fire right now so you can use the water to wash up if you'd like."

She nodded. "I will hurry."

"Take your time." He smiled at her, then went over to

the fire and, using the fire hook, grabbed the kettle from the back of the hearth. He set it on the stone base of the hearth and grabbed a towel to pick up the hot kettle. He hurried to his room and poured the water in the basin, steam rising as he did so. He went to his chest of drawers and pulled out bottom drawer, grabbing a towel. He laid it on the bed then left the room.

"I'll meet you out front when you are ready." He smiled at her, then placed the kettle on the stone near the fire to be filled again later.

She gave him a tiny smile, which made his heart soar, then went into his room and closed the door behind her.

NINETEEN

Abigail rode side saddle, in front of Nathan. She was relieved not to be in the wagon, even though being so close to Nathan was a little uncomfortable. She could not lean back against him because of her back. He seemed to sense her dilemma and had suggested she turn her shoulder towards him instead. She sat up as much as she could, given her situation. She grew tired, though, from keeping her back so straight.

"You can rest your head if you'd like," Nathan said, close to her ear.

Was she that obvious? Too tired to refuse, she leaned into him and laid her head against his shoulder. He was quick to adjust and move his arms comfortably around her. She breathed in his clean scent and felt something odd settle in her. Was it peace? She didn't know, really never had known what peace felt like. She had memorized the scriptures about God's peace as a child, but she doubted it was any more real than anything else He promised. She didn't believe much of what she had memorized as a child. How could she? She never saw or felt joy, peace, or any of the things supposedly promised to those who followed God. To her, God had been a selfish ruler. It occurred to her that Nathan had not mentioned anything about God since she met him. Did he believe in God? All she knew of him and his father, so far, was that they had been kind to her. Still, how far did that kindness go? When would it end? The fears and doubts overwhelmed her. She thought of Samuel, and panic rose like a stormy wave. Where was he? Could she find him if she went to Boston? She needed to figure out a plan, a way out. She was determined that she would not rely on a man for anything ever again. Her eyelids grew heavy, and the peaceful clip clop of the horse hooves lulled her into a sleep.

~~~

Nathan breathed in the scent of Abigail lying against him. She had fallen asleep on his chest. He kept Duke at a slow pace, wanting to let her rest, and enjoying the feel of her against him. It felt right, having her this close. He guessed that it wasn't because she trusted him that she laid against him but because she was too tired to sit up. She was still exhausted from yesterday. She had a hand on her belly as she slept. Nathan eased back in his saddle a bit, wanting her to be comfortable as they rode. He kept his arms around her, the reins loose in his hands. He felt the swell of her belly against his arm and it stirred his heart in a way nothing ever had before. He needed to find out the details about this child. It wouldn't change how he felt, but he wanted to know when the baby was coming and - when she was ready - he wanted to know the circumstances surrounding her child. *Jesus, give me wisdom. Show me how to help her.*

The outskirts of Weldon come into view and though he regretted it, he whispered to wake her. "Abigail. We are getting close."

She moved a bit but only snuggled closer into him, nestling her head under his neck. His heart stuttered, and warmth unfurled deep in his belly and spread all the way to his toes. He drew his arms tighter around her and leaned his chin against her head. Having her snuggled close felt right.

What was happening to him? What was this woman he had just met doing to him? He pulled Duke to a stop and sat a moment in the stillness. He wanted to sit there all day, just so he could keep Abigail close, and she could sleep. He looked down at her petite hands relaxed against her belly. How had she endured so much in her life? The trees rustled, and the sun spilled through the leaves onto them both. He closed his eyes and lifted his face to the sky, breathing deeply of the air scented with pine. The breeze was warm against his skin. Abigail moved again, her head sliding back on his shoulder. She gave a small moan, and her brows knit together. Was she dreaming? She moaned again - a sound of pain - and his heart twisted. Even in her dreams, she was burdened.

"Abigail." He whispered again, rubbing her arm a bit to wake her.

She opened her eyes and looked right into his. She sat up and looked around, still a bit dazed.

"We are close to Weldon." Nathan pointed ahead, and she followed his finger. He set Duke in motion again, at a slow pace, and thought to share a little about Weldon with her, hoping to set her at ease.

"Weldon sits close to the river. The town thrives on trade and being able to access Boston by boat. Many of our merchants have contracts with larger companies in Boston. Most families that don't have a trade of their own work for us at the mill."

He hoped she would enjoy seeing Weldon. He knew she had never left the village, so this would be a new experience. The familiar sounds of town greeted them as they entered. The docks bustled with men loading and unloading boats. Women hurried down the boardwalk with children in tow. The church house sat at the end of the town square with its tall, white steeple and bell used for signaling the church service and emergencies that came up in the town. The forest was dotted with the homes of those who lived in Weldon. It was a large settlement, and merchant shops lined the boardwalk on both sides. There was the dressmaker, baker, butcher and blacksmith. There were also men down by the docks who sold fish, shrimp and cod. Nathan breathed in the familiar smells of the bay.

"Is that where you bought my dress?" Abigail asked, pointing to the tailor's shop.

Nathan smiled. "No. I bought your dress from a friend who works out of her home as a seamstress. She is a widow and has three little mouths to feed. She lives between here and our cabin. She was happy to give you that dress. She said she wouldn't need it again because she isn't having any more babies." Nathan grinned, a twinkle in his eyes. "Of course, she could fall in love all over again, and then where will she be?"

He steered Duke towards the boardwalk, climbed down, and looped the reins around the post. He reached up to help Abigail down and she leaned into him as she slid off the horse. He saw worry in her face and wondered what was going on behind those blue eyes. He stepped away from her and led the way to Mrs. Hatchet's shop, which sat at the end of the boardwalk. He noticed the surprised glances he received from people passing by. Most people in Weldon knew him and Papa. They were responsible for a large percentage of the pay families received in Weldon. Papa was a good overseer, and he paid his workers well.

You would never know from how he interacted with people that Papa was the richest man in town. Still, Nathan had watched his Papa treat everyone like a friend and equal, and that had earned him a great amount of respect. Nathan nodded and smiled at those they passed. He recognized most faces, though some were unfamiliar. The colonies were booming, people flocking from all over Europe, and other parts of the world for a taste of life in this new land. New England was the most heavily populated colony, being that it was the first established in the last century. Most of the people who came here weren't after power or wealth. They simply wanted to earn a good wage, raise a family, and own a good piece of land to pass to their children. The Crown was pushing into dangerous waters with all the taxes they imposed from an ocean away. Nathan wondered how long it would be before Papa's prediction came to pass. Would the colonies really unite against the crown?

"Here we are." They stopped at a shop with a little wooden sign hanging out front that said, *Hatchet's Chandlery.*

Nathan opened the door and heard the bell jingle above them as they entered. He smiled when he saw Widow Hatchet straddling a big pot, with a large wooden paddle. She looked up at Nathan and her face beamed. "Well, it's a fine day indeed when a Bradford comes to call." Nathan grinned, wide. Widow Hatchet had come over to the colonies with her husband thirty years ago. They had raised two sons, both now merchants in Boston, raising their own families. Her husband had died two years ago from a fever. She had continued running their shop, even after he died.

Nathan made a show of removing his hat and bowing low to her.

"Milady. 'Tis an honor callin' on the prettiest lass in Weldon." He slipped into the brogue he knew so well.

Mrs. Hatchet chuckled, placing her hands on her hips. Nathan noticed she looked thinner. He hoped she wasn't working too hard.

"Oh, you and your flattery." She shook her head and chuckled again. "And who is this lovely creature?" she asked, wiping her hands on her aprons as she came around the counter.

"This, Mrs. Hatchet, is Abigail." He watched Abigail curtsy while keeping her eyes to the floor.

"Well, if you aren't the loveliest girl I've seen in a while." She peered at Nathan with a tease in her eyes. "What is she doing with you?" She asked, with a smirk.

Nathan feigned surprise then gave her a boyish grin. "Abigail is staying with us for a time, and we are in need of the finest soap and candles this side of Boston." He wouldn't go into the story. If Abigail wanted to tell people, it would be her choice.

"Only this side of Boston? I need to work harder, then." She smiled and went back behind the counter. "What kind are you after today?"

"Lye soap for cleaning, and whatever Abigail chooses for herself. I also need two boxes of candles." He looked at Abigail. "Pick whatever is your favorite." Her eyes were guarded, and he could tell she was afraid. "She has scented ones." He smiled and had to stop himself from grabbing her hand to squeeze it. He fisted his hand instead.

"Lye soap will be fine for me, too." She said still

refusing to make eye contact with Mrs. Hatchet.

"Oh, now you come look at these soaps. I'll not have such a beauty scrubbing her skin with lye soap when I have all these to choose from." Mrs. Hatchet's smile was bright.

Nathan was amazed that Abigail looked up and smiled back. Mrs. Hatchet wasted no time pulling out her sample tray and setting it on the counter.

"Come, find the scent you like best."

Nathan watched as Abigail hesitantly walked over to the counter. She waited a moment then, cautiously, as if she were afraid to do it, reached out and touched one of the soaps with a finger.

"These are lovely." She said, glancing up at Mrs. Hatchet.

"Have you never had scented soap, child?" She asked, softly.

"N-no. Only lye." Abigail smiled at Mrs. Hatchet.

Nathan stood there, watching intently, hoping for a clue about Abigail's life. Maybe Mrs. Hatchet could convince Abigail to take something. She didn't seem to want anything from him, but maybe that was because he was a man. He would understand that sentiment. She obviously felt safer with women. He watched her pick up a small sample and lift it to her nose to breathe in the scent. Her eyes opened wide and, for the first time since meeting her, Nathan saw pleasure in her face. He determined right then to do everything in his power to bring that look to her face as often as possible.

"Lavender." She whispered, closing her eyes. She opened them again and looked a Mrs. Hatchet. "Once, my father bought my mama a bar of lavender soap." She said it quietly, lying the sample back on the tray. "She loved the scent of lavender." She looked up at Mrs. Hatchet. "I'll take that one."

Mrs. Hatchet looked at her a moment, then with a slight tilt of her head said, "Wait here. I'll be back." She went behind the curtain to the back of her shop and Abigail turned and looked at Nathan.

"Thank you. This is a lovely shop and I like your Mrs. Hatchet."

Her smile was momentarily unguarded, and Nathan was mesmerized. "I'm glad," he said, smiling back. He was captivated by the way her eyes turned to sapphires when her smile was genuine. *Help her find your joy, Jesus.*

Mrs. Hatchet returned a few minutes later with a small package wrapped in brown paper, with a piece of purple ribbon tied around it.

"For you, Abigail. A gift." Nathan saw Abigail's brows knit together.

"B-but why?" She asked barely above a whisper.

"I happen to think God, in his way of working, sent you in here today, to remind you of your mama, who loved you very much." She looked intently at Abigail and placed her hands on top of Abigail's that held the soap. "Think of your mama when you use this, and remember that God cares about the little things."

Nathan watched the exchange, astonished. God had clearly orchestrated this little encounter. Mrs. Hatchet couldn't know all that Abigail had endured, yet she spoke right to her heart. He watched a lone tear fall down Abigail's cheek.

"Thank you," she said.

Mrs. Hatchet turned to Nathan then, her teasing grin back in place, but also a sheen of tears in her eyes. "And how is your papa these days?"

"He's good. Keeps busy with the mill. I'll tell him to stop in and say hello next time he's in town." He turned to Abigail. "We best be off. I want to stop at the baker's shop on our way out of town. There's something I want you to try." He smiled, and she nodded, fidgeting with the ribbon tied around her gift. He looked at Mrs. Hatchet and saw her brow raised and a tiny smirk on her face.

"Thank you again, Mrs. Hatchet. I'll treasure this gift," Abigail said, clutching the soap close.

"My pleasure. Come see me again, soon." She handed Nathan the small sack of lye soap and the two boxes of candles. He gave her a discreet wink.

"See you soon, Mrs. Hatchet." He ushered Abigail to the door and before he could exit behind her, he felt a hand on his arm.

"That child is in need of love, Nathan. Desperately in need of it." Mrs. Hatchet whispered, with tears in her eyes. "However, she ended up with you, it is clearly God's hand."

"I know. He sent her to us. Pray for her, Mrs. Hatchet. She's a wounded soul."

Mrs. Hatchet smiled a knowing smile and patted his arm. "And she's pretty, too."

With another wink, he kissed her cheek and left to the sound of her soft chuckle.

~~~

Abigail sat atop Duke, in front of Nathan, holding the soap Mrs. Hatchet had given her. She had received two gifts in one day, after a lifetime of never receiving a single gift. It was all overwhelming. When they had left Mrs. Hatchet's shop, Nathan had taken her to Cromley's Bakery. She had never seen so many pastries and breads. She thought of Mary and could just see her standing in the bakery, delighted at all the beautiful choices. She felt pain at the thought of her friend, still trapped in the village. Feeling a bit unsure about the pastries, she had chosen a simple biscuit. Nathan had wanted her to try one of the sweet pastries, but she was afraid. Even though she wasn't in the village, she still feared breaking their laws. She unfurled her hands a bit and looked at her soap.

"She's one of my favorite people," Nathan said softly.

She turned slightly, looking at him. "I can see why." Abigail had liked her instantly. She seemed sincere as if she truly cared about Abigail's memory of her mama. It all overwhelmed Abigail and made her even more cautious. Nathan, his father, Mrs. Hatchet -they showed her more kindness in one moment than she had experienced in a lifetime. Worry and fear crowded her mind, and she clutched the soaps in her lap, silent for the rest of the ride back to Nathan's cabin.

TWENTY

Abigail sat on the bench, in Weldon's meetinghouse, every one of her senses alert. She didn't know what to expect here, from these people. She was flanked on both sides by Ian and Nathan. Nathan had invited her to come to the Sunday service but hadn't insisted she come. She didn't know how he would react if she didn't come. So, she had said yes to coming, even though everything in her wanted to stay away. She kept her hands clutched in her lap and her head down. That's what she would do in her own meetinghouse, so she assumed that was the proper posture here. She heard murmuring and chatting among the crowd, and it set her heart to pounding. *Talking?* No one talked in her village gatherings. They came, sat, listened, then left.

"Good morning!" Abigail heard a man say and her head came up in surprise.

"Good morning," people in the room responded. Even a couple of the children responded with giggly good mornings.

Abigail looked around, eyes wide with shock. What was going on? The man up front looked to be about her father's age, but he had no beard, and he didn't wear anything to signify he was an elder, or whatever they would call him. The elders in her village wore special black robes, and they all had beards. This man was average height, but stocky. He looked like he could just as easily be sitting in the crowd, rather than leading the gathering. Abigail's eyes narrowed a bit as she continued to study him. Nothing about him reminded her of the elders in her village. He put his hands on his hips and surveyed the group, with a big smile.

"Well now, it looks like we've all come ready to receive whatever the good Lord has for us." He smiled a big smile.

Abigail stared, incredulous, as people responded with, "Amen".

"Let's pray before we begin." The man up front said.

Nathan leaned forward, resting his elbows on his knees, leaning his head against his fists. She cut her eyes to Ian, who mirrored Nathan with his stance. She saw others do the same, while some simply bowed their heads. She saw a blond, curly headed little girl, bring her hands together in front of her and look at her mama for approval. The little girl's mama smiled and nodded, doing the same thing her daughter did.

What kind of gathering is this?

These people were participating in this service. They weren't spectators. They were engaging in prayer with the man up front, who she assumed now to be their head elder.

"Gracious Lord, we've come as we are, today, knowing full well that your grace is sufficient. Show us how to love you, and love each other as we listen and think on your word. Amen."

Was that a prayer? Abigail assumed so since everyone murmured, *Amen,* then looked back up at the man. Nathan leaned in and whispered, "That's Weldon's Reverend."

She nodded, eyes glued to the man up front.

So, they call him, reverend.

"What is love, friends?" He walked out from behind

his modest, wooden podium, with one hand on it. "Can anyone really know it? Can we see it, touch it? How can we know love?"

The crowd sat silent, but Abigail didn't sense fear in this room. She sensed anticipation of what the reverend was going to say.

"I dare say none here would raise a hand and say they've figured it out." He smiled, looking into faces as he spoke. He walked over to where a family sat on the front bench, and…

Abigail unconsciously brought a hand to her throat as she watched the reverend squat down in front of a little boy. *What is he doing?*

"Do you know what love is, sir?" He asked the little boy, loud enough that everyone could hear. Then, he tweaked the boy's knee, and the boy elicited a little giggle. The crowd chuckled.

"Yes sir!" The little boy said.

"You do?" The reverend asked, looking as if the boy were about to reveal a great mystery.

The little boy nodded, vigorously, then, "My mama makes us cookies sometimes, as a surprise, because she loves us!"

"Ah! Of course!" The man stood. "Cookies made by a mama are definitely the definition of love."

More chuckles from the crowd. The reverend grinned, then went back behind the podium.

Abigail sat in astonishment. What in the world was this gathering? Was this how every Sunday gathering went? She felt no fear in this place. And children, talking? People participating? It all confused her.

"This is love, friends. That while we were still doing what we please, still living in sin, God chose to send his son, and let Him die in our place."

Murmured amens went up in the room, again.

"Just like a mama, who makes cookies for her son," he winked at the little boy. "She doesn't make those cookies because he never makes mistakes. She makes cookies for her son because she delights in him, loves to see him enjoy the gift of a cookie."

He looked out over the crowd, and then his eyes seemed to zero in on Abigail. "God's love is like that," he paused. "He gives us good gifts because he wants to, not because we never make mistakes."

Abigail's heart was beating wildly, now. Never in her entire life, had she heard such things! God didn't give good gifts! God expected penance for the sins of men. The balance between his acceptance and rejection was like walking a tightrope. If a person wasn't careful, they would fall off the rope, into the dark abyss below. God had never given Abigail a good gift. Never.

She listened, as the Reverend talked about sin as if everyone struggled with it, and it didn't need to be hidden. He talked about Jesus, and how he makes us worthy in the sight of God. He went on to share a story from his own life, of a time when he needed forgiveness and asked God for it. He said God gave it, freely, and he had felt peace flood his soul in that moment.

A God who forgave, freely? It sounded absurd and unrealistic. Jesus had never been someone she understood or heard much about in her village. All she knew of him was that, because he died, she was even guiltier of sin.

Nathan leaned back and stretched his long legs out in front of him, then crossed his arms over chest. Relaxed…that's how the people looked, here. They all looked at ease, comfortable with each other and the reverend.

Abigail rubbed a thumb over her knuckles, concentrating on the action while trying to think through all of she was seeing and hearing.

She startled when Nathan leaned over and whispered, "I'm glad you came today."

She turned her head enough to look into his emerald green eyes. *How are his eyes that green?* He smiled, and they lit up like a match being struck. She didn't respond, didn't smile or nod. She just turned back to the reverend and stared, until the end. Who were these people and what did they expect of her?

TWENTY ONE

"Would you like to help us gather apples today, Abigail?" Ian asked sitting up from his work beside her in the garden. They were picking beans, today. Abigail sat up on her knees, shielding her eyes from the sun. It was a warm, breezy day. Summer and autumn were blending together. Some days were warm, while others were crisp.

"If you like, I can show you my grandmother's apple pie recipe, tonight." He looked hopeful as if he would be disappointed if she said, no.

Why does he care?

Abigail wiped her hands on her apron. "Yes. I can do that." She had been with Ian and Nathan for one month, now. They had not changed their behavior towards her. They made no demands, constantly gave her choices. She felt her insides starting to relax around them as if she were truly breathing for the first time in her life.

"Good, then!" Ian jumped up and wiped dirt from his knees. "I'll go grab Nathan."

He put his hands on his hips and smiled that smile Abigail had come to expect. It lit his whole face as if he smiled from the inside out.

"Nathan has always loved apple picking." He grabbed his pail full of beans. "Mine is full, so I'll head on in and wash up."

Abigail nodded. "Mine is too. I'll just finish this row, then come."

Ian walked off towards the cabin, and Abigail sat there, staring after him. He was nothing like her father. She couldn't find a single thing they had in common. Ian smiled and laughed a lot. Abigail marveled at his interaction with Nathan. They were father and son, but they were friends, too. She had always felt like a burden to her own father. She released a deep sigh and hurried to finish the row she was working on. She stood and brushed the dirt from her skirt. Soon, it would be hard to sit and stand. Her belly was growing by the day. She saw Nathan coming around the house from the barn and met him as they were walking back towards the cabin.

"Let me take that," Nathan reached for her pail.

Abigail was reminded of the first time she encountered him when he had rushed to fill her water pail. He still rushed to help her when he saw the chance. He treated her like she was...special? She wanted to reject that idea. She couldn't, though. The more she got to know him, the more she found nothing to make her suspicious of his motives.

"I hear you're coming to pick with us!"

She smiled. "I am." She untied her hat and pulled it off. She had taken to wearing a straw hat rather than a coif, when Nathan had come in one day and offered it to her with the explanation that she might need it when working outside, to keep her face from burning. She still kept her hair wound tightly at the nape of her neck, but she loved her new hat.

"How's Duke, doing?" She knew how much Nathan loved his horse and that Duke had been struggling with some stiff muscles.

"Better. He needs some exercise. I think I'll take him for a ride later, today. Want to come with me?" His expression was hopeful.

"Well, Ian offered to show me his grandmother's apple pie recipe after we pick apples."

"Well, by all means, don't let me get in the way of that lesson! I can think of nothing tastier than my grandmother's apple pie." He closed his eyes and breathed deeply as if he could actually smell one baking out in the open air.

Abigail smiled. "Well, I doubt I'll come close to making one as good as she did, but I do want to learn."

"If you want to ride with me, we can go after the evening meal." He stopped and faced her. "I have a favorite spot I like to go and watch the sunset."

Abigail's heart skipped a beat at the tender expression on his face. She nodded.

"Come on, we have apples to pick!" He set off ahead of her, running like an excited little boy. How did he find such joy in life? Abigail desperately wanted to feel that way, but how could she? Her life had been one heartbreak after another. There was no joy in it. She did admit to herself that she was beginning to crave what she saw in Ian and Nathan…whatever it was.

~~~

Nathan peeked through the limbs down at Abigail. She was helping Ian pick from the low hanging limbs, and collecting the apples littering the ground. She was so beautiful. He caught himself, in moments when she didn't know, just gazing at her. She walked with grace and dignity, despite all she had suffered, and it amazed him. He had to stop himself often, from reaching out to her. She had never been touched by a man in a way that made her feel safe, and he didn't want to give her any reason to feel unsafe with him. So, he kept his distance. Papa did too. She looked up through the trees, and he grinned.

He nodded towards her basket that sat on the ground. "Basket's almost full. How are you feeling?" She worked so hard. Nathan had noticed that she didn't really allow herself to rest even though he knew she was often tired. She always looked completely exhausted.

She dumped a few more apples in the basket then looked up at him. "I'm fine."

She always said she was fine. He knew how good she was at keeping her feelings to herself. He hoped she would start being honest with him, eventually.

Ian walked over to her and looked up at Nathan. "I'll carry her basket back." Papa was good about discreetly taking care of Abigail.

Nathan smiled. "Sounds good, I'm about done." He looked back at Abigail. "Will you wait?" She nodded. Nathan found himself wanting to spend more time with her. He thought about her constantly. When he worked at the mill or here at home, he wanted to hurry through the work, so he could get back to her. Every time he walked into the cabin and saw her standing near the fire stirring a stew or at the table chopping vegetables, a longing filled him. It felt right, having her here in his home.

Papa hoisted her basket in one hand, and his own in the other, then set off towards the cabin, calling over his shoulder, "See you both in a bit!"

Abigail walked over to the edge of the orchard and looked off into the forest, with a hand to her belly. Nathan plucked a few more apples then, carefully, came down the ladder with his basket in hand. He set it on the ground and made his way over to her. She looked lost in thought and didn't seem to notice him. He stopped beside her and clasped his hands behind his back.

"Why are you so kind?" Her question seemed to barely make it past her throat.

Nathan froze. This was the first time she asked him anything outside of wanting to know how to do something, or what chores needed doing. The fact that she was asking such a question caused his heart to leap with joy. He shoved his hands in his pockets. Abigail folded her arms across her chest and looked at him. Was she trying to shore up her heart, guard it against him and what he might say?

The thought that she was afraid to ask him an honest question, yet asked, filled him with tenderness. He wanted her trust, desperately wanted it. He looked out into the forest, thinking about his answer.

"I've received kindness, and I know the power of it." His eyes connected with hers. After a moment she looked off in the distance, again.

"I've only seen kindness in three people…" She said.

Nathan waited, silently pleading that she would share her thoughts with him.

"My mama, my brother," her voice faltered, "and my friend, Mary." She turned towards him, her expression stormy. "All were taken from me."

Nathan's heart hurt for her. Every good thing had been torn from her life. She had no reference for lasting kindness. Nathan would be faithful to her if she would let him. "I'm sorry, Abigail," he whispered.

She turned around and looked towards the cabin. Nathan faced her, studying her profile. He saw the storm raging inside of her. She was panicked, thinking she couldn't accept his and Papa's kindness because it would not last. He knew better than to promise that she wouldn't suffer ever again - he couldn't make that kind of promise. He would be with her in any and everything, though, if she would let him.

"I know you're kind, Nathan. I think I believe that." She looked him in the eye. "But I know it won't last. How long will it be before you fade away?" Tears filled her eyes and her next words came out raspy. "I've never been able to hold on to anything good."

"I won't abandon you, Abigail. Ever." He took a small step forward, searching her expression for any sign that she believed him.

"Even if that is true it won't matter." She looked at the ground then back at him. "Because God will take it all away...eventually." She sniffled and wiped the tears from her face with her fingers. "He always takes everything away from me."

With that, she walked off towards the cabin leaving Nathan to stare after her. What was he supposed to say to her? He was at a loss, sometimes, as to what he could do for her. There wasn't an easy answer, no words that would make all the memories and pain melt away. Once she disappeared around the corner of the cabin he turned and walked off into the woods, frustrated. Lost in thought he suddenly found himself at the bank of the river. He picked up a couple of rocks and threw them, one at a time, watching them skip across the water. Abigail was hurting, grieving the deep kind of grief that has the power to swallow you whole. Nathan knew there was hope for her, but hope could easily be buried under the rubble of despair. Her life was one of deep sorrow and tragedy. He sat down by a tree and leaned against it, staring out over the river. Why did life have to be so hard? Why were people so cruel to each other? Those weren't new questions. Nathan had been asking those question all his life. He knew the answer was the same as it had always been: this world was decaying under the influence of darkness. Papa told him as a boy to hold tight to his compassion, to guard it like a treasure. It was hard, though, feeling the ache of hurting people. Abigail's pain was the most horrid he had ever encountered, and his heart broke with grief for her. He stayed there a while, thinking and praying about how he could prove to her that he could be trusted.

TWENTY TWO

Abigail stood at the table peeling apples for another pie. Cooking was becoming something she loved. She was learning how to make so many different dishes. The village law said that food should be simple and bland to avoid the temptation of earthly pleasure, so they boiled a lot of their vegetables and made a lot of porridge. Abigail realized she had never enjoyed cooking, until coming here. The first time she had tasted Ian's squash and potato stew, her eyes had widened. She had never tasted anything so good! Ian had been patiently teaching her, explaining how he made things and what different flavors were used for. She loved learning but - if she were honest - what she really loved was the time Ian spent with her. He didn't just instruct her in cooking, he talked to her, asked her thoughts on things and made her laugh with funny stories. She wondered if that was how a father and daughter were supposed to be together and then she wondered what it would be like if Ian were her father.

She paused, apple in hand, as her father's face came to mind. Then, she thought of Mary and their last conversation before both of their lives had completely unraveled. Mary had been excited to try new foods in Boston. Abigail felt a twinge of sadness. How was Mary? She looked down at the apple in her hand and also thought of Nathan and their conversation by the apple orchard. He was kind, she knew it, but she also knew it wouldn't last. Somehow, she would lose his kindness - lose him – and it scared her because Nathan was becoming important to her.

She knew God didn't see her as worthy of kindness, and that was the reason he always took it from her. Her mind was constantly spinning, trying to come up with a plan to get away from Nathan and Ian before they were taken from her – before here heart could be broken all over again.

She put a hand on her belly. Her baby had grown some in the weeks she had been here. She had let one pleat out of the dress Nathan had given her. The stage of sickness had passed, with only an occasional upset stomach and a little pain in her chest after she ate. The baby would come in autumn, and she needed to figure out a plan before then. She was sure Nathan and Ian wondered when the baby would come, but neither had asked her anything. They just took her in, without question, and provided for her needs.

She needed to find a way to Boston, to find Samuel. Every time she thought of him, panic filled her, and tears rose. She hadn't asked Nathan or Ian for help in finding him. She was afraid to ask them, and she wanted to be independent, to make a way for herself without relying on help from a single person. Even Nathan, as kind as he had been so far, would not be reliable in the end. No one ever was. No, she wouldn't ask anyone for help, ever.

She finished preparing the pie, then set it aside to be baked a bit later. She would need water for cleaning dishes after the evening meal, so she grabbed the bucket and made her way out of the cabin towards the river, arching her back a bit as she walked to stretch the tightness out of her muscles. She heard the faint sound of the mill saws in the distance. She was curious about the mill and thought it would be neat to see it. Maybe Nathan would take her. Both he and Ian were at the mill today. She allowed herself a leisurely stroll to the river. Her burdens were still heavy, but something in her was shifting as if a part of her burden had lifted. Maybe being here with Nathan and Ian was helping. She admitted to herself that she did feel safe here, with them. She didn't really know if she could trust them but for the moment, she did feel safe.

She weaved in and out of the trees, enjoying the peaceful sound of the wind rustling the leaves. She heard the river moving just ahead, and picked up her pace. She saw a flash of movement behind a tree and stopped.

"H-hello?" Had it been a person or an animal? When there was no answer she continued on, assuming she had seen an animal. Just as she reached the edge of the river, she heard the crunch of leaves behind her and whirled around.

"Well, well. If it isn't the runaway."

Abigail stared, eyes wide with shock and horror. *Thomas!* What was he doing here?

"I must say, you have quite the little picturesque scene out here." He came close and circled around her, hands clasped behind his back.

Abigail's heart began to pound in her ears. "What are you doing here?" She rasped.

"Why, I've come to check on you, my pet." He smiled, and the hair stood up on her arms. "Tell me," he stepped close and without warning, yanked her to him with an iron grip around her back. "Is he the father? Did you run away with your lover?"

She pushed him away, angry. "You know the answer to that! You are the father of this child." She stepped away from him. "You plotted everything out didn't you? You planted that paper in the village, to stir up suspicion, then lied about me to my father."

He stepped up and grabbed her braid. "What's *this?*" He spit out the question. "Breaking more rules, are we?" He pulled the braid, forcing her to step close. "Now, tell the truth, my pet. You miss my touch, don't you? Miss me, don't you?"

He held her braid in his hand and she couldn't back away from him. She narrowed her eyes, not thinking rationally.

"No," she said through gritted teeth. "I will *never* miss you, or your touch."

His eyes went dark, in the same way they did when she had told him the truth about the baby.

"Well...I shall just have to remind you of all that you've missed, won't I." He yanked her close and kissed her hard. She struggled, tried to push away, but she wasn't strong enough. He pushed her to the ground and she screamed, hoping someone was close by. He put a hand over her mouth. He had never done this in public. He must be going completely mad! She clawed at the dirt and tried to throw it at him, but he pinned her down with both arms.

"You can't fight me, pet." He leaned down and spoke in her ear. "I know you better than you know yourself, remember? "She twisted, kicked her feet. He might hurt the baby! If it were just her own safety at risk, she wouldn't care what he did to her, but she had to protect her baby.

Oh, God! Help me! She never asked God for help, but she was desperate, panicked. Thomas was going to rape her, while she carried his child.

~~~

Ian and Nathan were talking with Matthew outside the mill, when they heard a sound. All three stopped, listening. There it was again. A scream. Nathan's heart began to pound in his ears. *Abigail.*

"Go, Nathan! Go!" Papa said it and Nathan's feet took flight. He ran with all his might, back towards the cabin, listening for the sound again. It had come from the woods. He veered off the dirt road and ran through the forest, jumping branches and dodging trees. He stopped a moment to catch his breath, and listen. He heard a sound. It sounded like a laugh, a man's laugh. *God, where is she?* He stopped, breathing hard, his eyes darting in all directions looking for a sign of Abigail.

He heard a muffled cry and ran in the direction of the sound. He came to a clearing near the river and what he saw was like a punch to the gut. Abigail was pinned beneath a man. Fury like a blazing fire filled his veins, heating his blood to a raging boil. He ran towards the man and with a guttural cry from deep inside, grabbed the man's shirt and yanked him off of her. The man landed on his back but came quickly to his feet. Abigail scrambled to her feet and Nathan pulled her behind him. The man ran at Nathan with a predatory expression. When he got close enough, Nathan punched him in the gut and he fell to his knees. Nathan pulled Abigail from behind him and pushed her in the direction of home.

"Abigail! Go back to the cabin! Now!" He kept his eyes on the man before him but heard her running off towards the cabin.

The man stumbled to his feet, and Nathan wasted no time knocking him down again with a punch to his jaw. He felt the skin on his knuckles crack open, but he didn't care.

"You want what is mine?" The man spit the words out with blood from his busted lip.

Nathan grabbed his collar, still blinded by rage that gave him increased strength. "Abigail belongs to no one, least of all you!" He said through clenched teeth, bringing the man's face close. He pushed the man away and he stumbled backwards, falling to the ground. He clamored back to his feet and wiped the blood from his lip with his sleeve. "Abigail belongs to me, to us. We will come for her, just you wait."

Nathan was about to go after him again when he felt a hand on his shoulder.

"Son," came that steady, firm voice behind him. *Papa.*

Nathan took only one step forward. "If you ever come near her again, I'll do much worse. You have my word." Nathan's chest was pumping from the fight.

The man turned and ran off. Nathan wanted to run after him and pound him until he couldn't speak or move. He stood there, breathing hard through gritted teeth, fists clenched at his sides, body trembling with fury.

"Go to Abigail, Nathan," Papa said behind him. "Go, now."

Abigail.

Getting back to Abigail was more important than chasing down that wretched man. He turned and ran towards the cabin. He burst inside and found her huddled in a corner, rocking back and forth, weeping. His heart broke into a million pieces at the sight of her. He went over and knelt down in front of her, still breathing heavy from running and fighting. He didn't touch her because he wasn't sure of her frame of mind.

"Abigail," he spoke as calmly as he could. She put her hands over her head, shaking it back and forth, and continued to weep.

"Abigail." He said it more forcefully, trying to get her attention. She didn't respond. As a last resort, he reached out and carefully took hold of her arms. She gasped and twisted, then looked up at him. "Abigail." He said again, firm but pleading. "It's me, Nathan. I'm not going to hurt you." He searched her eyes, still glazed over from shock. "It's me," he whispered.

He saw when she snapped out of it. Her shoulders slumped, and her arms fell in her lap. Her legs slid out in front of her and he moved to sit beside her. Her cries became less fearful and more sorrowful, wrenching a hole in his gut. She fell against his shoulder and it was all the prompting he needed. He wrapped her in his arms, pulled her close and let her cry on his chest. He didn't say anything. Right now she was too consumed with shock and fear to talk. She just needed to cry. Nathan guessed that had been the father of her child. Never had he been so overcome with the desire to destroy something or someone. Never had fury filled him so possessively. He was almost blinded by his rage, and would've run the man down if not for Papa's steady hand on his shoulder. His voice had come to Nathan through the haze of anger and reminded him that running back to Abigail had been more important. The man had been crazy, looked possessed. Seeing the man who had done this to her made the pain in his own heart even more real. He was going to protect her forever, no matter the cost.

Papa came quietly into the cabin and when he saw them in the corner, gave a small nod and left again. Nathan knew he wanted to give Abigail space, not to overwhelm her with both of them in the room after such an experience. After a time, her tears quieted to soft sighs. Nathan pulled his handkerchief from his pocket and placed it in her hand. She sat up, wiped her face and her nose.

"He is the father." She rasped.

"I know," Nathan said, quietly. His gut had told him the truth.

"The baby is coming in the fall." She sniffled as she spoke.

Nathan didn't say anything, just listened, rubbing his hand gently over her back as she cried.

"He has used me s-since I was a girl. It's my earliest m-memory." Her voice broke on the words. Nathan felt sick. He clenched his fist to control his own emotion. What a depraved, demented man. He had raped her when she was a child? He leaned his head back on the wall, and closed his eyes, listening as she shared. She was trusting him with her rawest pain, and while it hurt to hear it, he was honored that she was willing to share.

"When I was a girl, I would try to hide in the corner from him." She sighed through her tears. "It never worked."

When she looked up at Nathan he saw the same sorrow he had seen that first day he met her. She carried a depth of heartbreak like none he had known before.

"I only fought him because of my baby." Her voice quivered, and she wiped her tears away with the sleeve of her dress.

He raised one knee and turned towards her. With one finger, he raised her chin, so she looked him in the eye. "You are worth fighting for, Abigail." He searched her eyes then said it again. "You are worth fighting for."

She didn't say anything, and she didn't look like she believed him.

"Thank you for saving me, again." She looked away. "He may come back."

"He won't ever hurt you again, Abigail. You have my word." He said it with such gravity.

"Are you really this kind?" She asked, searching his eyes for the truth.

He brushed the hair from her face that had come completely out of her braid.

"I'm not perfect, Abigail, but I do my best to be who God asks me to be." He looked down at his knuckles, swollen from the fight. "I try to be like Jesus."

She leaned her head against the wall and stared at nothing.

"I don't know about Jesus, or God. Neither of them have done anything for me. All I've seen of your God is rules and punishment."

"That isn't God," Nathan said, softly. "God is love, deep abiding love. You haven't seen that from the people in your life, but it is real, and He feels it for you, Abigail."

He knew she heard him, but he also knew that his words didn't settle in her heart. She didn't believe him, yet. Her head fell against his shoulder. He laced his fingers through hers and leaned back against the wall, closing his eyes. He would prove it to her, show her what real love looked like. He prayed silently, for her heart to soften and her eyes open to the truth; that Jesus' love for her was fiery and deep. *Show me how to love her like you do, Jesus.*

~~~

Later that night, Ian and Nathan sat at the fire, talking. Ian saw the war raging behind his son's eyes. Nathan had insisted Abigail go to bed after the evening meal. Exhaustion from all the trauma of the day weighed on her, and she needed rest. Ian watched the way Nathan cared for Abigail. He had always known that when Nathan gave his heart to a woman, it would be fully. He was fairly certain Abigail was that woman, and that she already had his heart in her hands. She just didn't know it, yet.

"She amazes me." Nathan stared into the fire, speaking quietly so as not to disturb Abigail. "How she keeps going, even after enduring such horror." He looked at Ian. "She doesn't know how strong she is."

Ian nodded, hands clasped together, elbows on his knees. "She is a fighter. That makes it all the harder to fight for her. She isn't used to having someone defend her. Do you think the man will come back?"

"I think he will come, but not the way he did today. He was crazy, Papa. I saw it in his eyes. I don't know what he will do, but we have to be on guard, for her sake."

Ian looked at Nathan thoughtfully, and asked the question he already knew the answer too. "Are you falling in love with her, son?"

Nathan didn't hesitate to answer. "Yes, Papa. She has already captured my heart," he whispered.

Ian saw the emotion move behind Nathan's eyes.

Nathan ran his hands over his face and through his dark hair. "She isn't ready to hear that, though. She still can't see past what's been done to her. She wouldn't believe me if I told her."

Ian nodded. "That's wise, son. Wait for God's timing and for her heart to be ready."

Nathan nodded, and they both sat for a time, staring into the flames, lost in thoughts of their wounded lamb, sleeping one room away.

TWENTY THREE

Nathan came in the cabin and Abigail looked up from the crust she was kneading at the table. She blew at the wisp of hair hanging in her eyes and smiled at him. He walked over and gently tucked it behind her ear.

"I have an invitation for us," he said. "Matthew and Millie would like us to come to dinner on Sunday, after church. Would you like to go?" His smile was hopeful.

It surprised her that he asked her opinion. "Why are you asking me?"

"Because I want you to choose." He placed his hands on his hips. "Shall we go, or shall we stay?"

She smiled at his boyish grin. How could she resist?

"I would like to meet this Millie I've heard about." Millie had not been at the meetings on Sunday's since Abigail had begun attending. Her family had been passing around a cold for a month, now. Abigail had met Matthew, her husband. He was friendly.

"Good! Millie is a great cook. She kept us well fed before you came along."

He turned to go, sneaking an apple slice from her pile. She narrowed her eyes in a playful tease and he grinned as he popped it in his mouth. She shook her head and smiled. He walked over to the door and before leaving, turned back towards her.

"You're beautiful when you smile, Abigail. Especially when you have flour smudges on your cheek." He winked and then was gone.

Her heart stuttered at his compliment. She reached up, absently wiping at the smudges. What was happening to her? Her stomach had begun to flutter when he came near, and not from the baby moving around. Sometimes, when she caught him looking at her, the look on his face would make her throat dry. He didn't look at her with a hungry look, like Thomas, nor with judgment like father. He looked at her...like what? What was different? She went back to kneading. It wasn't fear that caused these reactions to Nathan, which was new to her. Men had only ever incited fear in her, but Nathan was different. She wasn't sure what to make of it all, and not being sure made her very afraid.

TWENTY FOUR

Nathan saw Papa and Abigail were deep in conversation, and he was curious what they were discussing. Abigail had the shawl he had bought her around her shoulders. It was a dark color, like she was used to. He was aching to buy her a beautiful pink dress or maybe lavender, to highlight her eyes. He waited though. She still took his gifts hesitantly, and he didn't want to overwhelm her. She wore her hair in the braid that had become her everyday style. Did she realize how brave she was, how that simple act was a step towards freedom? He thought not. She had seemed pensive in church, today. She stared, eyes wide, at everything that went on. He suspected the church gatherings had looked very different in her village. She seemed at ease now, as they were leaving the church. If he didn't know better, he'd think she had been with them forever. She fit so well here, in their life, in his life.

"I was just telling Abigail about the Christmas celebration in Weldon." Ian smiled at Nathan. "She's never been a part of one."

"You're in for a treat, then. Weldon hosts a dance and there are tables laden with food." Nathan smiled at her as he helped her up into the wagon. "It's the best night of the year around here."

"It sounds nice…but I've never danced. We were not allowed to celebrate holidays such as Christmas," She said, hesitantly.

"Well, it is a joyous night of celebrating. I think you'll like it."

"I will have the baby then," she whispered.

She bit her lip, something she did when she was worried.

"Abigail?" He climbed up in the wagon beside her. Papa sat on the other side of her. "It's okay if you don't want to go. You don't have to do anything you don't want to do." He gave her an encouraging smile, wanting to set her at ease.

She didn't say anything to that but folded her arms and lowered her head. Nathan looked at Papa with a raised brow. Papa just shook his head as if to say, "let it go," so, he did. If she wanted to share what was bothering her, she would, when she was ready.

~~~

Abigail sat pensively next to Nathan on the wagon seat. She was nervous about meeting people and sharing a meal. Suddenly, she wondered if they knew that she carried a child and how they would respond if they didn't.

"Nathan," she whispered, turning to him.

He wore his crisp white shirt and blue button-down coat. He had his hat on too, which made him look very distinguished.

"Do they know…about me?" she asked.

"They know you carry a child, and that is all." He looked at her. "I wouldn't share anything beyond that, Abigail…ever. You can trust me." She saw in his eyes that he meant it. "Oh…I also have a surprise for you."

Her eyes narrowed a bit and he chuckled. "Don't like surprises, do you?"

"Depends," she said, folding her arms over her chest, brow raised in curiosity.

He grinned. "Mrs. Hatchet will be joining us today."

Abigail beamed, relaxing her arms in her lap. "Oh, that is a lovely surprise! I would love to see her again!"

"See," he whispered, leaning towards her, slightly. "My surprises are always good. And you're beautiful when you smile."

He winked at her and she felt that flutter in her stomach again. The baby also kicked, and she put a hand to her belly.

"Does the little one agree with me?" he asked.

"It would seem," she responded, caught off guard by the way he made her feel. He had taken to telling her she was beautiful every time she smiled.

Abigail had seen Mrs. Hatchet in passing at the Sunday meetings, but they hadn't talked. Abigail found herself to be withdrawn at the gatherings. She was afraid and kept her head down most of the time.

Nathan pulled the wagon to a halt in front of the cabin and Abigail took in the scene. The cabin was modest but inviting. The wide front porch was framed with rose bushes and the rocking chairs on the porch hinted at time spent together talking and resting, like Nathan and Ian did.

Abigail was nervous about this dinner. People in her village didn't gather for meals. She worried about what was expected of her. She hated not knowing what the expectations were. Nathan set the brake, jumped down from the wagon then turned to help her. Climbing in and out of the wagon was hard with her swollen belly.

"They're going to love you," he whispered close to her ear, as if he knew what was troubling her. She looked up at him, surprised that he could read her so well. He squeezed her arm before stepping away. He grabbed her basket from the back and handed it to her. He offered her his arm and she took it. The three of them climbed the porch steps, and Ian knocked on the door.

Matthew answered the door with a smile. "Ah! Welcome!" He reached a hand out to Nathan. "Good of you to come, Sir."

"Not your overseer tonight, my friend. Just Nathan will do." He grinned, giving Matthew a hearty handshake. He took Abigail's hand from his arm, keeping a hold of it as he introduced her. Abigail was surprised he kept hold of her hand, but she was grateful. She felt safer with him so close.

"Ma'am." Matthew nodded towards her. "We are very happy to have you join us this evening. Mrs. Hatchet tells us you've met, and she's looking forward to seeing you. And my Millie is looking forward to meeting you."

Abigail curtsied. "Thank you, Matthew. It's nice to see you, again."

Matthew shook hands with Ian, and Abigail noticed a little girl peering up at them from behind her papa's leg. Nathan chuckled and knelt down in front of the girl, tweaking her nose. "Hello, little one." She giggled, and Abigail smiled watching Nathan with her. He was a natural with children, it would seem.

"Shall we?" Ian asked, gesturing for Abigail to proceed him.

As they went in the cabin, Abigail breathed in the scent of roasting vegetables. She saw, who she assumed was Millie, leaning over the iron pot at the fire, stirring something. She was a petite woman with dark hair. She wiped her hands on her apron, and walked towards them.

"Nathan! Ian! So good of you to finally come." She gave them both hugs, and they both kissed her cheek. It caught Abigail off guard, the way these people treated each other; with genuine affection, like they were family.

"And you must be Abigail! I'm Millie." Millie reached out, pulling Abigail into a gentle embrace, and Abigail fumbled to respond.

"Hello," she said, softly. Millie stepped back, and Abigail immediately liked her. Her smile was authentic, and her brown eyes were friendly. Just then, Mrs. Hatchet came into the cabin with flowers in hand.

"Oh! As I live and breathe!" She walked hurriedly to Ian, and he embraced her with a chuckle.

"Hello, Mrs. Hatchet. Good to see you."

"And when will you stop with the 'Mrs. Hatchet' and just call me Lizzy? I do believe you are older than me?" She had a twinkle in her eye and Ian laughed loud. Everyone knew she was older than Ian, but she always teased that she was younger.

"Nathan, come give an old woman a kiss." He went over and kissed her cheek, then stepped back.

"Oh, Abigail! The one I really came here to see." She walked over to Abigail and wrapped her in a warm hug.

Abigail hugged her back. "Hello, Mrs. Hatchet."

Mrs. Hatchet held Abigail's shoulders and looked into her eyes "How are you? Are you well?"

Abigail was sure she noticed her very obvious belly, but she didn't mention it. "I am," she replied, liking the way this woman made her feel. She reminded her of mama.

"Do I smell lavender?" Mrs. Hatchet grinned.

"I love it, Mrs. Hatchet. Thank you again."

"Come and meet our Bethany, Abigail." Millie motioned for Abigail to follow her and she moved into a small room, off to the side of the kitchen and main living area. There on a settee, with a quilt tucked around her legs, was a girl who looked to be about fifteen.

"Beth, this is our new friend, Abigail."

Abigail didn't think she looked sick, but she didn't rise from the settee. She had large chocolate eyes, and hair to match. She looked to be only a few years older than Samuel. She reached out a hand to Abigail with a smile that seemed to light up her countenance. "Hello, Abigail. Nice to meet you."

Abigail took the girl's hand and smiled. "Thank you for having me," she replied.

"Mama, can Papa move me over to the fire? I think I need the warmth."

"Of course!" Millie hustled from the room and came back with Matthew on her heels.

Abigail stepped back near a corner, not sure why Matthew needed to come help his daughter. She watched as Bethany pushed the quilt back, and Matthew leaned over and scooped her up in his arms. Abigail tried to conceal her shock. Could Bethany not walk? Matthew carried her into the main room where everyone was gathered and set her in a chair right by the fire. Millie came behind with the quilt and helped Bethany situate it over her legs, again. Abigail stood in the doorway between the two rooms and watched as Nathan and Ian both went over and knelt down in front of Bethany.

"How are you, Beth?" Nathan asked, taking her hand in his.

"Well, I'm doing great now that two strong, handsome men are sitting at my feet!"

The whole room burst out in laughter, except Abigail. She just stared, eyes wide in shock. *She can't walk!* No one in Abigail's village would accept someone in Beth's condition. Anytime a child had been born in her village with any kind of defect, they had just disappeared, without a trace. Many had ideas about what was done to them, but nothing was ever said out loud. Abigail watched as Nathan took Beth's hand and kissed the top of it - as if she were royalty - then stood. His gaze found Abigail's and his brows furrowed in question. She looked away, not wanting to reveal anything in her expression.

Ian asked Bethany a question about her flower garden and Abigail watched Bethany's face light up as she told him all about the flowers she was growing. He listened and smiled and asked questions like he genuinely cared. *He cares about a girl who can't walk?*

"I brought an apple pie, to add to our meal," Abigail said, remembering the basket she had been holding all this time. She set the basket on the table and pulled the pie out. She was nervous about bringing the pie, but Nathan had convinced her it was a good idea and that her pies were delicious. She glanced at him and he gave her a wink that made her feel brave.

"Oh, Abigail. It's lovely!" Millie moved it to the center of the table, then set about finishing the rest of the meal.

Nathan, Matthew and little Sarah went back out on the porch. Abigail sat down at the table next to Mrs. Hatchet. Her gaze kept wandering to Bethany and Ian by the fire.

"These old bones tire quickly, these days," Mrs. Hatchet said, situating herself in the chair. She looked at Abigail and clasped her hands in her lap. "How are you, Abigail? How's the baby?"

"I am well. The baby will come in two months or so," she said, absently rubbing her belly.

"You have those two men send for Millie when the time comes," Mrs. Hatchet said.

"Oh, yes, Abigail! Please have them send for me. I'll be happy to come." Millie gave her a warm smile as she went about setting the table.

Was everyone outside of her village kind? She couldn't believe that to be true, but she kept encountering such kindness. No one in her village would have offered to help her with the birth of her baby. They would have stayed away from her for fear of being contaminated with her sin. These two women had not even asked her for an explanation. She just didn't know what to make of these people.

~~~

The night was full of laughter, and good food. Abigail watched the interactions, watched these people gathered around this table. Matthew had carried Bethany over to a special chair that sat at one end of the table. Everyone teased that she sat in the queen's chair and she laughed, calling them all her royal subjects. No one at this table treated Bethany as a lesser person. She was obviously loved and cherished. Abigail ended up sitting right next to Bethany, and the girl had been a kind host. She asked Abigail questions and listened intently, face bright, when

Abigail answered. She shared about her flowers, and raved about Abigail's pie, as did everyone else.

Abigail was seeing a pattern of people gathering outside of her village for the simple purpose of being together. There was no ceremony, no rule they were following, they seemed content to just be together. Her eyes moved to Nathan, which they seemed to do of their own will lately, and she watched him laugh at a story Matthew told. She allowed herself to study him a bit. He was handsome, there was no doubt, with his strong jaw and green eyes. He exuded strength, but it struck Abigail that he didn't intimidate her. He drew her in with his kindness and smile that stopped her heart because it was always so gentle. He was handsome, yes, but it was his nature that drew her to him.

She felt a hand on her arm and jumped a bit in surprise. She looked over at Mrs. Hatchet.

"You'll not find a better man." She gave Abigail a warm, knowing smile then turned to Sarah who had something to show her.

Abigail looked back at Nathan, thinking on what Mrs. Hatchet had said. She agreed. She had never encountered a man like Nathan. He had defended her like no other saving her twice, now. Still, doubt gnawed at her. He caught her staring gave her a different smile, an intimate smile, a smile that made Abigail feel special. She smiled back, then looked down at her hands in her lap, not sure what to do about all these feelings he was stirring. She hated men, didn't she?

They stayed until just before dusk. Mrs. Hatchet would stay the night then ride to town with Millie tomorrow.

Everyone moved to the porch to say their goodbyes. Mrs. Hatchet hugged Abigail. "I'm praying for you, child." She patted Abigail's cheek, like a mama would do, then stepped away.

Bethany was in a rocker on the porch, and Abigail decided to be brave. She walked over to Bethany and stuck out her hand, somewhat awkwardly.

"I-it was nice to meet you, Bethany. Thank you for such a wonderful time." Bethany looked up at Abigail, delight, and surprise on her face. She reached both hands up and grasped Abigail's.

"Oh, thank you, Abigail. It isn't often I make a new friend. I hope to see you again, soon." Then, she pulled a white rose from under her quilt and put it in Abigail's hand. "For you, my new friend."

Abigail looked at the flower and emotion welled up in her eyes. She blinked hard to stop the rush of tears.

"Thank you," she managed, then turned and went down the porch. The girl who couldn't walk had given her a flower. She didn't know what to think of it.

Nathan and Ian said their goodbyes to everyone, including Bethany, then Nathan helped Abigail into the wagon. Ian climbed in the back.

"Think I'll stretch my legs and enjoy the sunset," he said.

Nathan jumped up beside Abigail and took the reins. "A fine meal as always, Millie. Thank you for the food and the company." With a final wave, they made their way down the dirt road towards home.

"Now, that wasn't so bad, was it?" Nathan asked quietly, a bit later. Ian rested his head against the side of the wagon with his eyes closed.

"No. It was not bad at all. I had a wonderful time. The best time I've ever had," she whispered, tears stinging her eyes, again. She had gone her whole life and had never experienced anything like this. It saddened her to think of all she had missed, all her village missed by living the way they did.

"I-I've never met someone like Bethany," Abigail said, fingering the rose in her hand.

"She's special," Nathan said. "She hasn't been able to walk since a riding accident when she was a little girl. Matthew's family in England are horse breeders. She was learning to ride when a horse threw her. She was only five. I think Matthew brought his family to the colonies to try and start fresh, change the scenery. You would never know they are from high society back home."

Abigail took in everything Nathan said. Beth hadn't been born that way, it had been an accident. Still, what would her people say? She knew the answer. They would say Bethany had some secret sin, and that was her punishment. Everything always came back to sin. Abigail sat a while, thinking on all that, then she remembered Samuel.

"Nathan." She turned towards him slightly. "I have a... favor to ask."

He nodded but didn't speak.

"I want to find my brother," she whispered. She took a deep breath then, "Will you help me?" Asking for help was harder than she thought it would be.

"Of course. Tell me what you know." He said, instantly, keeping his eyes on the horses.

"He was sent to Boston to apprentice with a blacksmith. The one he was being sent to closed, so he was sent to another one. Father wouldn't tell me where, so I don't have any other information."

Nathan moved the reins to one hand and took her hand with his free one. "We'll do our best to find him, Abigail. I promise."

Tears of relief filled her eyes. "Thank you, Nathan. Thank you so much."

He squeezed her hand then released it, which left her feeling…sad? What was it about this man, about his nearness that affected her so? She had to be careful. She had offered her heart to Thomas once, only to have it mocked and trampled. She wouldn't make that mistake again. Nathan was her friend, nothing more. Besides, the more she saw his goodness, the more she realized she was not worthy of him, in any way. She was used, unclean, and damaged. If he really were as good and kind as he seemed, then he deserved better than her…much better.

TWENTY FIVE

Nathan watched Papa carve another spindle, by the light of the oil lamp in the barn. They were crafting a cradle for Abigail's baby. They worked on it in the evenings, after Abigail was asleep. They wanted to surprise her. Nathan worked on the piece of pine that he had shaped into the headboard of the cradle. He was carving small flowers into it, hoping that would bring joy to Abigail when she saw it. They were close to being done with it. The pine had been a good choice because it was durable and easy to work with.

He and Papa had been working on it almost every evening for a month. Abigail was growing by the day, the birth of her baby fast approaching, though she couldn't say exactly when the baby would come. Nathan stayed close to the cabin these days. Papa had suggested it a couple weeks back, saying one of them should try to stay near her from now until the baby came. The last thing they wanted to happen was for her time to come and neither of them be around to help her. Papa was spending more time down at the mill, and Nathan did more work here, on their land. There was always something to be done. Abigail had been working the past two weeks to get all the food from the gardens jarred and put away for the winter. Nathan had taught her how to store the meats, something she had never done.

"I think we'll finish soon," Nathan said, sitting up and wiping sawdust from his face with the rag in his back pocket.

Papa nodded as he continued his carving. "Only three

more spindles and we can start putting it together."

"I think she will love it. I hope she does. She seems more open to gifts for the baby. It's gifts for herself she resists." Nathan said as he studied the flower he had just carved.

"She doesn't think she deserves gifts. Nothing has been given to her out of love before," Papa said.

Nathan sighed. "I know. She takes every gift I've given her with suspicion." He rubbed his face again, then stuck his rag back in his pocket.

"Don't stop giving her gifts, son. One day, her heart will break open and it will all make sense to her."

~~~

Abigail woke to an uncomfortable pressure in her lower abdomen. She sighed. Each phase of carrying a baby came with its own set of issues. She was constantly needing to visit the necessary, lately. Thankfully, Nathan had discreetly placed a chamber pot in her room one day, so she wouldn't have to leave the cabin at night. She had been grateful, though she hadn't mentioned it to him, feeling like that was a bit too personal to discuss.

When she finished, she arched her spine, rubbing her lower back. She was thirsty. She rolled her eyes. Drinking meant more visits to the chamber pot. She grabbed her shawl hanging on the hook of her door and wrapped it around her shoulders. She pulled her door open and peeked out. She didn't want to disturb Nathan or Ian. She was surprised when she came from her room to find Nathan wasn't asleep in front of the fire. Ian's door was left ajar and he wasn't in his room. *Where could they be this late at night?*

A bit worried, she lit a lamp and went out on the porch. She heard a noise coming from behind the house. When she came around the cabin, she saw a flicker of light coming from the barn. She walked towards the barn and, hearing Ian's familiar voice, slowed her steps.

"Only three more spindles, and we can start putting it together," she heard Ian say. Curious as to what they were doing, she walked quietly towards the door and turned the lamp down, so she could remain anonymous. She peeked around the door of the barn, and saw different pieces of wood, lying about. Some had been carved into spindles, and she saw Nathan hunched over a piece of wood, working on it.

"I think she will love it. She seems more open to gifts for the baby. It's gifts for herself she resists." Abigail's heart began to pound as she realized they were discussing her.

"She doesn't think she deserves gifts. Nothing has been given to her out of love before." She covered her mouth, to stifle a gasp, at Ian's words. How could he know that? She was careful and guarded. She made a point of not revealing too much of herself. How could they read her so well?

"I know. She takes every gift I've given her with suspicion." She heard Nathan say. A tear trailed her cheek at his words. He was right. She assumed any gift he gave was conditional, and he would expect payment at some point.

"Don't stop giving her gifts, son. One day, her heart will break open and it will all make sense to her."

Abigail stifled a sob as she hurried away from the barn,

back to the cabin. Who were these two men, who wanted to give her gifts, with no expectations in return? Tears trailed her cheeks. Would her heart one day soften towards this type of kindness? Fear screamed at her to keep her guard up, that the moment she began trusting, was the moment all the goodness would be snatched away from her. She hurried back into the cabin and into her room. Ian said that one day it would all make sense to her. Nothing made sense in her life and she could not imagine a time when anything would. She wasn't thirsty anymore, so she put the lamp on the side table by the bed and climbed under the quilts, wiping the tears away with the sleeve of her gown. What had they been working on for her baby? She thought about the different pieces of wood she saw. The spindles...her eyes widened, and she sat up. They were making her a cradle! She laid back slowly on her pillow, deep in thought. Nathan had saved her life, and Ian had welcomed her into his home, with no questions. They had been gentle and kind, without fail. Now, they sacrificed sleep to make a cradle for her? They seemed to know, without her telling them, what was in her heart. She sighed as one last tear fell on her pillow. Right now, she felt confusion about her life. She still wanted to be independent, a woman of means...but she also felt safe, for the first time ever. Nathan and Ian made her feel safe.

Was it independence she craved, or safety?

She realized that she was quickly growing accustomed to Nathan and Ian in her life. Could she live without them? Did she want too? She still felt trapped, was still cautious. What if all of this was a lie? What if they really did expect her to pay them back in ways she didn't want too? She felt like a caged bird. If she could just escape the prison that was her life, she might be able to fly.

TWENTY-SIX

Nathan thought Abigail was more quiet than usual. She was so focused on every task she did, that she didn't even seem to notice him or Papa in the cabin. He and Papa had exchanged some concerned glances, that morning over breakfast, but neither said anything to her. He had seen so much change in her, lately. She smiled more, asked questions, engaged in conversations at the table…until the past week. She seemed to be shrinking back as if she were closing herself up inside a shell.

What's going on in her heart, Lord? Show me how to help her.

He watched her as he ate his porridge. She sat to his left and ate with her head down never making eye contact with him. Papa had risen and left early that morning. He was making a trip to Boston tomorrow. Normally, this would be a trip Nathan would make, but they both agreed Nathan should stay with Abigail. Papa was delivering some of their orders, as well as meeting with their contractors. He was going to try and find Abigail's brother, Samuel. He would be gone for three days. How would Abigail respond to being here alone with him for three days? There were men who would pay good money to be put in the same situation with such a beautiful woman. He would never take advantage of her, though.

"Papa leaves tomorrow for Boston," he said, downing another spoonful of porridge. Abigail made the best porridge he had ever tasted. She had become a wonderful cook. All the new foods she had encountered since leaving the village had overwhelmed her at first, and she had even struggled with whether or not it was okay to eat such things. She had overcome her fear, though, and was learning daily how to enjoy it all. Nathan was proud of her for that tiny victory.

She looked up, surprised. "Why?"

"We have orders to deliver, and contractors to see. He'll be gone three days." He took a drink of cider. "If there are any supplies you would like, that we can't get in Weldon, we can give him a list." He smiled, hoping to draw her out of whatever was keeping her distant.

"I can't think of anything," she said, eyes in her lap, again.

"He's going to seek out your brother, too, based on what we know." Maybe that would pull something out of her.

She looked up into his eyes. "Really?"

Nathan nodded. "Really." Was she surprised he was going through with his promise to help her? It saddened him to think she still didn't trust him or his word, even though he understood why she was so hesitant. He wanted her trust, more than anything.

He took one last bite then took his bowl over to the dish bucket. "I'll be out back for most of the morning, chopping wood. Winter is coming, and we need a hefty supply of logs." An idea occurred to him. "Would you like to go with me to the mill, after the midday meal?" He knew she was curious about the workings of the mill. Maybe that would draw her out of her shell. She looked up at him and he saw a tiny hint of excitement in those blue eyes, but it faded as quickly as it came.

"I have a lot of work to get done today."

Nathan wanted to reach out to her, but he put his hands in his pocket instead. "You can come, even if your work isn't done." He tilted his head slightly as he studied her. "The work can wait."

Her smile was guarded, hesitant.

He went for his hat, hanging near the door, and put it on. "If you need anything, come for me."

She rose with a nod and set about to clean up the dishes.

Nathan stood a moment more, with his hand on the door, watching her. Then, with a heavy heart, he slipped out of the cabin.

~~~

Abigail came to where Nathan was behind the barn, splitting wood. His shirt clung to his chest, and sweat ran down his temples. Cutting firewood was no easy job. In her village, the young boys were taught how to do it as soon as they were strong enough to use the axe. She was bringing bread and water out to him, along with some dried venison. He had been going at it for a couple of hours, and she thought he might need a respite. She also had decided to talk to him about finding work. She had toiled over her dilemma long enough. It was time for her to make her own way in the world. She didn't want to owe any more debt to these two men.

Nathan saw her coming as he was setting up another block of wood to cut. He grinned, and it went all the way to his eyes. Her heart skipped a beat, as it always did when he smiled at her. His smile was so…inviting…but not in the way that made her feel unclean. When he smiled at her she felt cherished. That was just another reason for her to take control. She didn't know what to do with all the emotion he stirred in her. She had been trained her whole life to control and hide her emotions. She was finding that harder to do in Nathan's presence, and she needed to get away from him.

"I thought you might need a break." She said after he sliced through the chunk of wood with flawless effort. It occurred to her just how powerfully strong he was and yet, he never seemed to intimidate anyone with his presence. Thomas and father used fear to their advantage, to make people conform. Nathan's strength made others feel safe, at least it seemed that way.

Nathan sunk the axe into the chopping block and grabbed the rag in his back pocket, wiping his hands and face.

"A break is just what I need." He smiled and came towards her. "Will you sit with me?" he asked, removing his gloves and taking the cloth-wrapped bread and jug of water from her.

She nodded and followed him over to a grassy spot in the sunshine. Nathan grabbed her hand so she could lower herself to the ground without losing her balance. Sitting down was hard to do in her condition. Nathan sighed when he sat. He uncorked the jug and drank his fill. He offered her the jug, but she declined. She needed to talk to him about her idea.

"Nathan, I want to find work." She hesitated, watching him for a reaction. Would he become possessive, start making demands?

He pulled the bread apart, offering her a piece. She shook her head.

"What is it you want to do, Abigail?" He asked.

She picked a blade of grass, fiddling with it in her lap. "I-I thought maybe I could find work as a cook or housemaid."

"And what about the baby?" He asked, looking off into the distance, arms draped over raised knees, bread in one hand. He didn't sound angry.

"I don't know. Perhaps I can find a place to work that will allow me to keep the baby with me." She knew that was a flimsy plan, but she was desperate to make a way for herself.

"You don't have to work right now, Abigail."

"I need too." She said, quietly.

"Why?" he asked, turning and searching her eyes.

Emotion clogged her throat, but she shoved it down, determined to be strong. "I don't want to depend on you and Ian for everything. I want to take care of myself. Maybe I can find work in Weldon, and a place to live." She worried about Thomas finding her in Weldon, but she pushed that thought aside.

After a few moments of quiet, Nathan stood and brushed the crumbs from his breeches.

"It isn't a burden for us to have you here, Abigail." He reached down and she took his hand so she could stand.

He walked back over to the chopping block, put his gloves on, grabbed the axe and set up another chunk of wood to cut. Abigail stood, becoming a bit defensive, and went over to him. She stood there and watched while he chopped wood, hands fisted to her hips. He was frustrated, she could tell. Good. She wanted to see him get angry, really angry. Maybe then, his true nature would come out, and her reasons for wanting independence would be justified. He picked up another piece of wood, set it up and raised the axe over his head, bringing it down hard. He threw the wood on his growing pile, then used his shoulder to wipe the sweat trickling down his face. After cutting a few pieces of wood into logs, he sunk the axe into the chopping block and turned towards her, chest heaving from the exertion.

"What is it you want most, Abigail?" He held her gaze, breathing hard.

He wasn't angry, she could tell. He was truly wanting to know. Abigail stepped back, folding her arms across her chest. He made her feel vulnerable, asked questions that made her feel exposed. She knew how to guard herself against anger and hate, but this gentleness he constantly offered her, it confused her. What *did* she want most?

~~~

Nathan noticed her retreating. She did not know how to respond to gentleness, so she withdrew from it. He stepped forward, slightly. She was going to see that he was not like them. He was going to show her.

She looked off into the woods. "I...I don't know what I want, Nathan. I feel like a small child, seeing the world for the first time. Except, I'm not unassuming like a small child. I'm confused." She looked at him, then, "I'm scared."

He knew that admission had been hard for her, and he was so proud of her for saying it. He wanted to take hold of her and assure her she was safe, here with him. He knew, though, that he could not promise her a life free of pain, and he wouldn't make promises he couldn't keep.

"You don't have to be afraid, Abigail." He looked up at the sun streaming through the trees. "God doesn't promise us a life free of pain." He looked at her. "He promises to be with us because he understands, he walked in our pain."

"Do not tell me God understands!" Abigail clutched her hands in fists at her sides and stepped forward, within inches of him.

He was surprised but pleased to see the fire in her. He knew the fire was there, it just needed to be kindled. He didn't move from where he stood but held her gaze with his hands at his waist.

"He *does not* understand what I suffered! All he does is punish! All he does is turn his face away from all the ugliness!" Her voice cracked, and tears formed in her eyes. When she let him glimpse the hurt inside, her eyes reminded him of a stormy sea. Right now they were raging.

He let her vent, let her say whatever she wanted to say. He wanted to take her pain, but he knew he couldn't. He wanted to grab her face with his hands and tell her to just let go of all of it and let him take care of her, but he knew he couldn't do that either. She had to walk through it, to the other side. That's the only way she would be free of her past. He could walk with her through it, and he would if she would let him. Being honest in this moment was a bigger step than she realized. Just her speaking out loud the truth of how she felt was a victory.

"What is it you want, Abigail?" He asked again, taking one step towards her.

Tears trailed her cheeks and she stepped back. "I want to earn my place." She whispered brokenly, looking away.

"Maybe if I work hard, I can earn my place in the world."

Nathan's heart hurt, hearing her say that. Nothing in her life had proved her worthy of love. No one had treasured her, ever. He did, though. She held his heart in her hands, and she didn't even know it. When he looked at her, he saw a beautiful, strong, courageous woman. When he looked at her, he saw his own future. She couldn't see past her wounds though, or the shame that held her captive. She thought if she earned her way in the world, she would be worthy of love. She couldn't see that he loved her as she was, that he was honored to love her wounded, broken heart.

"Abigail." Saying her name did things to his heart. He reached up, cupping her cheek. "You don't have to earn your worth. You are loved, as you are." He desperately wanted to tell her that he loved her, but he didn't. She wasn't ready to hear it. She needed to accept God's love, first. "God wants you, just as you are."

She shook her head, vehemently and backed away. "NO! I don't believe it! He has never accepted me! All he does is take! He didn't save me because I wasn't worth saving!"

Nathan's heart ached. She was so blinded by brokenness that she could not even see him, right in front of her, and what he offered; that he had been sent to rescue her, that she had been worth saving. "He was there. He cried with you, his heart broke with yours. He has never forsaken you."

She crushed her palms to her eyes, shaking her head fiercely, as a sob escaped. "No! He did forsake me!" She backed away some more as if she had to distance herself from his words.

"Abigail." There was an ache in his voice. She was beginning to break down again and he stepped close, so he could look deep into her eyes. He took her wrists, and gently pulled her hands away from her face. "You can never earn your worth, because you are priceless. You don't owe me or Papa anything, either. We want you here, we want to take care of you and your baby."

She pulled her hands from his grasp and looked off in the distance, cheeks red and eyes puffy. Nathan watched as the wind rustled the wisps of hair that framed her face. *Help her find you, Jesus.*

She looked back at him and he saw the despair in her eyes. "Nothing is ever free, Nathan." A tear slipped down her cheek. "Nothing," she rasped out. She turned and ran back towards the cabin.

Nathan watched her go, his heart heavy. She couldn't see the truth for all the lies that held her captive. Nothing had been free to her thus far, that was true, but that wasn't *the* truth. The truth was that Jesus loved her right now, completely, and that love came with no conditions…just like his. He turned around and grabbed his axe from the chopping block. He stayed there for a while longer, taking his frustrations out on the many logs that laid at his feet.

TWENTY SEVEN

Ian pulled the wagon to a halt in front of the stables. This was the last one he would go in, today. He had covered a lot of ground in his search for Abigail's brother but had made no headway. No one knew of a boy named Samuel. Really, searching for someone in a city the size of Boston was like searching for a needle in a haystack. He had to try, though, for Abigail. Somewhere in this city was a boy who had been abandoned by his own father. Ian's heart grieved at the thought. If he found Samuel, he would offer to bring him home, to Abigail.

Father, help me find him. I know he isn't lost to you.

He climbed down from the wagon, then walked behind the stable, where the blacksmith's shop was always located and heard the familiar clink of a hammer beating a piece of iron into shape. He walked into the shop heavy with heat and smoke. The blacksmith was pounding out iron, forming it into something useful. When he saw Ian he stopped and grabbed a rag from his work table. He wiped his face and hands, as Ian approached.

"Morning," the man said.

"Morning," Ian greeted the man with a handshake. The man's grip was solid, firm.

"What can I do for you?" The man asked.

"Names Ian Bradford, and I'm looking for someone. A boy, named Samuel. He was sent to work in Boston by his father. His sister is living with my son and me at the moment, and she doesn't know where he was sent."

"Samuel, you say?" Ian nodded.

"I had a Samuel working here a couple months ago."

Ian's heart quickened. *Please, Lord!*

"He was a young boy, about ten years I'd say. He came alone from a village."

Ian smiled and nodded. "Yes, that sounds like him! Do you know where he is, now?" The man spoke as if Samuel were no longer here.

"About a month ago, he quit working for me. Man came through town recruiting for the military and he signed up."

"But, he's just a boy." Ian said.

"They take 'em if they're willin' to go." The man said. "I told him he didn't have to do it, but he said he wanted too. I could see there was no changing his mind." He looked out past Ian a moment. "The boy was troubled, I could see that."

Ian's heart was heavy, now. A boy of ten years joining the military?

"Any idea where I might go to find him?"

The man shook his head. "Don't know exactly. He could've been shipped out for training to somewhere else."

Ian sighed. "Thank you, sir, for your help." He shook the man's hand again.

"I'm sorry I couldn't help you more. Didn't know he had a sister. He never talked much, but he was a hard worker. I was sad to see him go."

Ian nodded. "He has a sister. If he happens to come back this way, will you leave him a message that his sister is in Weldon, and she's looking for him."

"I'll do it." The man said.

Ian left the place heavy hearted. He dreaded telling

Abigail. She was still holding on to the hope that they would find him. This would crush her spirit.

Father, I know you see Samuel and love him more than any of us ever could. Watch over the boy, and if it is your will, bring him back to his sister one day.

He spent the rest of his trip tending to business, and then, as he made the journey home, he prayed for Abigail asking God to give her peace and comfort in her brokenness.

~~~

Abigail heard the wagon wheels coming down the dirt road towards the cabin. Ian! She was anxious to see him and ask if he had found her brother. Maybe Samuel would be in the wagon with him! Oh, how she hoped it would be so. She hurried out onto the porch, wiping her hands on her apron. She looked ahead trying to see if anyone sat in the bed of the wagon. She saw no one and disappointment sank in. Nathan came from the barn and greeted Ian with a big hug when he climbed down from the wagon. "Good to have you home, Papa."

"Good to be home, son." Ian sounded tired. He turned to Abigail then, and she saw the sadness in his eyes. He walked over to the porch and stopped just before climbing the steps. She leaned on the porch rail, one hand on her belly, the other wrapped around the post feeling the need to brace herself.

"Abigail…"

She heard the pain in his voice and her heart twisted with fear.

"I found the shop where Samuel worked." He said, putting a hand on the porch rail. She waited, her heart beginning to pound. "He wasn't there, anymore," Ian said, somberly.

"Where is he?" she whispered, afraid to hear the answer.

"I'm positive I found the one he worked at. The blacksmith described a boy of about ten that came to him from a village."

Abigail put a hand to her throat. Ian had found him, but she sensed there was more. "Where is he?" she asked again.

"He left about a month ago…" Ian looked down then up at her, again. "He joined the military."

Abigail's eyes widened. Samuel - her Samuel - in the military? "But…he is just a boy." She barely managed, voice trembling.

"I know. I said that, too. Apparently, they are taking them younger and younger, now." He stepped up on the first step, in front of her. "The blacksmith couldn't give me any details on where he went. He said he had probably been shipped away, for training."

She stared at him, numb with shock. Samuel was gone. Her father had sent him away and he would never come back. She stepped back, hands clenched in fists, her whole body shaking with rage.

"I hate my father…" she said it fiercely, wishing her very words could bring him destruction.

"And… I hate your God." She spoke with a dead kind of calm, staring Ian down with unaccustomed boldness. She saw Nathan move forward out of the corner of her eye. He walked up on the porch and she stepped back, out of his reach.

"Abigail," Nathan said.

"No! No, Nathan! I don't want to hear any of it!" She turned then, and ran back into the cabin, into her room, where she shut the door and leaned against it. Samuel was gone. She would never see her little brother again, and it was her father's fault. He had destroyed everyone who had loved him, and God had helped him. Thomas had ruined her, and father had finished her off. There was no such thing as love in this world, and she had been a fool to even begin to think that God cared about her. She wanted nothing to do with him and hoped that in her anger, he might just strike her dead this very moment.

"Go ahead and smite me, God!" She said it with such force, staring at the ceiling. "You already have, anyway. Why not finish the job!" She began to weep then, as her fury simmered into a cold dull ache in her chest. The display of emotion had drained her of energy and she stumbled over to the bed, curling on her side. She laid there weeping until there were no tears left. Once her tears had been spent, she laid there staring at nothing, not even aware when the sun eventually set, shrouding the room in darkness.

~~~

Nathan quietly opened the door to check on Abigail. Her weeping had subsided a while ago, and he wondered if she was asleep. He saw her laying on the bed, curled on her side, an arm around her belly. He went over and pulled the quilt up over her. Her braid had fallen apart and her golden hair fanned out around her face, giving her the appearance of an angel. He picked up a strand and ran his fingers over it. Her nose was red from crying and, even closed, he could see her eyes were puffy from weeping.

Her life had been so devastating. He knew she had clung to hope that Samuel would be found. His heart had shredded into pieces as he had listened to Papa tell her the news. Watching the hate and anger pour out of her brought tears to his eyes. He didn't have any answers to her rage against God. Sure, he could tell her "bad things happen" or "this world is not perfect" but those words wouldn't heal her heart. She had spoken from a place of raw hurt and deep brokenness, and all he could do was grieve with her. He trailed a finger over her cheek then left the room, pulling the door closed behind him.

He went over to the fire and sat in his chair, opposite Papa. "She is asleep."

Papa had his Bible open in his lap. "I hated bringing her that news," he whispered, leaning his head back against his chair, and closing his eyes.

"I know, Papa." They both sat for a time, staring into the fire, saying nothing. The air around them was filled with sorrow, and both knew there was nothing to be said.

"We must watch over her, closely. She will be vulnerable."

Nathan nodded, still staring into the flames. "I will stay close to her over the next few days. Maybe she'll be up for visiting with Mrs. Hatchet, or Millie and the girls."

"Pray, son," Papa said, voice thick with emotion. Oh, how they both had come to love this woman.

Nathan nodded, emotion clogging his own throat. He prayed for her then, when he was out of words, Papa prayed. They stayed there a while, crying out for Abigail's heart to be made whole.

TWENTY EIGHT

Abigail ran, as fast as she could, Samuel beside her. She heard Thomas behind her, taunting her. "I'm coming for you. You can't get away from me." He laughed a low, throaty laugh as he chased her. He was getting closer, and she knew she couldn't outrun him. She kept a tight hold on Samuel's hand and didn't stop. She couldn't stop, couldn't think about what he would do if he caught them. The woods were thick, and she kept her free hand up to protect her face as she ran. Suddenly, she tripped over a tree root and cried out as she fell. She lost her grip on Samuel. As he tried to scramble back towards her, he began slipping into a hole in the ground. She screamed his name, chest heaving, gasping for air as she reached for him. Then, Thomas was there, laughing as he came closer. He grabbed her waist, as she still tried to get to the hole, and she screamed as he pulled her hard against his chest.

"You can't run from me." He whispered in her ear, breathing hard. She kicked, twisted, did everything she could to try and break his hold. Samuel kept sinking, yelling for her to help him and she screamed his name. Then, Thomas threw her to the ground and straddled her. She began to cry. He leaned down over her, putting a hand over her mouth, and bringing his mouth close to her ear.

"You are mine, and I will have you anytime I please." He laughed a bold, raucous laugh. He began pulling at the buttons on her dress, ripping it apart, laughing the whole time. She squirmed, kicked her feet that were pinned under him. She bit his hand and he released his hold over her mouth. She let out an ear-piercing scream…

Abigail sat up, breathing hard, sweat pouring down her neck. She put a hand to her chest, shaking all over. The cabin. She was in the cabin. He wasn't here, hurting her. She felt as if Thomas had been here in her room, the nightmare had been so real. Then, the other reality sank in. Samuel was gone, she hadn't been able to save him. He really was gone. She clutched the quilt in both hands and brought it to her face to muffle the weeping she couldn't control. Thomas had done those things to her. He had hurt her, used her, and he might come back for her – he would come back for her. Samuel had been the only person who really loved her, and now he was gone. She carried Thomas' child and could never be rid of him. She felt sick as memories rolled over her, wrapping her in their invisible chains. The need to be clean, to try and rid herself of the dirt she felt her soul was caked in brought a sense of panic. She threw the covers back and jumped up. She ran from her room and unlatching the cabin door, ran down the porch towards the river. Sobs wrenched from her with such depth she could barely breathe through them. She ran hard, fast, hands clutching her bulging belly. She felt so dirty, she wanted to claw her skin off to rid herself of the dirt. She tripped over a branch and cried out as she fell to her knees. She climbed up and kept running. She felt as if something were running beside her, dumping dirt on her, rubbing it deep into her skin, her soul. Every time Thomas had touched her, he had smeared more dirt inside of her, so much that she knew there was no hope of being clean again. The nightmare had reminded her of her shame, making her desperate to try and cleanse herself or to just be done with this life. She couldn't raise a child; she couldn't live a normal life. She would never be normal. Escaping this life was the only answer.

She came to the bank of the river and ran straight into it, crying out from the icy cold water as she stumbled and fell to her knees. She gasped as she scooped the frigid water, mixed with mud and rocks, and began scrubbing at herself. Her arms, her face, her mouth. She wanted to scrub until there was no skin left until she was raw from scrubbing. She sank down in the river, knowing it could harm the child, but not caring at that moment if they both died. She was ready to die. Who could ever love her? Who could ever want her? Who would ever love her child? She thought of Nathan and his kindness. She didn't deserve any goodness. He would see that, soon. She cried out in anguish. God didn't even want her, couldn't look on her with all her shame. He had looked away, was ignoring her. She kept scrubbing, her skin starting to bleed in places where rocks and mud pierced her skin.

~~~

Nathan walked around the cabin, having come from the barn. He woke from a sound sleep and when he couldn't get comfortable, he had gone out walking, praying, and feeling restless. He had been worried after his encounter with Abigail earlier that day and then the news Papa had brought. He had checked the horses, the cows, made sure they were comfortable. It was a very cold night. Their first snow was probably right around the corner. He walked up on the porch, careful not to make too much noise, so as not to awaken Abigail or Papa. He went quietly into the cabin and set the lantern on the table. He saw Abigail's door open and went over to check on her. Her bed was empty. He looked around the cabin. He froze in place. His heart rate picked up, instantly. Where was she? He walked quickly to papa's room, pushing the door open. Papa slept soundly, and Abigail wasn't in there. A sense of danger rose inside him. He hurried out on the porch, searching in the dark for any sign. He ran back inside for the lantern then came back out on the porch. His spirit was giving him warning signs that something was wrong. *Where did she go?*

The River.

Nathan's feet took flight and he ran, fast, hard. *Please, Jesus! Get me to her in time!* He felt the urgency in his spirit. She was in danger, he knew it. She was still so wounded, so afraid, and he feared for her life. He didn't stop running, and it was the sound he heard that let him know where she was. He stopped, holding the lantern out in front of him, breathing hard. She was sitting in the river! She was sobbing the deepest, most heartbreaking sobs, and she was scrubbing at herself with her bare hands.

"Abigail!" He yelled to her.

She didn't respond. He ran ahead, hanging the lantern on a tree branch then waded out into the river. She was so consumed with her sobs, with her scrubbing, that she did not even notice him. He felt the cold water on his calves, then his knees as he continued towards her. How long had she been here? She could die, her baby could die! He came to her and, without a word, scooped her up. She gasped when she felt his arms come around her. She didn't speak, only looked up at him through a haze of tears and anguish. He felt the presence of evil like an oppressive blanket over her.

"Jesus…" It was all he knew to say, but it helped. He felt the evil slither back. Her head fell against his chest and he held her as close as he could. He began wading out of the river, legs hurting from the needle pricks of cold water on his skin. Her tears did not stop, and she clutched Nathan's neck with icy fingers. He came to where the lantern hung and knelt down, laying her on the ground. She curled into a fetal position, and her sobs abated as she began to shiver uncontrollably. He noticed scratches on her arms that were bleeding. He pulled off his coat and scarf. He scooped her up with one arm, and draped his coat around her with the other, wrapping his scarf around her middle, trying to give the baby added warmth.

"J-just l-l-let me die." She said as the shivering increased. "I-it wil-l be e-easier that way."

"No, Abigail! I've got you, I'm not letting you go! Hold on to me." He scooped her up again, and she laid her head against his chest, clutching his shirt with her bluish hand. He would come back for the lantern later. Right now he needed to get her inside near the fire. He walked as fast as he could with his own legs wet and cold.

Jesus. Please…

When he neared the cabin, he quickened his step, and ran up on the porch, kicking the door open with his foot. He hurried over to the hearth and gently laid her on the floor. He hesitated for a moment. He needed to get the wet gown off of her, but he knew she most likely had nothing but a chemise on underneath. He saw the tinge of blue around her mouth, and it spurred him to action. He pulled the gown from over her head, doing his best to keep his eyes averted.

His eyes caught her swollen belly and his heart twisted with panic for her and the baby.

He ran and grabbed blankets from her bed and piled them on top of her shivering frame then tucked them around her to keep the cold out. He stoked the fire, then added more wood, causing it to blaze brightly within a minute. He laid down on the floor beside her, giving no thought to his own breeches, wet against his leg. He wrapped his arm around her and pulled her as close as he could with her wrapped in all the blankets. She still shivered, violently.

Jesus, save her, save her baby. Please save her!

"S-so sleepy," she stuttered, her eyes closing as she spoke.

Nathan knew that was a warning sign. "Abigail! You can't go to sleep!"

His Father came quietly into the room then, his eyes widening as he took in the scene.

"What happened, son?" He asked, coming quickly to Nathan's side.

"I found her in the river. She is frozen through." Nathan was breathless, his voice raspy. He pushed the blankets up to her knees and began rubbing one of her legs vigorously trying to get the blood flowing. Next thing he knew, his father was kneeling beside him, doing the same thing with her other leg.

"Stay with us child," Ian whispered in a soft tone. She moaned then mumbled something.

"Abigail!" Nathan cried out, afraid. He moved closer to her, took her arm from under the blankets and rubbed vigorously the side that wasn't scratched up with cuts. She turned towards him, but she didn't open her eyes. He grabbed her face with both hands and leaned close.

"Stay, Abigail! Stay with me!" He pleaded, his voice cracking as tears ran down his cheeks. He pressed his cheek to hers and whispered in her ear. "Please, stay with me."

"Nathan…" she said his name, and then her eyes rolled back in her head and she fell into a deep sleep. Nathan pulled back, looking at her face. He cried out, afraid he was losing her. He pulled her close and felt his father's hand on his shoulder.

"Stay with her, son," Ian whispered, softly. He brought a pillow over and laid it close to the fire. Then, he brought over the cloth to wrap her arms. They each took an arm and carefully wrapped the cloth around the wounds she had given herself. Nathan heard Papa whispering scripture over her as he worked.

"He heals the brokenhearted, binding up their wounds…"

Nathan cried while he worked, afraid of losing Abigail, afraid of losing his heart.

"The lantern." Nathan turned to Papa. "I left it down by the river."

"I'll take care of it," Papa said. "Stay and share your warmth with her." Nathan laid down and tucked Abigail close to him, keeping the blankets snug around her. Papa draped a quilt over Nathan and left to fetch the lantern. Nathan stared into the fire and prayed. *Jesus, please…please leave her here with me. Please let me show her what real love looks like! Let her child live, Lord! Let them both live!*

Surrender her, beloved.

No! Jesus, no! Please don't ask me to give her up!
Tears flowed, as he held the woman who now held his
heart. He knew if God wanted her nothing he said would
matter. He pleaded with God, to let her stay with him, to
give him the chance to honor her, to love her, to show her
how treasured she was. He prayed for her baby, for the
chance to love her child as his own. He drifted to sleep with
prayers for them both on his lips.

~~~

Ian came back into the cabin, having found the lantern.
He put it on the table, then went to his chair, easing slowly
into it. He watched his son, curled protectively around
Abigail. He prayed for Nathan, ever the warrior, who had
already given his heart to Abigail. He prayed Nathan would
have the strength to let her go if it was required of him. He
prayed for Abigail, the wounded lamb brought into their
home, that she would be restored, made whole. He prayed
protection over her and her baby, as he sensed more and
more that she would need it in the coming days and
months. They were both so young – children, really – from
his perspective.

Late into the night he sat there, keeping vigil over them,
praying for peace and grace to reign in their hearts.

~~~

Abigail opened her eyes and saw the fire blazing before
her. Where was she? She looked around, realizing she laid
on the floor in front of the fireplace, bundled in blankets.
She felt something over her and turned enough to see
Nathan, sleeping soundly beside her, his arm snugly around
her belly. Her heart stuttered at his nearness, and then the
memory came back. He had come to her, had come to the

river and saved her, this time from herself. The nightmare had been so real, it felt as if Thomas had literally been in the room, hurting her. Was her baby okay? Shame enveloped her when she thought of how she risked her baby.

"Nathan," she didn't recognize the raspy sound of her own voice.

He stirred, slowly opening his eyes. When his found hers, he stayed there a moment, arm snugly around her. "Abigail?" His voice was groggy with sleep. He raised up on an elbow. "How do you feel?" It was dark out and the fire cast a glow on his features.

"You keep saving me," she whispered, a tear trailing her cheek and dripping to the blanket tucked under her chin.

"Always." He brought his forehead down to meet hers.

Abigail felt the baby roll around and she let out a breath. "The baby just moved, Nathan!' She said, as loud as her hoarse voice would let her. "The baby is alive!" She cried then, overwhelmed by it all, and relieved that her baby was alive. "I'm so sorry, Nathan. I'm so sorry."

"It's okay, Abigail." He turned her, still bundled up, towards him and held her close. He pressed his lips to her hair while she wept. She felt like she could cry forever.

"I feel so dirty, Nathan. I don't think I can ever be clean, again…and S-Samuel is g-gone. Father s-sent him away." The admission brought forth cries from deep inside her. The stains were so deep, there was so much dirt on her soul, and now grief all but drowned her at the loss of her brother. The sobs poured out and Nathan just held her, murmuring soft words into her hair.

"S-Samuel…he's gone, Nathan…he's gone." Nathan continued to hold her, letting her cry until the sobs subsided into soft cries. She pulled back from him a bit. "I'm s-sorry. I c-cried all over you." She hiccupped on the leftover tears.

He looked into her eyes as he spoke. "I'm honored to wear your tears, Abigail."

His eyes blazed with warmth. "I want to take the burden from you, but I cannot. I can only show you the way. Jesus can heal all of your pain, Abigail. He can take every stain away. And he does see Samuel, wherever he is and cares for him, too." Abigail watched a tear trail his cheek.

"I don't know if I can believe that," she whispered, brokenness bleeding through her words. "I don't know if I can believe in him after all that's happened."

Nathan slipped his hands into her hair and brought her head close to his heart. "He loves you, Abigail. He believes in you even if you don't believe in him."

She stayed nestled in the crook of Nathan's arms and admitted to herself that if Jesus were anything like this man beside her, she might be able to believe. Was Jesus like Nathan? The God she had known her whole life had been distant and callous. He hadn't loved her, hadn't cared about her…at least that's how she saw it. He was to blame for letting her suffer so much, wasn't he? The God Nathan talked about was different than the one she knew. Nathan said He was gracious, that his love was deep and wide and that Jesus is proof of it. He said that bad things still happen, but that Jesus defeated death, and we will have freedom one day from the burden of this world. He said that Jesus promised to be with us in this world, to never leave us. She had tried to free herself of this world hours ago. It hadn't felt freeing, though. She had been defeated and overcome with grief. She had acted out of that defeat. Had God send Nathan to save her? She remembered Mrs. Hatchet and the gift of soap. Had God orchestrated that encounter? How was any of it possible? How could God love a woman with all her stains? And what about Samuel? Why did God let him be taken from her? She didn't have any answers but, looking into the eyes of this man who had been kind and compassionate to her, she became desperate to believe that real love did exist...and that maybe she could find it.

TWENTY NINE

"Nathan!" Abigail stumbled and fell to the ground as she called out his name. He came running from the barn, and as soon as he saw her hunched over on the ground he ran towards her.

"Abigail!" He dropped down beside her just as she cried out. "What's wrong?! Is it the baby?"

"Y-yes." She gritted out through the pain of a contraction. "It's time."

Nathan wasted no time scooping her up. She wrapped an arm around his neck and clutched his shirt with the other hand.

"I've got you, Abigail. It's going to be okay."

She groaned, fisting his shirt so tight her fingers turned a pasty white. Nathan hurried to the cabin, climbing the porch steps and kicking the door open with his foot. "Papa!" He called out.

Ian came from his room and moved quickly to Nathan's side.

"It's the baby," Nathan said.

"It's time," Ian spoke calmly and smiled at Abigail, who looked like a frightened doe. Her face was pale, and beads of sweat had already broken out on her forehead and upper lip. Ian reached out a hand and gently cupped the side of her face. "We are going to be with you, Abigail. We aren't going to leave you alone."

He spoke with assurance, and for a brief moment, Nathan saw peace in Abigail's countenance. It was as if Papa's words were a cool drink of water for her. The momentary peace evaporated, though, as a pain slashed through her belly.

Nathan moved to his room and lowered her gently to the bed. He helped her out of her cloak, tossing it on the chest of drawers nearby, then helped her get onto the bed. He leaned over and spoke quietly to her. "What do you need, Abigail. Tell me how to help."

She rolled as another contraction gripped her, and came up with her elbow, holding her swollen belly with one arm. Nathan grabbed her hand, and she squeezed it tight until the pain subsided.

"She needs to breathe, son. You stay beside her and help her concentrate on breathing."

Abigail and Nathan looked at Ian, surprised by the command. He gave them a crooked grin.

"I was there when you came into this world. I haven't forgotten everything. Besides, I've birthed enough foals and calves to know the necessities."

Nathan knew the necessities of giving birth also, but with Abigail, he couldn't seem to recall any of it. He was thankful for Papa.

Ian left the room and put a pot of water on to boil. Abigail clutched Nathan's hand tight again as the pain started to build. Nathan was kneeling by the bed now, his face close to hers.

"Breathe, Abigail. Deep breaths." With one hand he brushed the hair back from her forehead, and with the other, he held her hand close to his heart.

"I'm scared, Nathan." She said, through the quick breaths that followed her contraction. "My mama died this way." She laid back against the pillow and Nathan saw a tear trail her cheek onto her pillow. He caught another with his thumb, kissing it to his lips.

"Yes, she did…but that doesn't mean you will. Today, we make a new memory." He smiled. "To replace the bad ones."

"But, the baby. I'm so scared to bring a life into this awful world." More tears came, and she closed her eyes tight as another pain began to build.

"Breathe…" Nathan continued to rub his fingers through her hair, soothing her with his voice. "This baby is going to be a piece of your heart, Abigail. The sorrow, the pain you've suffered, it is going to be redeemed…today…it is being redeemed." She cried out as the contraction came on strong. She let go of Nathan's hand and gripped the quilt on either side of her. The pain wrapped around her middle like a vise. She heard Ian through a haze of agony.

"I think it will be quick. Her pains are coming close together."

She fell back on the pillow, as the pain subsided, taking deep breaths. Ian came and knelt beside her, taking her hand in his.

"Abigail, I don't think we have time to go for Millie. This baby is anxious to enter the world." He gave her an encouraging smile. "I would be honored to help you deliver this baby. Will you let me help you?"

~~~

Abigail stared at Ian. She saw in his eyes that he really would be honored to help her. There was no disdain, no disgust. He genuinely wanted to help her. She didn't have a choice, she knew, but he was still asking her, giving her a choice. She didn't feel shame, either, at the thought of Ian knowing her so intimately. Maybe that was just the desperation to get this baby out, talking. She gave a timid nod.

"Nathan is going to be here, right beside you, and I will do the rest." She nodded again, and Ian stood, letting Nathan take his place at her side. Abigail gasped and sat up, as a rush of warm liquid seeped from her body onto the bed.

"It won't be long, now," Ian said.

~~~

The pains intensified once Abigail's water broke. She labored for what felt like an eternity. There were moments when the pain felt like it would suffocate her.

"Nathan!" She cried. "Please. Just make it stop! Make it stop!" The pain forced her head back into the pillow.

Ian checked her, seeing the crown of the baby's head.

"It's time. Nathan, get behind her, and hold on to her." Nathan moved into action, gently lifting Abigail so he could slide behind her. He pulled her up against his body, straddling her with his legs. She rested her head against his chest.

"I can't do it, Nathan." She said through clenched teeth, tossing her head back and forth in pain.

"You are doing it, Abigail. You are bringing life into this world." He spoke close to her ear, covering her hand with his and lacing his fingers through hers. "Don't give up. Hold onto me, and squeeze as hard as you need too."

Suddenly a pain gripped her that was unlike any she had felt thus far. She lurched, pushing back against Nathan who held her tight against his chest. She screamed, a sound that pierced the air and sent Ian into action.

"Almost there. You're almost there, Abigail." Nathan's voice was gentle. She laid her head back against him, breathing hard. With barely a moment to catch her breath, another pain came on stronger than the last. She felt an overwhelming amount of pressure and then her body, of its own instinct, began the work of pushing the baby - her baby - from that sacred place inside her womb.

"That's it, Abigail! Keep pushing!" Ian was focused on the task, towel in hand, leaning in to help bring this baby forth.

"Push, Abigail! Push! It's coming, it's almost here!" Ian directed, remaining calm but firm.

Abigail leaned forward, legs bent, hands clutching Nathan's legs on either side of her. Leaning in so she could hear his voice, he covered her hand with his.

"You are beautiful, Abigail. What you are doing right now is beautiful. I'm with you, you aren't alone."

Abigail heard him through the haze of pain, screaming and pushing this life out of her. Then suddenly, she felt a blissful release and fell back against Nathan.

Ian raised the baby for Abigail to see, laughing and crying. "A girl! It's a girl!" He exclaimed. He quickly wiped the baby down, using the warm water to clean her off.

The sound of her baby crying brought forth a cry of joy from Abigail. Never had she heard anything so beautiful. Ian quickly cut the cord from the baby and tied off the nub still attached to her belly.

Abigail cried and laughed, so overcome with emotion. Nathan laughed and brought her fingers to his lips. "You are breathtaking."

Abigail felt the wetness of tears on his cheek as he pressed her hand to it.

Ian came around the bed, and sat down beside Abigail, the baby in his hands, wrapped in the towel. He leaned in, and kissed her little forehead, tears trailing his cheeks. "She is perfect."

He spoke with such awe and wonder. He turned and carefully laid the baby on her mama's chest.

Abigail began to weep as she clutched her hands around her baby girl. Perfect. Her baby was perfect in every way. Ten little fingers, ten toes, perfect little lips. Beautiful. Her baby was perfect and beautiful. She didn't look at her and see any of the darkness of this world. She didn't look at her and see the pain she had carried all these years. She only saw a perfect, beautiful little girl that needed a mama to love her.

Nathan's hand came up around Abigail, and he placed it gently on the baby's forehead. "What will you call her?" He asked. Ian set about to clean up the afterbirth and soiled towels. She looked up at Ian, at the foot of the bed, and the name came to her.

"I will call her Grace." She knew it was the right name, though she wasn't sure where it had come from. When she said it, something that might be peace settled over her. She saw tears streaming down Ian's face. She pulled her baby close and breathed in her scent. She leaned in and gently kissed baby Grace on her forehead. Exhaustion overwhelmed her and she laid back against Nathan.

Nathan slid out from behind her and, gently, lifted her and her baby in his arms so Ian could clean the bed and change the sheets.

"I can stand," Abigail said, softly.

"Yes, you can," Nathan said, giving her a teasing grin and a wink that made her heart stutter.

Abigail leaned her head against his chest and looked up at him. "Thank you," she whispered, her voice fragile.

"Thank me? You did all the work," he said, softly.

Tears welled in her eyes and Nathan leaned his forehead down to meet hers. "I'm so proud of you." He spoke with such tenderness, his breath warm on her face. "Look what beauty you have brought to the world today." He looked at Grace and Abigail saw a glistening of tears in his eyes. "She is so perfect, love." He kissed Abigail's forehead and she closed her eyes, savoring the moment and the peace she felt being in Nathan's arms.

Ian finished with the bed and then Nathan lowered her down, carefully, on the side of it. He went to the chest of drawers and pulled out a fresh gown for her. She hadn't even thought about being soiled or dirty when he was holding her.

"If you will allow me, I'll take her and introduce her to the sun and the wind while you get changed and back into bed." Nathan held his arms out for baby Grace and Abigail did not hesitate to hand her over. She watched as he took the baby, pulling her in close, holding her like the most precious treasure he had ever held. Then, in the most tender moment she had ever witnessed, he brought the baby up and leaned his cheek against her tiny forehead.

"You are our Grace," he whispered. He nestled her in the crook of his arm and gave Abigail a smile that made her feel beautiful, despite how she knew she looked.

Nathan and Ian left quietly, closing the door behind them to give Abigail privacy. She quickly changed into her fresh gown then slid down into the clean bed, sighing a deep sigh. Her body was sore, but she had never felt more alive, more complete. She heard Grace start to cry, and it pierced her heart in a way nothing had, ever before. She started to rise just as the door opened.

"Are you dressed, Abigail?" Nathan didn't come in until she responded. "I think someone is hungry," he said, coming into the room, grinning. Grace's cries were growing stronger.

Ian chuckled as he poked his head around the doorframe of Abigail's room. "Nothing wrong with those lungs!"

Nathan laid Grace beside her mama and gave her some privacy, so she could adjust to feed the baby. He left the cabin with Ian and all was quiet and still for a time. Abigail marveled at how easily everything happened. She didn't know what she was doing, and Grace didn't either, and yet, they figured it out. As if none of this was unexpected or surprising. There was some pain at first, as she helped Grace find her breast, and begin to nurse. She stared, completely in awe at this little life she held that needed her so desperately. Her heart filled with what must be the purest kind of love. The peacefulness of the moment settled over her like a warm blanket, lulling her to sleep.

~~~

Nathan came back into the cabin and into Abigail's room. Seeing her eyes closed, he quietly set the cradle on the floor by the bed. He couldn't wait for her to see it. He stood there a moment, staring down at the two most beautiful creatures he had ever seen. Abigail had Grace tightly wrapped in a blanket and held her in the crook of her arm. Both slept, peacefully. Nathan marveled at all that had just happened. He had already given his heart to Abigail, and seeing her do this today, well, it just made him love her even more. She looked like an angel laying there, Grace snuggled close. *I want to love her, Lord. I want to protect her, take care of her, forever.*

Surrender...

The word seemed to carry on the wind and grip his heart. *What does that mean? How do I surrender her? You sent her to me to be her warrior, her protector. Please don't ask it of me, Jesus.*

He watched her, intently, pleading with God to let him be her warrior, let him keep her safe. What did God want from him? Why would he send her to him, then take her back? He heard the front door open and left the room, shutting the door quietly behind him. Papa came over and sat in his chair, close to the fire.

"It's cold out today." He spoke softly, not wanting to awaken Abigail or Grace.

Nathan sat and leaned forward, hands clasped between his legs. "Yes. I think a heavy snow is coming." Ian looked at him a moment, then leaned forward as well. Nathan knew he had something to say by the look on his face.

"You can't be her everything, son. You have to let her find Jesus." He said it plainly, but with understanding.

Nathan sat back, rubbing his hands over his face. "I know." His heart broke on the words as they came forth.

"Jesus will be for her what you can never be." Papa said.

Nathan looked at his father. He wanted to fight for her. *Let me fight for her, Jesus!*

"You can't be her redeemer."

Tears came to Nathan's eyes. He knew the truth. She needed to find Jesus, to meet him face to face. Jesus wanted to give her his heart, to show her how deep and wide and endless his love is. Nathan knew that he could never heal the deep places of her heart. Only Jesus could do that. Still, he didn't want to let go.

"Why send her to us, if He meant for us to give her up?" His emotions were at war, his heart on the line.

"We are the doorway. Jesus sent her here to show her the door. She must go through it, and find him on the other side." Ian sat back, staring into the fire and rubbing his beard like he always did when he was thinking about something. He stopped abruptly, and looked at Nathan.

"She is going to leave us." He said, his voice raspy with emotion.

Nathan just stared, and his heart began to pound. He knew that look, knew his Papa had just spoken from the Spirit within him. He felt the lump form in his throat. He stood, pushing a hand through his hair when what he really wanted to do was crumple to the floor and weep.

Why? Why God? She has my heart! If she leaves, my heart leaves with her!

He looked at Papa, clenching his jaw to control the emotion welling up. What was he to do? He wouldn't close his heart off to her, wouldn't stop loving her. It wasn't possible. She held his heart in her hands, and if she did leave - when she left - she would just take it with him. Without a word, he left the cabin. He had some wrestling to do with a God he loved, about a woman he loved...a woman who held his heart.

THIRTY

Abigail sat in the rocking chair, near the fire, watching Grace sleep. She had grown so much in six weeks. She ran a hand over Grace's fuzzy blond head. She had not realized how much her heart would soften when she looked at the face of her own child. She thought that she might, for the first time in her life, understand what it meant to love someone unconditionally. It hurt, though, to realize that her own father couldn't love her the way she loved Grace. She could not imagine doing to Grace what her father had done to her…or Samuel. He had obviously never loved either of them. That revelation was a knife to her heart.

She stood, and took Grace to their room, and carefully laid her in the cradle Nathan and Ian had made for her. She loved it and was amazed by the craftsmanship. It was beautiful. She looked at her baby as she slept and was overwhelmed again with awe that this beautiful child had come from her body. How could something so beautiful come from something so terrible and ugly? Grace had blond hair, blue eyes, and pink lips. Abigail smiled when Grace's little tongue peeked through her lips, and she started sucking on it. *She is mine…my little girl.*

Nothing had ever been truly hers.

She left the room, needing to make preparations for the evening meal, and knowing Grace might not sleep for very long. There was a chicken roasting over the fire and she needed ti add the squash and carrots. She stifled a yawn. Exhaustion seemed to always be tapping on her shoulder these days. Grace woke every two or three hours to be fed, so the nights were long.

Nathan came in just as she sat down to start chopping carrots. She looked up, giving him a tired smile. He carried a package and she eyed it curiously as he removed his hat, gloves, and scarf from around his neck. He left his coat on. Winter had found its way to Weldon earlier than usual, with the first snow just over a week ago.

Nathan came over and took a chair beside her, setting his package on the table.

"How are you, Love?"

He had taken to calling her that since Grace was born, and it warmed her every time he said it.

"Tired." was all she said. She knew better than to lie to him. He could read her so well. He reached up and tucked a wisp of hair behind her ear.

"You have reason to be tired. Is Grace asleep?"

"Yes, I just put her down." She said. "What's in the package?"

His face lit up. "Something for you."

"Nathan. Why do you keep bringing me gi-" He put a finger to her lips to stop her protest, and her eyes widened. His finger on her lips felt like a flame, sending heat through her cheeks. Why did he have this effect on her?

"This is from Millie and Mrs. Hatchet. They insisted."

She looked down at the package, even more curious now, as to what was in it.

"They said every new mother needs a little spoiling." He grinned. "Open it."

She took the package and pulled the ribbon off. The package fell open in her lap, and her eyes widened. There inside was the most beautiful, lavender linen she had ever seen. "It's beautiful." She picked it up, admiring it.

"It's for the celebration," he said, softly. "For you to make yourself a new dress."

She stared at him. "B-but, I've never worn something this color…never been allowed." Her voice trailed off as she thought about her childhood and all the restrictions, all the rules.

"Do you want too?" He asked.

She didn't answer right away. Did she want to break the law she had grown up with? Could she? Should she? She reached up and touched her braid, thinking of how even that was breaking the law she had known. She loved it, though, and she knew Nathan loved it.

"I promise you will not be the only one in a colorful dress. All the ladies will wear their finest, and prettiest dresses," Nathan said.

"I'll do it," she said as if she were resolving right then to break away from what she had known her whole life.

Nathan's smile lit up his face. "I'm so glad!"

He reached out and took her hand, lacing his fingers through hers. Her heart skipped at his touch. Everything about her had begun to respond to everything about him since the night he rescued her from the river. His voice, his smile…his touch. It confused her.

"You will be the most beautiful woman there; I have no doubt."

She looked down, embarrassed by his compliment. He seemed to give her more compliments since the night he saved her at the river. He was tender and kind in everything he said, and she knew he meant his words, that they weren't just for show. With every kind thing he said to her, he tethered her heart to his and drew her closer. Did he know he was doing it? Did he know he was capturing her heart with his soft words and kindness? She suspected that he knew, but he didn't hold it over her head as if it gave him power over her. He treated her as a treasure and said he was honored every time she shared a piece of her heart with him. She often would come sit by the fire during the night to feed Grace. He was careful to give her privacy while she adjusted her nightdress and covered herself for feedings. He would sit in the chair across from her, and they would talk about things. She shared stories from the village, and things from her own home. She told him about her father and Samuel. She told him some of the things her father had done, how he had treated her. She even talked to him about Thomas. She had shared much with him these past six weeks, and in all that she shared, he had listened, intently. He never looked at her with shock or disgust. His eyes were always steady, filled with compassion. Every time she would finish feeding Grace and stand to go back to bed he would rise, come to her, lean in, kiss her forehead then whisper the same words...

"I'm honored that you choose to share your story with me, Abigail. Thank you for trusting me."

Somewhere along the way she *had* begun to trust him. Maybe it was his calm, steady nature, or the way he looked at her, always with compassion in his eyes. She wasn't sure why or even how she had the courage to share with Nathan all she had, but every time she did, she felt more security, rather than less. It made no sense, she would admit that, and fear still gnawed at her that this wouldn't last, that it was too good to be true.

She ran her hand over the linen, then looked at Nathan. "I will do it. I'll make myself a dress of lavender to wear to the celebration."

Nathan stood, and offered a hand to her. "Will you let me show you a dance?"

Her heart forgot to beat for a moment. "I-I don't know, Nathan." She looked down at the fabric, absently rubbing her fingers over it. "I will probably not be any good at it."

He knelt down in front of her and covered her hand on top of the fabric. "Please?"

She could hardly resist him, and the tender hope in his eyes. "Very well…" She moved the package to the table and they both stood. Nathan took her hand and drew her out away from the table. He didn't let go but pulled her close. He slipped a hand around her waist and raised the other between them.

Breathe. Remember to breathe. She looked at his chest, feeling fire everywhere they touched. What was happening to her? She had determined to despise men, forever, yet this one made her throat dry and her heart forget to beat. She had never known anything but fear with men. Fear of Thomas and all the horrid things he did to her. Fear of her father's harsh rules and punishments. Fear was the only emotion she ever attached to men. But Nathan….

"Abigail, please look at me." He said.

She slowly lifted her eyes and their gazes connected. She didn't feel afraid of him, but…what did she feel?

"Does this make you uncomfortable?" He searched her gaze, dropping his hand from her waist. "We don't have to dance at the celebration. We don't have to do anything you don't want to do." He backed up a step, giving her space.

She searched his eyes and saw that he actually meant what he said. If she said "no" he would never mention it again. He wouldn't make her do anything she didn't want to do…ever. "I-I want to try."

Light filled his eyes as he smiled, and he put his hand to her waist stepping close again. "Just follow my lead."

She breathed in his woodsy scent and noticed how small her hand looked in his large, work-worn one. She didn't look at him but kept her head down, trying to watch his feet and follow. She didn't want to step on his toes. She didn't want to mess up. He moved slowly around the table, keeping her close and leading her gently through the dance. Nathan stepped back and raised her hand in the air, spinning her once, then pulled her close again. Their eyes connected in the exact moment that he drew her close and everything seemed to go perfectly still.

"You are beautiful." He whispered.

He always called her beautiful, but in this moment, standing so close to him, it felt different. Standing in his arms as he said it made her feel wanted. He brought her hand to his heart and kept it there. Who was this big, strong, timber man that always treated her with such tenderness? She searched his eyes and she saw something in them that she hadn't noticed before, something she couldn't label. It didn't scare her, though. Everything she saw in Nathan's eyes only ever made her feel safe. When in her whole life, had she ever felt safe? *Never…until you.*

He reached up and tugged her braid. "You're a fast learner." He grinned.

"Thank you." She didn't look away but stayed there, searching his gaze, overwhelmed by this man and what he was becoming to her. He leaned in and kissed her forehead. She closed her eyes and they filled with tears. His kiss felt like a warm blanket being draped around cold shoulders. His gentleness made her want to weep.

Nathan leaned back and looked at her. "Tears?" He asked, softly.

She nodded, unable to speak past the lump in her throat.

Nathan brushed a tear from her cheek with his thumb and brought it to his lips. "Your tears are treasured, love."

She smiled at him through the fresh ones that fell, too overcome to speak. Why would he treasure her tears?

After a moment, Nathan squeezed her hand then went to the door, grabbing his hat, gloves, and scarf. "Thank you for saying, yes," he said. Then he left, closing the door quietly, behind him.

She stared at the door, glued to her spot. *Thank you for saying yes to me.* Something about those words stirred something deep inside of her. She had only said yes to him showing her the dance, but it felt like more. She felt like she had been saying "yes" to Nathan for a while now, and he had been thanking her again, as he always did, for trusting him with the tiny pieces of her heart.

THIRTY ONE

Nathan glanced at Abigail beside him on the bench. She seemed more relaxed now in their Sunday gatherings. The first time she had come her eyes had been wide and her face pale the whole time. Now, she seemed to be listening to what Reverend James had to say, with a look of curiosity. She often had a question for him on the way home from church about something she had seen or heard. Today's message was about God's grace. He smiled to himself. *I'll bet she has lots of questions about that, Lord.*

He thought often of what Papa said, the day of Grace's birth. He still pleaded constantly with Jesus to let him be Abigail's protector. He never heard an answer, but he didn't stop asking. He didn't close his heart off to her either, even though he knew what might loom ahead. How could he? He loved her, completely. There was no way he could just stop giving her his heart. He could only plead with Jesus to give him the grace to take what might come. He spent many nights alone in the forest, crying out to God for her soul and his own heart. He looked down at Grace sleeping peacefully in Abigail's arms. He marveled at them both. Abigail had taken to motherhood without question. She loved her baby, fiercely. It amazed him, how a woman who had been through all she had, could still love unconditionally. There really must be nothing like a mother's love.

"And so, friends, what do we say to all this? Do we keep living in our old ways, doing what we know is wrong, so that grace can abound?"

"No, reverend!" Someone up front responded.

Nathan grinned. He loved how the people responded to the reverend's words.

"No, indeed!" Reverend James said." It is because of grace that we walk away from our old ways." He walked out from behind his wooden podium and stopped in front of it, looking out over his congregants. "Grace must become the foundation of our lives. When we discover the greatness of grace, our hearts are turned towards God, not away from him. We no longer worry with how we will mess up, or fear that he will turn away from us. Grace reveals to us the depth of His love for us, and that love sets us free. Grace draws us towards God." He stepped forward a bit, clasping his hands in front of him. "We know we will make mistakes…unless there is one among us who can say they have managed to live without mistakes?"

The crowd chuckled a bit. Reverend James smiled.

"We rest in grace, friends. We pray, we seek to be like Jesus and we rest in grace when we fail, because we know Jesus covers our mistakes."

He scanned the crowd with a warm smile, and then his eyes found Abigail. Nathan glanced at her again and saw that she was sitting completely still, wide eyes glued to Reverend James.

"We rest in grace." Reverend James said again as if he were telling Abigail, specifically. He motioned for the congregation to rise then led them all in a prayer, thanking God for His grace and asking Him to show each heart how to rest fully in it. Nathan slipped a hand around Abigail's free hand and squeezed her fingers. She looked up at him, eyes puffy with unshed tears. He smiled at her then leaned down, bringing his mouth close to her ear. "God's grace is just like that sweet baby you hold. She knows your voice, your touch, and your scent. Just as she always wants you above anyone else, his grace is always seeking you out, always wanting you."

She leaned her head on his shoulder and he brought his arm across her back, leaning his jaw against her hair. She shuddered with soft cries.

Tears are good. Let her tears bring her healing. He looked at Papa who stood on the other side of Abigail. He smiled at Nathan. They both knew that today had been a God orchestrated moment, just for Abigail.

Please, Jesus. Save her…and let me keep her safe. His eyes filled with tears. He knew he needed to leave that last part off, but he couldn't help it. He wanted her, so desperately, and he wouldn't stop asking God, ever.

~~~

Abigail followed behind Nathan as everyone filed out of the meetinghouse. Reverend James' words had left her with many questions. Never in all her years had she heard anyone talk about grace and say that we all make mistakes and that it was okay. The elders in her village talked about all the things people must do to rid themselves of their sins. Grace was never part of the solution. She had been taught that Jesus died for the elect, and the elect must work hard to stay in good standing. She walked out of the church behind Nathan and Ian, shivering a bit when the icy air touched her skin.

"Ah, and how is our favorite little girl, today?" Reverend James asked, giving Abigail a kind smile.

"She is well, reverend."

"And you, Abigail? How are you these days?" He searched her eyes as if he really wanted to know.

She looked down at Grace. *Does he really care?* "I-I am well," she whispered.

He put a hand on her shoulder, and she looked up at him. "It was good to see you both today."

She thought he meant it. "Thank you."

Reverend James turned to Ian and asked him how things were down at the mill. Nathan led Abigail down the steps towards their wagon. They waved and greeted friends as they passed them. Normally they might mingle for a while, but no one wanted to linger in this cold weather. Ian caught up to them and took Grace, so Abigail could climb into the wagon. Once she was settled Abigail reached out for Grace.

"Can she sit with me mama, in the back?" Ian asked, holding Grace close.

Abigail smiled. These two men sure did dote on her baby. "Of course she can."

Ian slid into the back of the wagon, then turned Grace in his arms so she could see all around them. He made sure her bonnet was down snugly around her ears then tucked her close. Abigail smiled at how gentle a big timber man could be with a baby girl. Nathan climbed up beside Abigail, grabbed the reins, and set the horses in motion.

He nudged her playfully with his shoulder. "So…any questions for me today?"

She had so many questions, so many things she didn't understand. "I've never heard someone say that mistakes are allowed." She looked at Nathan, pulling her coat close around her neck to block out the cold air. The dirt roads had been cleared from the most recent snowfall, but the forest was still blanketed in white, making for a beautiful, peaceful scene. "All this talk about God's grace doesn't really make sense to me. How can a God who expects us to be sinless also offer this grace that excuses us?"

"Grace doesn't excuse our sins. It paid for them."

She looked out ahead as they rode along. Payment for sins was something she knew well. "So, you're saying that God doesn't excuse our sins, but he found a way to pay for them, so we don't have to. That is grace?"

"That is grace" Nathan responded, nodding.

"It sounds too good to be true," Abigail said, skeptical.

"I know. I thought that too, at one time. Then, I thought about my Papa," he motioned behind him to Ian. "He has always loved me, and that hasn't changed based on my mistakes. That's the same kind of love God has for us. He keeps loving us and wanting to be close to us, no matter what we do. He wants to be in a relationship with us."

"So, you think God wants a relationship with me?" She put a hand to her chest.

"Very much, love," he said, softly.

"And you have a relationship with Him?"

Nathan nodded. "I do. I spend time with Him by reading his word and praying. Sometimes, I just share what's on my heart. Other times I sit in stillness and listen for His voice."

"And He speaks to you?" She asked, incredulous.

Never had she heard of being in a relationship with God and talking to Him. He was always a God who couldn't be reached by people like Abigail. The elders were the ones who supposedly knew God and what He expected.

"He speaks to me in different ways. Sometimes, through a verse, or story in his Word. Sometimes, I hear His truth from Papa. Then, there are times I just know the answer deep in my heart, like His spirit has just come along and written it there." He looked at her. "He longs to be in a relationship with us. So much so, that He sent his son to die in our place. We can't add to what Jesus did by punishing ourselves for our mistakes. We can only accept that God is a loving papa and that His only son was willing to take our place."

"And anyone can be forgiven?"

"Anyone," Nathan said.

She stared at him a moment, then looked back at Grace and Ian, who sat snuggled up. She turned back and stared out over the horses, pondering everything Nathan and Reverend James had said. It made no sense, talking to God as if He were a friend. How could it be? She felt the shame of her past tapping on her shoulder, reminding her of how impossible it was for God to see her and want her. Nathan didn't have the stains on his soul that she did. He was easy to love, with his kindness and compassion for others. No, it wasn't possible for God to look at her and love her. He had never come to her rescue, never saved her from all the horror she had experienced. Where had His grace been for her, then? It didn't seem to her that God had ever been on her side. Grace must be only for those who deserve it, and she knew that she did not.

THIRTY TWO

Abigail stared at herself in the mirror. The dress she had made for tonight's celebration turned out better than she expected. She loved it. The fitted sleeves and high collar trimmed in lace were so beautiful. She could hardly believe she was looking at herself in the mirror. There had even been enough fabric left to make a baby gown for Grace who laid on the bed, kicking her feet out in front of her. Nathan assured Abigail that all the women would be wearing dresses of all colors. She had hesitated about breaking away from her traditions and laws, but seeing herself now, she was glad she had said yes.

She grabbed the skirt of the dress and twirled a bit, delighted at the way it swished at her feet. She had braided her hair starting at her crown and gathered it all the way down her back. She let tiny wisps fall around her face and was pleased with the way it looked. She wasn't courageous enough to leave it completely down. She had seen the light in Nathan's eye when she wore it in a braid, so she chose to do so hoping to see that light in his eyes, again. She admitted to herself that she wanted his approval. She sat down on the bed beside Grace who smiled when she saw her mama and made a cooing sound. Abigail smiled and leaned her elbows on either side of her sweet baby, and kissed her chubby cheek.

She then went about putting on her boots and lacing them up.

"Well," she turned to look at Grace again. "I guess this will be a first for both of us, baby girl. I've never been to a dance, either." She stood up. "I'll be back for you in just a bit." She had barricaded Grace with pillows, even though she knew she wasn't quite old enough yet to roll over.

It was time to go out and show Nathan what she had created. Why was she nervous? It was just Nathan, and she knew he would be kind. He was always kind in everything he said and did. "Here we go." With that, she opened the door and stepped out into the main room.

~~~

Nathan stood up as soon as he heard the door open, excited to see Abigail in the dress she had been working on for a couple of months. He was not prepared, though, for what he saw when she emerged from the room. He stared at her, knowing he was staring but helpless to stop. His mind scrambled for the right word to describe her. The dress fit her perfectly. The fitted sleeves and high collar were trimmed in lace. The bodice tapered into her waist, then fanned out around her hips. It highlighted her petite curves beautifully, and the lavender color gave her eyes an almost violet hue. She wore her hair in a braid that hung over her shoulder, and tiny wisps curled around her face. *She is breathtaking.*

He had told her not to worry about standing out among the other women because all would be dressed in different colors, but the vision he saw before him now would draw every eye at the dance. Nathan heard Papa clear his throat, and it snapped him out of his trance. He walked quickly to where she stood and reached for her hand.

"You are beautiful, Abigail," he whispered, wanting to infuse her heart with the truth of his words. He placed a gentle kiss on her hand, then squeezed it. "I am honored to have you next to me, tonight." *Oh, Jesus. Don't take her from me...please...*

She lowered her gaze as she always did when he gave her compliments. He knew they made her uncomfortable and shy because they were foreign to her.

"Thank you."

Papa came over and Nathan stepped back a bit, extending Abigail's hand in his. "She is lovely, Papa, isn't she?"

"Indeed! You will outshine the rest, Abigail." He smiled his warm, comforting smile, and she gave him a little curtsy, a grin filling her face. Nathan knew that Papa's praise always gave her courage, even though she didn't realize it. They both bowed dramatically before her, causing her to giggle.

"Now, where is my Grace?" Papa asked.

"She is all ready for you," Abigail said, smiling. She let go of Nathan's hand and went back into the room. She came out a few seconds later with Grace in her arms, turned out so they could see her in her new gown. Grace saw Papa and the kicks and coos increased.

And how are we tonight, little one?" She wasn't reaching for people yet, but if she could, she would be reaching for Papa, Nathan was sure of it.

"Well aren't you just the prettiest thing," Papa said as Abigail handed Grace over. Nathan shook his head with a laugh. "I do believe she has you wrapped around her finger, Papa."

"Both our girls do," he said with a wink to Abigail who blushed slightly. "I love you Nathan, but I've been missing out all these years without daughters to love."

Nathan laughed at that statement. Papa wandered out onto the porch with Grace, leaving Nathan alone with Abigail. He stepped over in front of her again. "You look lovely, Abigail." He caught the subtle fragrance of lavender and gently lifted her braid in his palm. He closed his eyes and breathed in the scent of her. When he opened his eyes he saw a sheen of tears in hers.

"Tears?" he asked, knowing if this woman had tears to shed there was a good reason. Everything good that came her way seemed to bring up more pain, more memories.

"I feel...pretty." A lone tear trailed her cheek as she said the words. "I've never felt pretty...ever." She whispered.

Nathan caught the tear with his thumb and brought it to his lips. He cupped her cheek. "You're beautiful." He meant every word. Abigail was enchanting but didn't know it. Life had made her believe she was less than beautiful. He was determined to show her the truth. He saw a shadow cross her face. "What's wrong, love?"

"I..." She looked away, hesitant, he could tell, to finish her thought. He gently tipped her chin up with a finger, searching her eyes. "Tell me, please?"

"I just don't want anyone to think poorly of you or Ian for taking in an unwed girl and her baby." More tears trailed her cheek and she bit down on her bottom lip.

Nathan cupped her face with one hand and brought her other hand up next to his heart. "I care nothing for what others think, Abigail." He looked deep into her eyes. "I will stand beside you with joy in my heart." She let out a half laugh, half sob at his words.

"There is no place I'd rather be," he whispered. He brought her close and kissed her forehead. Oh, how he wanted to communicate his whole heart to her with a real kiss, but this wasn't the time. She needed to believe she was cherished without the physical intimacy that had always brought her pain. For tonight, he would cherish her with his words and deeds.

"I would be honored, fairest maiden, if you would allow me to be your escort tonight." He made a grand show of bowing as he spoke, hoping to bring out her beautiful smile. He wasn't disappointed. She wiped the leftover tears from her face then, with a quick intake of breath, grabbed Grace's little bag of necessities and favorite blanket from their room. Nathan extended his arm and she took it with a smile on her face. Tonight he was going to treat her like royalty because, as far as he was concerned, royalty, she was.

THIRTY THREE

Abigail took in the scene of the meetinghouse. The women all looked so beautiful. She had never seen so many colors in one place. Nathan had been right. The women of Weldon had brought out their finest for this night. She saw dresses of purple, pink, green and blue. All the dresses shimmered in the light of the many candles around the room. She didn't stand out at all in her dress and she was relieved. She glanced at Nathan next to her, so handsome in his black breeches, crisp white shirt, and cravat tied at his neck. He was one of the tallest men in the room, and he stood out whether he wanted to or not. His navy blue coat with gold buttons down the front fit snugly over his chest and flared from his hips to his knee. He wore his finest tricorn hat, the one he saved for special occasions, because it didn't have sawdust all over it. He had even shined his shoes, she noticed. He caught her staring and grinned, then leaned in close to her ear.

"This thing is choking the life out of me." He tugged at his cravat and she covered a giggle when he stuck his tongue out to mimic choking.

Abigail knew he was trying to put her at ease by being silly. It did help, and she felt the knot in her stomach slowly begin to release. These people were not like the ones in the village. She didn't have to be afraid here. Nathan wouldn't leave her side. She untied her cloak and handed it to Nathan. He took it over to the little area set up for hanging hats, coats and cloaks. Abigail glanced behind her and saw Ian had been held up by a couple of little elderly ladies.

While she stood waiting for Nathan her gaze roamed the meetinghouse that had been transformed for the celebration. There was one area with a long row of tables, laden with more food than Abigail had ever seen at one time. Colorful ribbons trimmed the doorway and streamed between the columns in the room. A few men sat together at the front of the room, tuning their instruments. Her village would call this unforgivable – having a party in a meetinghouse. She had a hard time believing this was a sin, though, as she heard the sounds of laughter and saw the joy on people's faces. These people were celebrating life. There was nothing serious or somber about this Christmas celebration. She saw Millie, who waved at her from across the room. Ian stood there, showing off Grace to all the ladies. He was beaming over all the attention Grace was getting. She waved back with a smile. Millie had become her friend here in Weldon. She thought of Bethany, home tonight with her little sister. She didn't come to many gatherings in the winter time. Millie had mentioned that the cold weather caused Bethany pain, so she stayed home near the fire in these long, cold months.

The men on stage began a sweet melody on their stringed instruments.

"Care to dance, milady?"

She felt Nathan's breath on the back of her neck as he whispered in her ear. What was happening to her? Every time he came near, her stomach did flips and her heart skipped. This was Nathan; her defender, her friend. She didn't have the right to feel anything else for him. He deserved much better than her.

"I don't know how to dance like them, Nathan," she said quietly, feeling insecure about her lack of knowledge on something that clearly every woman in Weldon knew how to do.

"Don't worry, you can stand on my feet." Nathan teased. "We can stay on the edge in case it gets too confusing. If so, we can easily slip away."

She couldn't think with him this close. "Fine. We can try one dance."

If only her father could see her now: wearing a dress of purple, dancing in a meetinghouse. She shook her head at the irony of it all. Nathan took hold of her hand and led her to the dance floor, keeping to the edge, as he promised. He put a hand around her waist and held the other one out from him a bit.

He applied a little pressure to her back drawing her closer and said, "Now, this one is easy. We practiced, and you can do it. Just follow my lead. I'll move slowly, I promise."

He winked and gave her that trademark smile. She kept her eyes on his, letting him lead the way and was amazed at how smoothly it all went. It was as if, as long as she held his hand and let him lead, she couldn't miss a step. He led her in two dances, one of them completely new to her. He seemed to sense her every move and when she started to step wrong, he gently corrected. No one was the wiser. When the dance finished, everyone clapped, then dispersed.

"Grace will be hungry, soon," she scanned the room, looking for Ian and Grace. She spotted him sitting next to Mrs. Hatchet on one of the benches that had been moved to the side of the room for the celebration. Grace sat against

Ian's chest, chewing on her fingers while taking in the scene. Ian threw his head back with laughter at something Mrs. Hatchet said. She appeared to be amused, too.

"I think I'll go out for a breath of fresh air before I feed her." Perspiration dotted her forehead from both the dancing and the crowded room that was quickly warming up. Nathan took her hand and they weaved through the crowd, toward the door. They stopped occasionally, to speak to people. She watched as Nathan gave everyone he spoke to his full attention, asking questions about their families and various things he seemed to know about them. He treated everyone with the same kindness she saw in him daily.

She needed to hurry so she could get back to Grace and feed her. She stepped up behind him as he was speaking to an elderly lady and whispered in his ear. "I'll be back."

He squeezed her fingers letting her know he had heard, and she slipped away towards the exit. She walked out onto the porch of the meetinghouse breathing deep of the frosty air. Her skin began to cool, immediately. It had warmed some in the past days but still, the air was crisp. The sounds of music and laughter came through the doors out into the open air. She went down the porch and walked a few steps away, craning her neck to take in the stars above. There were so many, too many to count, all shimmering and twinkling as if they winked at her from above.
Suddenly, she felt the hair on her neck stand up, then just as quickly felt a hand come around her waist.

"Well, well." His voice singed the hair on her neck. She tried to turn around, but he pulled her against him. She didn't want to make a scene, so she didn't resist. At least

Grace was safe inside, with Ian.

"Breaking all the rules, now, are we?" He whispered into her ear.

"What do you want?" She asked, keeping her voice low. How had he known she was here? Did he always know where she was? Dread filled her. He knew exactly where she had been all these months.

"Why, I've come to see you pet." His hand tightened on her waist and she felt bile rise in her throat. "It's almost time for you to come home," he leaned his head in right next to her ear and spoke in a low, gravelly voice. "It's almost time for you to repent of your sins."

Her eyes widened then she closed them tight, breathing deeply. *Nathan.* She needed him, now. *God. I need Nathan, now!*

Almost as if in response to her silent plea, she heard footsteps on the meetinghouse porch. She faced away from the meetinghouse, and Thomas stood behind her, so she couldn't be sure who it was that had come outside.

"I'll be back for you…very soon." He ran his free hand down her braid like a snake slithering down her back. Then…he was gone.

She whipped around, fast, scanning the darkness. He had faded into the night so fast she couldn't make out anyone. Then she saw Nathan.

He came down the steps and spotted her. She didn't move…couldn't move.

"There you are! I was coming to ch-" he stopped, able to see her face now that he was closer. He put his hands on her shoulders. "Abigail? What's wrong?" He searched her face.

She stared, paralyzed by fear. "T-Thomas…" She managed to say.

Nathan's eyes widened, and he looked all around. "He was here?" He asked, fiercely.

"He is coming back for me, Nathan." She didn't cry. She was too numb with shock and fear to cry. "He's coming for me…soon."

Nathan pulled her to him, her body like a stone as he wrapped his arms around her.

"He came…said he would be back…then he was gone." She spoke muffled against his chest.

"I'm sorry, Abigail. I'm sorry he got to you tonight." He gripped her closer, one hand to her head and another around her back. He pulled back, cupping her face and searching her eyes. His face was illuminated by the glow of the moon. "He will not hurt you again, Abigail."

She knew he meant it. He would do anything in his power to protect her. Still, she knew Thomas, and she was afraid.

"H-he is clever, Nathan…he will have a well thought out plan." She started to tremble.

"Abigail." He spoke with passion and ferocity, gripping her tight. "He *will not* hurt you, again. I promise you, he will not."

She did trust Nathan - he and Ian were the only people she had ever trusted - but she knew how evil and clever Thomas was. She feared Nathan's kindness and compassion would be the weakness Thomas used against them both. Nathan wanted to be her warrior, wanted to protect her. He had been her warrior, saving her many times. How much would that cost him? She had cried out for him, silently, just now, and then he had been there as if he had heard her. He was her savior, but she feared he couldn't stand against Thomas.

She nodded in response. "You have been my savior so many times. Thank you." Then, she remembered. "I-I need to feed Grace."

He stepped back and looked at her as though he were shocked by what she said. "I-I am not a savior, Abigail. I'm just a man." He said it as though he were in pain. He searched her eyes a moment, then lifted her hand and placed a kiss in her palm. His gentleness in every moment made her want to weep, especially in this moment. She steeled herself, though, against emotion. If she started crying, she would become hysterical, start to panic. Grace needed her, and she needed to stay calm. Nathan turned and led her back into the meetinghouse. They found Ian standing near the entrance, holding Grace. Nathan stopped in front of them, and when Grace saw Abigail she started to fuss. Abigail took her. "I'll just go find an empty corner, so I can feed her." She took the blanket from Ian, then quickly made her way through the crowd. The music, the laughter, it all sounded different after seeing Thomas, as if it all mocked her now. There was to be no joy or peace for Abigail. Her life was one battle after another. It was just a matter of time until the next tragedy came for her.

It was only a matter of time.

~~~

"What happened?" Ian asked, concern etched on his face.

Nathan still felt the heat of fury pumping through his veins. Thomas had been here! Had he touched her? The thought of him anywhere near Abigail sickened Nathan. He stared off into the crowd, jaw set, eyes blazing. "Thomas was here."

"Jesus…" was all Papa whispered.

"She went out for some air, and he must have been lurking around." He turned and looked at Papa. "He said he was coming back for her…soon."

"We will protect her, son," Papa spoke with authority and certainty.

"Papa…" he was terrified if he were being honest. Abigail had become his heartbeat and he couldn't handle the thought of losing her. Then, when Abigail had called him her savior, the truth had become crystal clear to him. She saw him as her savior, and if she didn't find Jesus, she would turn him into her god. He realized in that moment that letting her go was the only way she would find Jesus. His eyes filled with tears. He would protect her with every fiber of his being. As long as she was with him, he would fight for her. "I'll do whatever I have to."

"I know, son…I know." Papa searched his eyes, then looked off into the crowd.

They stood there a long time, staring into the crowd, both consumed with their thoughts. Nathan felt like he had been tossed into the middle of a storm. He was filled with fury over Thomas showing up and sorrow over Abigail's words. He had been careful not to show Abigail any of his anger. He didn't want to scare her. He realized his hands were fisted at his side and he relaxed them a bit. He felt Papa's hand on his shoulder.

"We'll stay close to her, son. Don't let her go to the river alone."

Nathan nodded, jaw still clenched.

"I have a feeling when he does come back, we will put an end to this madness." Papa looked at Nathan, his brow furrowed.

Nathan didn't know exactly what that meant, but he wanted there to be an end. He wanted Abigail to be safe, once and for all.

THIRTY FOUR

Abigail sat in the rocking chair near the fire, knitting a new hat for Grace. Grace sat on the floor beside Nathan who was stretched out on the rug, playing with her. She could sit up with a little help, now. Nathan had put a fortress of pillows around her, so she wouldn't fall over and hit her head on the hard floor. Ian sat in his chair, reading his Bible.

The winter weather had started to fade, and spring was knocking on the door. Abigail was ready for springtime. She wanted to take Grace into the forest and let her experience all the life that bloomed in it.

She heard a faint noise and turned her head a bit to listen. "Did you hear something?" She looked at Nathan.

He sat up, listening. There! She heard it again. Nathan got up and went to the window and pulled back the curtain. Abigail left all her knitting on the chair and went over beside Nathan. There were lanterns off in the distance, but it was too dark to make out anything but the tiny dots of lights. Abigail felt a prickle of unease crawl up her spine, and she looked up at Nathan who put an arm around her shoulder, then kissed her temple. She walked over to where Grace sat on the floor and picked her up.

"It's a crowd, coming this way," Nathan said, peering out the window. He turned to Abigail. "Thomas is leading them."

Her eyes widened in fear and she gripped the chair next to her. They were coming for her; Thomas was coming, just as he said he would. Nathan came over and took her hand from the table, lacing his fingers through hers and bringing it up next to his heart. With the other hand, he cupped her cheek.

"I'm going to protect you. Will you trust me?" He asked, his voice steady, no hint of fear.

Panic seized Abigail. "How?" She choked out, face ashen with fear, her grip on Grace tight.

"Don't be afraid." He whispered, rubbing his fingers through Grace's downy, blond hair.

Ian stood and came over to them. Grace kicked and cooed when he came close, and he reached for her. She went to him, willingly.

Nathan pulled Abigail close, with his arms around her, and she laid her head against his chest, right next to his heart. She was trembling with fear. How was Nathan going to protect her? How was he going to fight off an entire mob?

Nathan whispered close to her ear. "I will fight for you, Abigail."

The words filled her, causing a tidal wave of emotion. No one had ever protected her…ever…until Nathan. Her cries increased.

"Abigail." Every time he said her name it drew her gaze, as if when he said it her heart couldn't help but respond. "I will not abandon you," Nathan said.

He caught one of her tears with his thumb, kissing it to his lips.

"I will fight for you." He said again with firm resolve.

Her heart wanted to believe him, but fear screamed that he couldn't, or that he wouldn't, in the end. Still, she nodded. There was nothing she could do, nowhere else to turn.

"I want you to stay inside, no matter what. Promise me you'll stay in here, with Papa."

She stared at him a moment, then, "I will stay inside. I promise."

He moved a hand to her shoulder and leaned his forehead against hers. She brought a hand to her mouth, stifling the sob that wanted to escape.

"It's going to be okay, love."

She nodded, gripping his shirt in her fist.

"No matter what happens, stay in here." Nathan pulled her close, kissed her forehead firmly, then stepped away.

~~~

Nathan turned to Ian. "Papa." He didn't have to say anything else. His Papa put a hand on his shoulder, the other holding Grace snug against him.

"I know, son. I know you have to do this...for Abigail and Grace."

Nathan saw the sheen of tears in his eyes. "Though, as your papa, I don't want to send you out there, into danger." He gripped Nathan's shoulder, tighter. "This madness ends tonight," Papa said with more intensity than Nathan had ever heard. "I will be in here with them," he said. "I won't leave them."

"Thank you, Papa." Nathan gripped his shoulder and they stared at each other for a fraction of a second. Papa had taught him to defend the weak, to fight against injustice. Nathan knew he was doing the right thing.

Nathan leaned in and kissed Grace's temple. He went and grabbed his rifle, hanging over the mantle and headed for the door. He paused and looked over at Abigail. She stared at him, looking much like she did the day he rescued her; helpless and afraid. Every fiber of his being wanted to rush over, take her in his arms and hold her until she believed he was hers and she mattered to him more than his own life.

Instead, he asked the question always present between them. "Will you trust me, Abigail?" He watched her, willing her to believe he was trustworthy, that he would protect her. He cared more that she believe it than he cared what happened to him tonight. She nodded and Nathan looked back at Papa once more, then left the cabin, shutting the door firmly behind him.

He stood on the porch, rifle in both hands, and waited. They came close, and Nathan's eyes connected with Thomas'. His spirit quickened and reminded him of the dreams he had of Abigail - before he rescued her - where she had been cornered by a figure in black.

Thomas.

Thomas was the figure in black in Nathan's dreams. He was the one who had oppressed her all these years. Nathan was flooded with the realization that those dreams had been from God, preparing him for this moment. He closed his eyes and leaned into the one voice he needed to hear above all else. Then certainty flooded his soul, and he knew; tonight he would fight for Abigail but not with a weapon. He looked at the rifle in his hand, and slowly leaned it against the porch railing.

We fight with weapons, not of this world.

Truth flooded his heart. Tonight, he would fight for Abigail with his own life.

"Jesus…" He only knew to call on his Savior in this

moment, when darkness pressed in from every side. "Be my strength."

The mob came close to the porch and stopped, the torches they carried highlighting the darkness in their faces.

"We've come for what is ours." Thomas said, "Just hand her over and we will leave you alone."

Nathan scanned the faces before responding. He didn't see her father among them.

"No. She doesn't want to go with you." He paused. "And I will protect her, if necessary."

Thomas laughed a sinister laugh that made Nathan's skin crawl. *This man is the very presence of darkness.*

"You will protect her? From us? You cannot stand against all of us! Don't be a fool! Give us what is ours!"

Thomas was spitting as he spoke. His eyes looked crazed, possessed. "She must pay." He spoke in a low, gravelly voice.

"Abigail belongs to no one. Go home. I don't want any violence." Nathan spoke with calm authority even though his nerves were strung tight and sweat trailed his back.

Thomas suddenly came up on the porch and stepped close to Nathan. "Abigail is ours," he said.

Nathan didn't flinch or look away from Thomas' eyes. Anger coursed through his veins, at the thought of all the evil things this man had done to Abigail. He warred with what his flesh told him to do and what he knew he must do. *Jesus, help me.*

Just like the day he had rescued Abigail from the mob, he would try speaking to the crowd; the one's easily swayed. He stepped away from Thomas, over to the side of the porch. "Why do you come for her? Why do you want her back?"

The crowd began to murmur, then someone shouted, "We need to complete her purging, so we will be restored to God! She left our village unclean!"

Nathan marveled at the absurdity of these people. Their view of God was so distorted, so completely wrong. "Friends, God doesn't need you to punish yourselves! He took the punishment for all our sins!" He wanted to reason with them, hoped he could.

"Don't listen to him! He speaks lies! We must continue to earn our favor with God! We must continue to seek retribution!" Thomas shouted.

The crowd began to murmur and shout agreement. Nathan felt the presence of darkness like a thousand little insects crawling up the porch, surrounding him. *Jesus, they won't listen this time! What do I do? How do I protect Abigail?*

Surrender...

The truth became clear the moment that word whispered through his soul. They wanted retribution, thought they needed a sacrifice. They would not leave without Abigail, even if it meant cutting him down first. He knew what he must do.

He would offer himself in her place.

"Take me, in her place! I will stand in place of Abigail and take the purging." He spoke calm, steady, looking into the faces of the mob. There was no fear in him, only love for Abigail and it filled him with courage. He knew without a doubt that Jesus had been preparing him for this moment. The mob could very well kill him tonight, but Abigail and Grace would be safe.

The crowd stirred with murmurs and exclamations, confused and shocked at his declaration. Thomas still stood on the step near him. He looked over at Nathan, and Nathan saw a shadow of surprise on his face. Then, the crazed look returned, and he smiled a crooked, filthy smile.

"Yes." He whispered with delight, leaning close to Nathan. "We will take you in her place." He turned to his followers. "He will stand in her place! We will purge him and then finally be restored to God!"

The crowd shouted agreement. Thomas then moved quickly behind Nathan and shoved him off the steps, into the mob. Nathan fell into the dirt and was immediately attacked by the crowd.

"Take him!" The mob became violent, grabbing at Nathan as if he were an empty sack. They pulled him by his hair, drug him by his legs through the dirt. He didn't fight it, he let them take him away. They beat him, causing him to cry out more than once. He could have fought them off, but he didn't. He was choosing to surrender.

I can do this...for Abigail.

He saw her face in his mind even as the crowd was beating him, and he knew he could do this. He knew Papa would watch over Abigail and Grace until he was free to come back to them. And if he didn't make it back, he knew Papa would take care of them, forever.

Once he was beaten and bloodied to their liking, the mob hoisted him up and carried him off towards the village. It seemed like forever that they carried him, his body becoming heavy with pain. They threw him down on the ground and beat him, then dragged him some, before they would hoist him up again and carry him like a pig about to be thrown on a fire. They were chanting some low mournful sound. Finally, they came into the village.

"Tie him to the purging post!" Thomas shouted, in a high-pitched voice. The mob threw him down in front of the post, and his head smacked against it, causing pain to explode behind his eyes. All he could think of in this moment was that Abigail had suffered here, that these people had imprisoned her with their twisted form of religion.

No more. The thought beat through his head like a drum. Abigail would be free, never to suffer like this. He was making sure of it. Tonight, he was sealing her future. Someone yanked his arms hard and he groaned in pain. His eyes were swollen to small slits. He only saw the blur of figures as they crowded around him. They tied his arms to the post and he felt someone rip his shirt off. His whole body was on fire from being punched and kicked so many times. Thomas came to stand beside him. Then without warning, Nathan felt and heard the whip crack across his back. He cried out in pain, squeezing the post, with arms wrapped around it. The whip cracked against his flesh, over and over, blood running down his back and dripping to the ground around him. He was barely conscious, but he knew when the whipping stopped. He hung from the post like an animal stripped of skin, too weak to hold himself upright.

"He is purged and now we can be restored to God!" Thomas shouted to the mob.

The shouts of gladness went up all around and faded in Nathan's ear as everything went black.

THIRTY FIVE

Abigail checked on Grace, asleep in her cradle, then left the room, closing the door behind her. She walked to the window and looked out into the darkness. Her eyes were on fire from all the tears she had shed, and her throat ached. She began pacing again, too nervous to sit still. Ian sat in his chair near the fire, Bible open in his lap, his head leaning against his hand. They had watched from the window as the mob drug Nathan away. She had screamed, wanted to run after them, but Ian had kept her there beside him with his arms around her. He told her to stay, that Nathan was fighting for her, and she must let him. Tears had rolled down his cheeks as he said it. She felt sick with worry and panic. They were purging Nathan instead of her. They might kill him! She went over to the chair opposite Ian and sat down.

"Ian…I'm so afraid." There wasn't much else to say. She was terrified; terrified of losing Nathan, because he had taken her place. Ian set his Bible aside, and leaned forward, clasping his hands between his legs.

"I know, dearest. I know…"

A loud thumping sound outside brought both of them to their feet. They rushed outside and found Nathan laying in a heap on the ground, shirtless, covered in blood and dirt. Abigail cried out when she saw him. Thomas stood at the foot of the stairs, with another man from the village. Abigail stared at him, horrified. She gripped the door frame, to terrified to move.

"We're returning your lover to you, so you can see the

price for your sin." Thomas' face was void of emotion when he spoke, as if it were of no consequence that a man lay near death at his feet. "He took your place. Your debt to the village is paid." His eyes roved over her, then narrowed slightly. "There's no need for you to ever return to us." With that, he and the man with him turned and mounted on their horses then rode down the road into the darkness.

Abigail crumpled beside Nathan, turning him so she could see his face. He was bruised all over, and she could barely make out his features from all the swelling. He looked nothing like the strong, handsome man she knew. She cried, gingerly touching his cheek. His eyes opened, just small slits. He was only barely conscious.

"A-abigail." He rasped.

"Nathan," she said on a sob. "Oh, Nathan! What did they do to you?" She leaned in and her tears fell on his face.

"You are s-safe." He barely had the word out before his eyes rolled back in his head.

Abigail cried out and looked up at Ian, frantic.

"My son!" Ian cried out, voice breaking on the words as tears trailed his cheeks into his beard. Ian knelt down and scooped his son up into his arms, cradling him like he was a little boy.

"Help me get him inside, Abigail." Together, they managed to hoist him up and move him. They carried him to Ian's room and laid him on the bed, on his side.

"Abigail set water to boil. We need to clean these wounds."

Abigail hurried to the fire and set the water to boil in the water pot. She pulled a sheet from the small cupboard and began ripping it into small strips. She hurried back into the room with the rags she had made and came to stand on the other side of the bed. Ian sat beside his son, hand on Nathan's head.

He is praying. Abigail saw his lips moving and knew that's what he was doing. He opened his eyes a moment later, and when he looked over at Abigail, his face was full of sorrow but also peace.

"He will live." He whispered. He looked at Nathan. "My son will live."

Abigail began to cry again. She ran back to the kitchen, briefly checking on Grace who slept peacefully on their bed, oblivious to everything around her. She went to the fire and using her apron, hoisted the water pot into her hands. She carried it back to the room and set it on the floor by the bed then went over to Ian.

"I will clean the wounds." She whispered, voice thick with tears.

Ian took her hands in his. "Abigail. He chose this. Remember that. He chose you." His words brought more tears to her eyes, and all she could do was nod. "We will need more water. I'll go to the river and bring some back."

Ian gently turned Nathan, so he laid on his stomach, then rushed from the room to fetch water. Abigail soaked the strips of cloth in the hot water, then began cleaning out his wounds. There were so many cuts, so many gashes. Her tears fell to his back as she cleaned his wounds. He had taken a lash for her that first time he rescued her, and now…this. He would carry scars from these marks. She carried one scar on her back, but he would carry many…because of her. She stopped crying abruptly and pulled her hands from his back, eyes circling wide.

He loves me.

The revelation was a balm to her soul, but it also filled her with fear. Nathan couldn't love her. She was not worthy of his love. He laid here, barely alive, because of his love for her.

I love him.

She had not realized it until this moment. She was in love with Nathan…and he was in love with her…and this was the result of it. She closed her eyes. Everyone she had ever loved had died in some way. First, her mother, then the father she knew as a girl had died, replaced by the village elder. Finally, Samuel had been torn from her side. She had even believed for a time that she loved Thomas, that he would marry her someday, make everything right. The thought sickened her now. No, she couldn't share love with Nathan. She was stained and dirty, and those stains followed her, would follow her, forever. She couldn't love Nathan, and she couldn't let Nathan love her. *I can't stay here.* She had to take Grace and leave. For Nathan and Ian's sake, she had to leave them.

Ian returned, with ale to help disinfect the wounds. He doused some of the rags in it, then laid them, carefully, over the wounds on Nathan's back. He probably had broken ribs, if the discoloration was any indication. The rest of his wounds would heal, but the lashes could turn to infection if they weren't careful. The next twenty-four hours would be critical.

Ian and Abigail took turns keeping vigil over Nathan. He was delirious and mumbled often during the night.

Many times, he mumbled Abigail's name, and every time he did, it felt like a knife in her heart. Oh, how he had suffered, for her.

They changed his bandages often during the night. Abigail had dozed off in the rocking chair near Nathan and stirred from her sleep when she felt a warm hand on hers. She opened her eyes, foggy from sleep, and turned her head towards Nathan. He was awake! She leaned in, clutching his hand with both of hers. He laid on his side, facing her.

"I'm thirsty." His voice was raw and raspy.

Abigail jumped up and poured a cup of water from the pitcher beside the bed. It was a challenge helping him drink while on his side, but he managed to get it down. He laid his head back, breathing hard. Abigail knelt beside him.

"Oh, Nathan. I'm so sorry. Please forgive me." Tears dripped off her chin. "This is my fault." She said, through heaves and sobs.

"Abigail." His voice was hoarse. She pushed the hair back from his eyes and cupped his cheek.

"Why did you do it, Nathan?"

He reached out with an unsteady hand and caught a tear on his thumb then brought it to his lips. "Because I love you."

She closed her eyes, feeling so many things at the sound of those words coming from him. Her heart yearned for him, but she was afraid. She loved him too much to stay and cause him any more pain. She had to let him go. She felt his hand go slack in hers and saw that he was dozing off again.

"I love you, Abigail," he whispered the words on a sigh as he fell into a deep sleep.

"I love you too, Nathan." She whispered to his sleeping form, fear and sorrow heavy on her heart.

THIRTY SIX

Abigail packed Grace's small bag first, then her own. She wanted to leave before anyone stirred. There was no way she could leave if Nathan or Ian knew she was leaving. She had decided she would go to Weldon and ask Mrs. Hatchet for work. Maybe she needed help in her shop. She wanted to go to Boston and start over, but she would have to earn enough to get there, first. Maybe she could live in Mrs. Hatchet's spare room, and pay rent. She knew she might run into Nathan and Ian living this close, but at least she wouldn't be under the same roof. At least there would be distance between her and Nathan. It had been just over two weeks since Nathan's beatings and he had been slowly healing. He was able to move around a little, though he could barely get up from the bed without tiring out. Some of the wounds on his back were still healing. His broken ribs would take the longest to heal. Abigail had taken care of him as best she could, staying close by if he needed her. She would catch him staring at her sometimes with a sadness in his face as if he knew what was going on in her heart. He probably did know – he always seemed to know. She had waited until she knew Nathan would be alright, before deciding to leave. She knew this was the best thing, the right thing. She also knew Nathan couldn't come after in his condition so now was the time to go.

Nathan said real love was about giving up your own desires for someone else's. If that was true, then she was proving her love for him by leaving. She had fed Grace a bit ago and bundled her up, now. It would take her only a couple of hours on foot to reach Mrs. Hatchet. She put her coat on and buttoned it up. She made a little nest for Grace with her shawl tied around her shoulder and waist, then snuggled the baby down in it. Grace was getting heavy and it would be a challenge carrying her all the way to Weldon, but Abigail was determined.

She pulled her mittens on and wrapped her scarf around her neck. She gathered her bag and Grace's, then came quietly out of the room. She didn't hear any movement and was relieved. Nathan had taken over Ian's bed and Ian insisted on sleeping in the corner, on a cot he rigged. So, they both slept in Ian's room, making it easier for her to slip out. She tiptoed to the door and lifted the latch as quietly as possible. The cold, winter air hit her hard and she shivered, pulling Grace closer, checking to make sure she was bundled well. She pulled the hood of her long cloak snug around her head, tucking it down into her scarf, and moved quickly down the dirt road. The sun was just starting to dust the sky with pink, and she knew Ian and Nathan would stir, soon. Neither of them slept past dawn. She felt her heart squeeze tighter with every step away from the cabin. She told herself over and over that she did this to protect Nathan because she loved him. She had left a note on her pillow that said simply, "I love you." She knew Nathan would come for her when he was well again, so she didn't give any indications of where she was going. She knew he would come to Weldon looking for her, but by then she would be set up hopefully, with Mrs. Hatchet. Eventually, she would find a way to go to Boston, to find Samuel. In time, Nathan would move on and find someone else to love, someone clean and pure. The thought of him with another woman made her sick, but she told herself it was the best thing.

~~~

The sun was up when Grace finally stirred. Abigail calculated she had been walking for over an hour, so they should be over halfway there. She would wait until Grace started fussing to stop and feed her. She adjusted her coat, so Grace could see the trees and the sunshine. That seemed to capture her attention for the time being. She kept walking, just waiting for the sound of a horse coming her way. She purposefully didn't walk on the dirt road, but stayed a little deeper in the woods, in case Nathan or Ian came down the road. She would ask Mrs. Hatchet for work. If Mrs. Hatchet would hire her, she would work hard and save as much as she could. Then, she would go to Boston and try to find Samuel. She knew Nathan and Ian had tried, but she still hoped that he was there, somewhere…that one day she would find him. She kept her pace until just outside of Weldon. Grace fussed to be fed, so she stopped by a big tree that would block her from the road and dropped her sacks to the ground. She sat down with a deep sigh, weary from the pace she had kept all morning. She quickly adjusted, the shawl, and her dress so Grace could nurse. Leaning back against the tree, she looked out at the river in the distance. A part of her was proud of herself for being brave and setting out on this journey. Before leaving her village, she would have never done this. She had been planning and plotting to go to Samuel, but she knew now that she would have never left had she not been taken out by Nathan. She saw his warm smile, his eyes the color of spring grass, and her heart ached. How she loved him. He had been kind to her, had shown her what real love looked like. She would carry her love for Nathan, and his for her, for as long as she lived.

~~~

Abigail felt relief rush through her when she saw Mrs. Hatchet's shop sign. Her feet ached from the journey and her back hurt from carrying Grace. She had done it, though. She had made it to Weldon, all by herself. Feeling like she couldn't walk another step, she pushed open the door to Mrs. Hatchet's shop. It was still early, and there weren't any customers about. Grace slept again in her little nest, and Abigail was grateful. She didn't think she had the energy for anything but sitting down. She was beginning to wonder if anyone was here when Mrs. Hatchet came through the curtain. Her eyes widened when she saw Abigail.

"Abigail!" She hurried around the counter and took Abigail's satchels. "What's wrong, why are you here at this hour? And where's Nathan?" Concern etched her face. All Abigail wanted to do was sit down and cry.

"Oh, Mrs. Hatchet." Her voice faltered, and Mrs. Hatchet led her behind the counter, and past the curtain.

"Come, sit and tell me what's happened." Abigail sat on the chair she offered and sighed a deep heavy sigh. She looked down at Grace, who slept still.

"I-I'm in need of work, Mrs. Hatchet…and a room to rent."

Ms. Hatchet's brow furrowed in confusion. "Why? Abigail, tell me what's wrong?"

Abigail proceeded to tell her the story. Mrs. Hatchet stopped her once, to help her untie the shawl and pull Grace out. Abigail slumped from the relief of the missing weight. Mrs. Hatchet ushered Abigail into her small parlor, where she had a fire going. She laid Grace on the settee and pointed to the chair close to the fire for Abigail to sit in. She hurried out of the room and came back with a cup of steaming tea for herself and Abigail. She sat in the chair across from Abigail and motioned for her to continue. Abigail told her everything. She told her about the village, and her father, and Thomas. She told her about Samuel, about her purging, and how Nathan came to her rescue. Then she told her what happened to Nathan, that he had been purged in her place. Mrs. Hatchet listened intently.

Tears trailed Abigail cheeks and she didn't try to stop them. "I had to leave Mrs. Hatchet."

"Abigail, I think you can call me Lizzy. All my friends do." She smiled and gave a gentle pat to Abigail's hand.

"I have to make my own way and protect Nathan from the danger that comes with loving me."

"So, you believe loving you will continue to bring Nathan harm, and that because you love him, you need to leave him?"

Abigail nodded, and wiped her nose on the handkerchief Mrs. Hatchet -or Lizzy, rather- had given her.

"What else can I do?" She asked. "Nathan deserves better."

"Better than you?" Lizzy asked, softly.

Abigail nodded, and her face crumpled again. She sat for a time, waiting on Lizzy to respond. Lizzy crossed her arms in front of her, staring at Abigail in contemplation. Then, she leaned forward, as if she had suddenly made a decision. "Alright, then. You can come to work for me. It's no secret I need some help in my old age. I have an extra room you and Grace can have. I have one condition, though." She raised her brow. "I'll not take rent. You'll work for your wage, but for your rent, you can help me with the cooking."

Abigail was grateful for this kind friend she had met on her second day with Nathan. She nodded her agreement as tears continued to fall.

Lizzy stood. "Very well. And what will we tell Nathan when he comes looking for you because we both know he will?"

Abigail stood next to her, raising her chin a notch. "I will tell him the truth. That he needs to find someone more deserving, someone, who won't bring him harm."

Lizzy sniffled. "Well, then, it sounds like we have work to do. You have a lot to learn. Grace can stay with you for most of it. We'll rig a little box for her, so she will have a place to play on the floor where you are."

"Thank you, Lizzy. You don't know what this means to me."

"Oh, I think I do, Abigail. I think I do." She gave Abigail a warm hug. "For today, you rest. You can start tomorrow."

Abigail was relieved. Her body ached from the travel, and she wanted to fall into bed right this minute.

"Come, I'll show you your room, and then you can eat something, and rest awhile. If you feel up to it later, you can help me with dinner."

Abigail scooped up Grace, who was starting to stir and followed Lizzy down a narrow corridor to a door at the end. "This is your room. Mine is just there," she nodded to the door on the left side of the corridor. "Get settled and then come have some breakfast. You saw the kitchen when you came through the curtain. I have biscuits and fried apples. Then, you can rest awhile."

Abigail thanked Lizzy again and went in the room to get settled. This plan was going to work. For the first time in her life, she was taking care of herself. Her heart ached for Nathan, but she knew that with time he would move on. If she would, was an entirely different story.

THIRTY SEVEN

Nathan sat silently, staring into the fire. "I love you." Those were her parting words. Papa had come from her room with the note he found and handed it to him. "I'm sorry, son." He had whispered, knowing the grief it caused. Now, Nathan sat with his heart bruised and broken, like his body that was still healing. He had known this was coming, so he wasn't shocked. It still hurt, though...really hurt. She had become a part of him in almost every way. She had taken his heart with her when she left. She hadn't taken a horse, so she couldn't have gone that far. She could have found a ride to Boston, though. The thought made him antsy, made him want to go search for her. The irony of it all was that he couldn't go after her in his condition. He couldn't even mount up on Duke and ride. She could very well be somewhere close by, and he couldn't go find her. It was as if God planned it this way, to keep him from going after her. Papa kept telling Nathan they weren't meant to go after her this time. Nathan couldn't rescue her, this time. She needed to meet Jesus on her terms, in her way. It all frustrated Nathan.

"Son, come eat." Papa put a hand on his shoulder.

"I'm not hungry." He stared into the fire, face set in stone. If he wasn't aching inside, he felt the heat of anger. Either way, he was miserable.

"I know, but your body needs the nourishment."

He knew Papa was right. He had not been eating much these past few days, and he hadn't bothered to shave or bathe. He looked the way he felt; worn and haggard.

He stood, slowly, needing Papa's help to get to the table. His ribs were still healing, and he couldn't move very fast. He shuffled over to the table and sat down, gingerly. Papa put a bowl of stew in front of him and Nathan saw the potatoes floating in the creamy broth that he usually loved. Papa reached out a hand and Nathan took it, almost mechanically. He ached to have Abigail here holding his other hand and Grace, cooing in the little play-box he had made for her. Moisture filled his eyes, and he slumped over on the table. Papa prayed for peace, strength, wisdom and protection over their lost little lambs. Nathan clutched Papa's hand and wept. The woman he loved had left him and taken the little girl he loved with her.

"Why, Papa?" He pounded a fist against the table, causing pain to shoot through his side. "Why would God bring her here only to take her away?" He continued to weep, so much that his wounds and his ribs began to hurt, but he didn't care. He preferred physical pain to the pain of a shattered heart. He felt Papa's grip on his hand tighten.

"I know it hurts son, but remember what I told you. We are only the doorway. She has to find Jesus on her own, in the way that will draw her to him. We can trust him to take care of her and, if it's in his will, bring her back…and Grace."

Nathan heard the crack in Papa's voice and realized that he was aching too. He loved both of them like daughters, and losing them hurt him too. He sat up and rubbed his face with his hands to wipe the wetness away and clutched his head in his hands. "I'm sorry, Papa. I know this hurts you, too. You love them like your own."

Papa nodded, eyes glistening with tears. "I do,

son…but I know that God loves them more than I. He did not bring them to us to abandon them, now. Just as the shepherd left the ninety-nine sheep to go find the lost one, God will not forsake our two little lambs. He will find them. He will make a way." He wiped the wetness from his cheeks. "We must trust Him. He is working on Abigail's heart. I know it. I saw it in her countenance. And she loves you, with her whole heart. I saw that, too." He smiled at Nathan, his eyes warm with compassion. "Hold on to that, son. God loves her more than you can. He will not fail."

Nathan nodded, then forced himself to eat the meal, knowing his body needed nourishment. He wished he could as easily nourish his broken heart.

THIRTY EIGHT

Abigail sat at the large barrel, dipping a cluster of candles in tallow to be hung and dried. The days had blended into weeks since she had come to Mrs. Hatchet's shop. She thought her pain would lessen with time, but it hadn't. She ached for Nathan as much as she did on the day she left him. In a small way, though, she was proud of herself. She was being a somewhat independent woman. She was earning her own money, for the first time in her life and she was providing for Grace, without the help of a man. She paused in her work, staring out the shop window, her thoughts wandering to Nathan, as they always did. Was he recovered from that awful night? She pictured his warm smile, his emerald green eyes, his gentle kisses on her forehead. She closed her eyes and breathed deep, refusing to be overcome with emotion. She needed to toughen herself up, figure out how to move on with her life. Nathan would move on, she knew it. He was too good, and handsome, and wonderful not to find someone else to love.

She saw a wagon stop in front of the shop out front, and her eyes lit with surprise when she saw Millie climb down from the wagon. She stood and went to the counter just as Millie came in, the bell above door chiming at her entrance. She saw Abigail, and her face filled with bright warmth.

"Abigail!" She reached her hands out across the counter and Abigail took them, smiling.

"Hello, Millie." Abigail's smile was genuine.

"Are you working here, with Lizzy?" Millie asked, searching Abigail's face for understanding.

"I am," Abigail said. *Please don't ask me any more questions.* She didn't have the emotional stamina to explain her situation to her friend. She looked down at the tray of sample soaps and absently started adjusting them on the tray. She expected them to know what had happened. How could it be a secret? Nathan was known and loved by everyone in Weldon. They probably all knew about his purging and blamed her.

"I see," Millie said, hesitantly. "And how is little Grace? I do miss her so…and you. I haven't seen you lately."

Abigail looked up and put on her best attempt at a smile. "I've been here, learning everything about soap and candle making."

Millie's eyes narrowed a bit then warmed. "Abigail," she said softly. "Ian told Matthew what happened."

Abigail tensed, waiting for the condemnation to come.

Millie leaned over the counter, clutching Abigail's hand tight and spoke with intensity.

"No one faults you, Abigail. Nathan defended you because he loves you." She stood up straight again.

Abigail stared, speechless.

"I'm glad to see you here. In fact, my Bethany has been asking about you. She loved talking with you. She asked me to talk to Nathan about having you all over again for a meal."

Abigail's heart skipped and she looked down at her hands on the counter, fiddling with her nails.

Millie paused a moment then, "But since you are here, let's set up a date. Oh, and bring little Grace. Bethany loves babies!"

Abigail looked up and saw the hope in Millie's face. How could she say no? "W-we would love to come. I can bring Lizzy, too, if you like."

"Oh, of course! Can you come Sunday, for the afternoon meal?"

Would she invite Nathan and Ian? Abigail did not want to see them yet, no matter how determined she was.

"Um, well, how about Saturday? Sunday isn't the best day for us."

"Saturday, then," Millie didn't hesitate to say. "Oh, and I came in for a box of candles."

Abigail grabbed a box from under the counter and slid it across the counter. "I'll add it to your account," she said, smiling at Millie.

Millie surprised her by reaching out for her hand, again. "I can see you are burdened." She searched Abigail's eyes. "I don't know all that has happened to you, but please know that I will be praying for you…and that we all care for you, deeply."

Abigail could only nod, unable to speak past the lump in her throat. Millie squeezed her hand, then grabbed her box of candles and left the shop.

Abigail stared out the shop window, watching Millie climb in her wagon and head further down the street. She thought of sweet Bethany, and something in her stirred. She wanted to see the girl again. She genuinely did. At least this would give her something to look forward to.

THIRTY NINE

Abigail was proud of herself for learning how to drive a wagon. Nathan had taught her a little, and of course, Lizzy seemed to be an expert at it. Abigail steered the two horses down the dirt road that led from Weldon to Matthew and Millie's house. Lizzy sat next to her, with Grace on her lap. Grace was teething and gnawed on everything in sight. Right now, she sat up straight, eyes bright and observant, with a finger shoved as far back in her mouth as she could get it.

Abigail came around a bend in the road and Millie's house came into view.

"It's a beautiful spring day, isn't it?" Lizzy asked, leaning in to kiss Grace's cheek. She had become like a grandmother to Grace.

"It is. I'm grateful for the warmer weather. Winter can be long." Abigail said.

"Indeed."

Abigail pulled the wagon to a stop in front of the cabin. She wasn't prepared for the flood of memories that assailed her. She remembered coming here with Nathan and Ian, and the way Nathan had treated her, staying close and whispering encouragement in her ear. She clutched the reins in her hands, staring at them.

"Abigail?" Lizzy looked at her, concerned.

"I'm fine." Abigail looked out at the forest. "Just remembering." She gave Lizzy a sad smile and Lizzy gave her hands a gentle pat.

Matthew came out of the cabin. "Abigail! Mrs.

Hatchet!" He hurried down the porch steps and came over to them.

Abigail let him help her down and smiled up at him. "Hello, Matthew. It is good to see you." She wasn't as afraid, this time, of visiting people as she had been the last time she came. The thought gave her some courage. She wasn't the same woman who had come from the village. She had changed, some.

Matthew smiled, then went around to help Lizzy down. "Well, hello miss Grace!" He said. He took Grace from Lizzy and helped her climb down, then walked back to where Abigail stood. She reached in and grabbed her basket from the wagon bed. Grace stared up at Matthew with curious blue eyes. Then, her little lip poked out a bit, and she started to whimper.

"Oh, now don't start that. This is Matthew. He's our friend," Abigail said. Grace was just entering the phase of not being too sure about strangers. Apparently, she had not been around Matthew enough to consider him a friend. Matthew handed Grace over to Abigail and took the basket from her.

"That's alright. I'll have her warmed up to me in no time." He reached in and tickled her belly, eliciting a baby giggle from her.

"Come on in, Millie just about has the meal ready."

The ladies followed Matthew up the porch and into the cabin. They found Millie setting a big pot with a roasted chicken in it at the center of the table. Little Sarah was busy setting the table. Abigail's eyes automatically scanned the room, looking for Bethany. She must be in the other room.

"Abigail! Lizzy!" Millie hurried over and hugged them

both. "And look at you!" She leaned in so Grace would see her. Grace kicked and cooed when she caught Millie's eye.

"Oh, fine. I see where I stand." Matthew said, giving Lizzy a wink.

"She knows what she likes, that's for sure," Lizzy said, just like a grandmother would.

Millie reached out and Grace went right to her. Millie propped her on a hip. "Now, let's go say hi to Beth," she said.

Abigail and Lizzy followed Millie and the rest of the family into the room where Abigail had first met Bethany. She found her in the same place, on the settee, with a quilt over her legs.

When she saw them her face lit up. "Oh! You're here!" She went about twisting herself around so that her legs hung over the settee. She moved the quilt off to the side. Millie came over and knelt down in front of Beth with Grace.

"Oh, aren't you just the prettiest little thing," Beth said, clasping her hands together as she spoke.

"Abigail. Come sit with me!" She said with a bright smile.

Abigail sat down beside her, and Beth immediately grabbed her hand and squeezed it. "I'm so glad you came and brought this little angel for me to meet."

Beth had not been able to attend the gatherings much on Sunday's in the winter time and Abigail hadn't been in a while, either, so she hadn't met Grace yet.

Abigail smiled. "Thank you for having us, again."

Beth leaned in and took Grace's chubby little hand, shaking it like she was an adult. "It's nice to meet you, miss Grace."

Grace eyed Beth a moment, then gave her a gummy grin and leaned towards her. Beth laughed in delight, and Millie handed Grace over. Beth adjusted Grace on her lap and hugged her tight.

Abigail marveled at this girl. She was full of…what? The word that came to Abigail's mind was light. That was what she thought of when she looked at Beth. She seemed to radiate light.

"Hello, Mrs. Lizzy," Beth said. She always seemed to notice everyone in a room.

"Beth," Lizzy said with a gentle nod. "You look lovely."

She did look lovely in a pale pink dress with a high collar. Her chocolate-colored hair hung down her back in a braid, and her cheeks were rosy.

"Let's leave these girls to talk some, and finish preparing the meal." Millie rose and went into the main room, Lizzy following behind her.

Suddenly, Abigail wasn't sure what to say. What could she talk about with this girl who couldn't walk but radiated light?

"How are you, Abigail?" Beth asked, searching Abigail's eyes.

"I'm okay." She might as well tell the truth. She wasn't great, but she was okay. "How are you?"

"I'm well. I'm grateful for these warmer temperatures. It is easier on these lifeless legs."

She grinned, as if talking about her lifeless legs were not a problem.

Abigail didn't say anything but looked down at her hands.

"I'm sorry, Abigail. Does it make you uncomfortable for me to talk about my condition? I forget that some people aren't used to it, and don't know how to respond."

Abigail looked up, taken aback that Beth was apologizing. She was the one who couldn't walk, and she was apologizing.

"No...it's okay. I just..." Abigail looked out the window at the cypress tree budding with fresh new life. *Just be honest, Abigail. Just tell her exactly what you are thinking.*

"I just have never met anyone like you." She looked into Beth's eyes, waiting for her to get angry. She didn't, though. Instead her eyes warmed with compassion.

"Tell me about yourself," Beth said, absently rubbing Grace's back.

"I'm from the village outside of Weldon." Grace began to squirm and Abigail took her and sat her on the rug at their feet, where she found new things to explore. "I had never left the village until the day Nathan brought me out." She shifted as if saying his name caused her pain.

"Nathan is a very kind man," Beth said.

"Yes," Abigail whispered.

"Can I ask why you came without Nathan today and why you seem so troubled?" This young girl seemed to have the ability to read people, just like Nathan.

"Oh, Beth. It's such a long story." She gave a sad smile and could see that Beth was waiting for more details.

"I live with Lizzy now and work for her." Abigail reached down and helped Grace untangle herself from her gown. "I have been living with her for a little over a month."

"I see," Beth said. "And do you visit Nathan?"

Abigail didn't look at her, couldn't. "No…no I don't. I left for his own good."

"How is it good for him that you left?" Beth twisted herself a bit, so she faced Abigail more fully. "He is in love with you. That was clear from the one visit we all had together. His eyes barely left you the whole time you were here."

A tear escaped and slide down Abigail's cheek.

"Oh, Abigail. I don't mean to make you cry. I'm just trying to understand." Beth reached over and squeezed Abigail's hand.

Abigail wiped at her nose with the back of her hand. "Loving me is dangerous. I'm not…whole, Beth." She rasped out through tears.

Beth sat back against the settee and Grace started fussing. As if on cue, Lizzy came into the room and picked Grace up from the floor. "Come, little one. You can help us in the kitchen." She left, closing the door quietly behind her. Abigail stared after them lost in thought.

"I understand about not being whole, Abigail," Beth said, softly. "I've struggled with that my entire life." She stared out the window as if she were thinking back. "And I've been angry about my condition more times than I can count. I've asked God many times why He let this happen. Why didn't He stop it? Why didn't He heal me?" She looked back at Abigail with a stormy expression. "I still wrestle with that, sometimes." She gave a sad smile.

Abigail waited, sensing she would say more.

"Jesus has become my strength in a way I wouldn't know if I had never suffered."

Abigail stared at Beth, surprised. "How?"

Beth's smile seemed to become warm again. "Because I read about his suffering, and all He endured by dying on the cross, and I realize that He really does understand my struggle."

"But why, Beth?" It made Abigail angry, thinking that God allowed all of this. "Why does He allow it all if he supposedly is good and has the power to stop it?"

Beth tilted her head a bit, her expression thoughtful. "Well, He is a God of promises. He keeps all of them. As much as I wish He sometimes didn't, He does. That includes allowing sin to reign on this Earth because of humanity's choices. Jesus doesn't promise to make the world around us perfect, or even these human bodies. He promises that we will struggle in this life, but that He has overcome it all, because of His sacrifice. He promises to be with us for the rest of forever."

Abigail stared at Beth, overwhelmed. This girl, who couldn't walk, was talking about Jesus being her friend, and she wasn't bitter or angry.

"Even though I can't find a perfect answer for why I sit here unable to walk, I can tell you that Jesus' love for us is passionate, and deep...deep enough that He died, for me and you." A tear slipped down Beth's cheek. "Oh, Abigail! I'm so sorry for whatever you suffered to make you feel unworthy." She leaned in, clutching Abigail's shoulder.

"But, take it from the girl who can't even get up and walk to the table to eat that our wholeness doesn't come from these earthly bodies and what is or isn't done to them. Our wholeness comes from the inside." She put her hand over her heart. "He has made me whole in here, and when I finally get to Heaven, this body I'm trapped in will be made well again." Her smile was as bright as Nathan or Ian's. Abigail stared at her, amazed.

Millie came into the room, and announced that dinner was ready. Grace finished eating and Abigail adjusted her dress, then hoisted Grace to her shoulder. Matthew came in the room and Abigail moved over so he could pick up Beth. She followed behind them, trying to process everything Beth had said.

Was it possible that God loved people from the inside out, instead of the other way around? She had been taught her whole life that he looked at how she acted, then determined her worth. Could it be possible that she was completely wrong, that her whole village had been completely wrong? Had it come from anyone else, she might not believe it. Coming from Beth though, she couldn't rationalize it all away. This sweet girl who radiated light despite her affliction said that Jesus loved her from the inside out. Abigail felt like a match had just been lit inside her heart - a heart that had been cold forever - and a tiny spark started to burn.

FORTY

Abigail was busy with customers all morning. She needed to work on a batch of lavender soaps, but between tending to Grace and customers, she hadn't gotten to it, yet.

"Now, who is happy as can be?" Lizzy came through the curtain with Grace on her hip. "I do believe having this angel around is giving me back some years."

Abigail smiled at the two of them. Grace loved Lizzy, and Lizzy doted on Grace.

"I need to get to work on the lavender soaps. That seems to be the most popular these days."

"I'm doing the bookwork so Grace can come with me," Lizzy said, giving Grace a pat on the back. She went back through the curtain, and Abigail went to put on her apron. She was just collecting supplies when the bell above the shop jingled. She held back a sigh. She might not get these soaps made today.

"Hello, Abigail." Whirling around, Abigail dropped everything she held at the sound of that voice.

"Nathan?" she whispered in shock. "W-what are you doing here?"

He smiled that warm smile she missed. "I do believe this is the best place for buying soap and candles isn't it?"

"Oh. Y-yes." She went about collecting the things she had dropped, then came over to the counter. Just having him standing on the other side of the counter caused her heart to pound and made her ache to touch him. She drank in the sight of him. He looked like he had recovered from the purging. She could tell he had lost a little weight, but he looked well. Shame coursed through her at the memory of what he had suffered because of her. *It should have been me.*

Her gaze traveled over him, soaking him in like water on dry land. He was still the strong and handsome man she remembered, but he looked tired and worn down. She noticed the dark smudges under his eyes. Was he still in pain because of her? She didn't expect him to just come walking in the shop. She knew she would see him eventually, but she realized in this moment she was nowhere near ready to face him. Now that she saw him, she doubted she would ever be ready.

"What can I get you?" she asked, refusing to look up into those eyes that always drew her in. She fiddled with her apron and the samples set out on the counter.

"Two boxes of candles, and a bar of lavender soap," he said, the calm in his voice not matching the rattle in Abigail's.

Her head shot up before she thought of it, and she locked gazes with him.

"W-why do you want lavender?" She asked cautiously, afraid of his answer.

He looked at her with such intense longing that it took her breath away.

"In case the woman I love decides to come home." His reply was gentle, his gaze warm and steady.

She stared at him, swallowing hard. *Home.* Yes, Nathan had felt like home, had felt safe. "I don't have any lavender at the moment." She looked down, away from his eyes. She needed to be strong.

"I'll come back for it then."

She closed her eyes thinking she couldn't handle any more encounters with him.

"Nathan," she whispered, brokenly. She willed herself not to cry. Crying seemed to be all she did since leaving the village, and she was determined to toughen herself up. She couldn't, however, stop the one tear that slipped free and trailed her cheek. She felt Nathan's thumb rub across her cheek and she looked up in surprise and saw him press it to his lips. She squeezed her eyes shut to block out his tenderness.

"We miss you," he whispered. "I miss you."

She infused determination into her voice. "We miss you both, too. How is Ian?"

"He is well. Working a little harder than normal, lately. I think he's trying to keep his mind occupied," he said with a sad smile. She knew what he meant.

"So, you work here now?" His eyes never wavered from hers.

She guessed that he had known that before coming in, but he asked anyway.

She nodded. "Yes. Grace and I stay in Lizzy's spare room. She is kind to us. She has been teaching me everything she knows."

"I'm proud of you Abigail. Look how far you've come. A brave and strong mother striking out on her own."

Abigail wasn't sure how to respond to his praise. She had expected him to lash out, to be angry with her, but encouragement? He never acted the way she expected. She reached down into the basket under the counter for the boxes of candles. The sooner she filled his order, the sooner he could leave her life again. She needed him to leave, needed the distance to stay between them. She wasn't strong enough to resist him if he were near. He didn't speak while she put his soaps in a bag and collected the two boxes of candles. She slid the items across the counter in front of him. "The lavender soaps will be ready in a day or two."

He slid his coins across the counter. "I'll come back, then."

Just then Lizzy came through the curtain. "That baby girl is just too -" She stopped short when she saw Nathan. She looked to Abigail, then back to Nathan. "Well, here we are, finally." She put hands on her hips. "Abigail, Grace is fussing to eat."

Abigail nodded but kept her head down. "Please give Ian our love, Nathan," she whispered, then hurried behind the curtain to escape his presence.

~~~

"Don't be discouraged, Nathan," Lizzy said, coming around the counter to stand by him. He couldn't even describe the pain in his heart.

"I miss her," he rasped, as a sheen of tears filled his eyes. He looked at Lizzy. "I love her."

"I know." Lizzy placed a hand on his arm. "God led her here to me, to help her find answers. She knows love finally, in you and Ian, but discovering love for the first time is scary. She is afraid."

Nathan took Lizzy's hand. "Thank you for being another open door. I know God sent her here to you." His smile was sad. He had heard from Matthew where Abigail was, and after giving himself a lot of time to fortify his heart, he had come to visit. He realized though, at one glimpse of her that his heart would never be fortified enough to be near her but not be free to love her.

"Papa and I pray for her every day…and Grace." His voice wavered.

"Don't stop. Her heart is completely broken, which means she is open to the truth. When the time is right He will show her the way back home."

Nathan smiled, and breathed deep, "Thank you." He leaned in and kissed her cheek. "Thank you, for taking in our two girls. I have some peace knowing they are here with you."

"It is my pleasure. Now, you get on home and tell that Papa of yours I said hello. One day, we will all dine together, again." She squeezed his arm, and her eyes glistened with tears. He nodded and left the shop. He felt like a desert, desperate for a drink of water. He was depleted and exhausted. He stopped and looked up at the sky. *Where are you?* His mind screamed the question. From the moment Abigail left he had searched for a sign that everything was going to work out. He had surrendered, done what God wanted. Now he wanted to know if it would be okay.

Silence was all he heard. He made his way to Duke and mounted up, angry and wounded, then set off towards home. He had given his heart away, and he wasn't sure if he would ever get it back.

FORTY ONE

Abigail cried, hard. She wanted to escape, to get away from him, but she couldn't. She wasn't strong enough to open the door, and he knew it. She ran around the room, looking for a hole in the wall, an open window, any way out. Suddenly, he lunged for her, grabbing her hair. She cried out as he threw her on his bed, and she clawed at the sheets trying to get away. He came in close enough that she felt his breath on her face. She turned her face away, and suddenly she caught sight of something. In the corner was a man surrounded by light. He wore a white gown and she saw blood dripping from his side and running down his leg. There was agony in his eyes and tears running down his face. He lifted his hands up toward her and she saw blood dripping from two holes in his wrists. The man on top of her didn't seem to notice the other man as he pulled at her clothes, consumed with his lust. She kept her eyes on the man in the corner though, so drawn to him that she forgot to be afraid. How was he bloodied and beaten but also surrounded by light? Her eyes caught sight of a figure shrouded in black, slinking across the floor toward the bleeding man. She wanted to warn the man, but he noticed the dark figure on his own. He moved in front of it, reached down and grabbed it with his bloodied hand. The faceless figure squealed and squirmed like a pig. Then, the bleeding man spoke...

"Leave!"

His voice echoed around the room and Abigail felt the force of it push her back into the bed. The figure continued to squeal as it scurried away, then vanished into the darkness…

Abigail sat up, breathing hard, sweat rolling down her chest. She still heard that voice as if it were here in the room. She looked in all the corners of her room, convinced that man was here. She still saw his face - his sorrow-filled eyes - so vividly. His bloodied side, his wrists…who was he? She tossed the covers back and sat on the edge of the bed a minute, looking out her window and seeing the light of dawn approaching. She leaned over and checked on Grace who slept peacefully. She got up and donned her robe, then left the room quietly, heading toward the sitting room where a low fire burned. Lizzy must already be up and moving. Abigail went and sat in a chair near the fire, her heart still slowing down from the dream. She stared into the flames seeing the dream as vividly as if it had really happened. She hadn't made out the face of the man on top of her, but the man in the corner, she had seen him clearly. His eyes had been filled with so much sorrow that Abigail teared up just thinking of him. Then he had reached for her. He told the dark figure to leave, and it did. She sat up straight as realization flooded her.

This was the first time a nightmare had come to her but didn't leave her terrified. She thought back to the dream. The faceless man had been on top of her and she had been afraid, but then she had seen the man in the corner and everything else had faded away. She didn't feel afraid now as she thought about it. She felt…she wasn't sure what she felt. The man in the dream had been powerful. She knew because with just one word the walls had shaken, and the dark figure had vanished. Who was he? Lizzy came into the room and looked at her a moment before sitting down in the chair near the settee. Abigail stared into the fire, completely consumed with the picture of the man in her dream.

"You're up early," Lizzy said softly, situating herself, a cup of tea in hand.

"I-I had a dream..." Abigail looked at Lizzy, her brows furrowed in thought.

"Care to share it?" Lizzy asked.

"There was a man, hurting me..." she paused. "But then, I saw another man in the corner. He was bleeding from his side and his wrists, and his face was full of sadness." She looked into the fire, seeing his face so vividly. "But he was surrounded by light."

Lizzy sat forward abruptly, setting her tea on the little table by her chair.

"Jesus..." she whispered.

Abigail looked up sharply at Lizzy's whispered word. "Is that who I saw in my dream?" She asked, searching Lizzy's face for an answer. "There was a dark figure that came towards the bleeding man and when it got close, he grabbed it with his bloodied hand and said just one word."

"Yes?" Lizzy sat on the edge of her chair, staring intently at Abigail.

"Leave," Abigail whispered it, her skin tingling at the memory of the power she had felt in her dream.

Lizzy got up and knelt down in front of Abigail. "Child, that dream was no accident. You've had a dream of the Savior." She clutched Abigail's hands, searching her face. "You've dreamt of Jesus," she whispered in awe, eyes glossy with tears.

Abigail just stared at her, unable to comprehend it.

Lizzy didn't say anything for a time, then she finally spoke. "You've been here for almost three months and I think it's time for us to have a talk," she said, standing and going back to her chair. She sat up straight in the chair with her hands in her lap. "I'm going to say something that you may or may not agree with."

Abigail looked at her, waiting, still dazed.

"God sent you here to me. He loves you enough, that even in your wandering, he brought you to another safe place. You cannot run from his love child. There is nowhere you can go that his love will not find you." Lizzy clasped her hands in her lap. "You cannot become worthy enough to be loved, and he is not waiting for you to earn it. Love is a state of being for God, not an emotion he chooses based on your actions."

"But...I don't deserve that kind of love, Lizzy. I am damaged, unclean. How can a perfect God love me with my past?" She looked down at her hands.

Lizzy stood and hurried out of the room. Abigail watched her go, confused. She returned quickly, a candle burning in her hand and walked around the room closing the curtains. Once she finished the only light in the room was the light of the candle and the low fire burning in the hearth. She came and stood in front of Abigail.

"I can add as much darkness to this room as I want, and it will never put out this light." She knelt carefully in front of Abigail and placed the candle in her hand. "The more darkness you bring into this room, the brighter this one candle will be."

Abigail looked at Lizzy through the glow of the candle uncertain of her meaning.

"You cannot cover up light with darkness, ever. The darker the darkness, the brighter the light." Lizzy's said, voice full of emotion.

Abigail thought of her dream, and how much light was around the man in the dream. Had she seen Jesus? His light had filled the room despite the darkness around her and on her.

Lizzy put a hand to Abigail's cheek. "God's love is the same child. Your past, all the darkness you think makes you unworthy, it does the opposite. It all makes His love for you go deeper and wider. The more pain you lay at His feet the more love He has to give." Tears began to slip down Abigail's cheek, and Lizzy pulled a handkerchief from her pocket. "Jesus is the form of God's love in flesh. It was because of His deep love for you, Abigail, that He came to this Earth." Lizzy reached up and blotted at the tears on Abigail's cheeks.

Abigail listened, seeing the man in her dream so clearly as Lizzy spoke.

"You cannot run from His love child, and you cannot run from Nathan's. He loves you like Jesus does. Your story only makes Nathan love you more. Your pain only brings him closer to you. You cannot run from this love no matter what choice you make."

"But…where was He when I suffered so much? He didn't come to my rescue; He didn't save me." Her voice choked on the tears as the words poured out. She had felt abandoned her entire life, especially by God.

"Oh, dearest. God did not abandon you." Lizzy grabbed her hands and squeezed them. "Jesus was there, suffering with you in all of that. That's what was happening in your dream. Jesus was showing you that He has always been there, grieving and hurting with you…and fighting off the darkness."

Abigail's eyes were wide and puffy now.

"He knows the road of sorrow, Abigail. That is the story of the cross. Jesus knows our human struggle and shares in our burdens." She spoke with such passion and conviction. "He sent you Nathan and He gave you that precious baby." Tears began to stream down Lizzy's face. "He gave you Grace for all the sorrow. Don't you see? You named her Grace, not even knowing that grace is the foundation of God's love for you. For all your ashes, He will give you beauty." She wiped her own face with the handkerchief she had given Abigail. "You need only to reach out and take His hand."

Abigail stared at her a moment, overwhelmed by it all. Was it true? Did this candle, burning brightly in this dark room represent God's love for her? Was He not the God she had known all those years in the village? Was He good? Was He loving? She thought of Beth and how she radiated light. She thought of Nathan and Ian and their constant kindness. Had she seen Jesus in her dream? He had looked exactly like she had always felt: broken and bleeding. Could it be that He was here now wanting to help her?

"God can love me just like I am?" She asked voice full of brokenness and uncertainty.

"He loved you first, Abigail. He loved you before you knew to love Him." Lizzy took the candle and set it in the candle holder on the little table by the settee, then hurriedly wiped the tears from her cheeks. "Jesus is desperate to fill you with His grace, Abigail. Just as Nathan was willing to sacrifice himself for you, to take the purging your village thought you deserved, Jesus did take your place. He did give up His life for you, for me, for all of us. This is love, Abigail; that He loved us first, and that while we still lived for ourselves, doing what we pleased, He took our place and paid the price for the sins of humanity."

"He loves me," Abigail said it, eyes wide as if she were discovering a treasure. Lizzy's words were pouring into her heart, and she felt as though the light of that little candle was filling her up and beginning to seep from her pores. Everything began tumbling into place, making sense. She thought of Nathan and how he had treated her all these months. He had been just like Jesus, loving her no matter the cost. She looked over at the little candle burning beside her. Nathan had shown her Jesus' love all these months, and she had been afraid, worried she didn't deserve it, or that it was conditional. It wasn't though. Jesus loved her, expecting nothing in return. She had seen Him in her dream, suffering with her and fighting the darkness. She realized that He had sent Nathan to rescue her. Nathan and Ian had been God's love on display! She looked at Lizzy and put a hand to her mouth. "He loves me, Lizzy. Jesus loves me!"

"Yes, child! Yes! He loves you completely!"

"What do I do, Lizzy? How do I let Jesus know I accept His love, that I want Him to be in my life?" She needed that man, bloodied and broken but surrounded by light. She needed Him to come and show her how to be like that; broken but full of light.

"Oh child," tears streamed anew down Lizzy's face. "It is so very simple. All you must do is tell Him you want Him in your life. He listens to your voice, and He will always come near when you call on Him. I can pray with you right now. You can begin a relationship with Him this very day." Abigail could only nod, to overcome with emotion to speak.

Lizzy bowed her head, and Abigail did the same. Then, by the light of that one little candle burning bright, Abigail received the prayer Lizzy prayed over her. When Lizzy finished, Abigail prayed, for the first time in her life, to the God who she now knew loved her. Jesus had rescued her, and now He was restoring her heart, filling all the broken pieces with His perfect love.

When they finished Abigail looked up at Lizzy filled with wonder. "Is this what peace feels like, Lizzy?"

Lizzy nodded, smiling. "Yes! Jesus gives you peace as a part of His gift of salvation. His peace is with you, no matter where you go or what happens." She cupped Abigail's cheek again. "You are a new creation now. Every old thing is gone, and you are filled with the newness of Jesus."

"I-I feel it, Lizzy," she whispered, in awe of what had just happened. "I feel new." There was still the memory of her life, the sorrow of everything that had happened, but she felt hope, for the first time in her life, she felt hope, and it made her feel new. Then, revelation flooded her soul.

"I can go back to Nathan, Lizzy! I can let him love me, and I can love him!"

Lizzy jumped up bringing her hands together in excitement. "Yes, Abigail! You can, because Jesus is at the center of that love. It is a never-ending stream of flowing water."

Abigail thought of the river, and how she always loved the sound of the water moving, and how it flowed constantly, pushing impurities downstream. Jesus loved her that way and so did Nathan!

"I will return to Nathan and Ian!" Ian had loved her like a father, she saw that now. His gentle, quiet presence had always brought her comfort. He was the example of a Papa she never had. She felt what must be pure joy fill her soul at the thought of Nathan and Ian. She no longer feared their love, and she was free to love them in return. They were a gift to her, from a God who loved her completely. She thought of Grace. She was a gift too, and a living, breathing example of God's grace. "Oh, Lizzy. It's almost too much to take in!"

"Indeed. God's grace and mercy are overwhelming, and it will be until the day you die." She reached out for Abigail's hands. "You are loved, child, and will always be loved. Now, go pack your bag and return to the place where you belong."

Abigail paused. "But, Lizzy…what will you do? I don't want to leave you here alone."

Lizzy chuckled. "I don't live here alone. Jesus is with me just as He is with you, and He will send me someone who needs me as much as I need them."

Abigail smiled, then reached out and hugged Lizzy.

"Oh, Lizzy! I can never thank you enough for what you've done."

"No thanks needed. Knowing you've found peace, and that you are returning to Nathan is thanks enough." She pulled away and went over to open the curtains and let the sunshine back in. Abigail squinted as her eyes adjusted.

"Now off with you!" Lizzy said with a grin. "Hurry home. You've got a lifetime of living to do with that handsome young man of yours." Abigail saw the twinkle in her eyes. "And I want you to get busy bringing those beautiful babies into the world that the two of you are sure to make."

Abigail's cheeks warmed, and her eyes widened. "Lizzy!"

Lizzy laughed loud, and shooed Abigail from the room. She hurried towards her room, grinning from ear to ear. She was going home to Nathan clean, whole, ready to be his bride. *Oh, Jesus!*

I love you, Abigail.

She stopped with a gasp and brought a hand to her heart. Was that God whispering to her? Yes! She knew in her heart He had just spoken her name. The God of the universe knew her name and had whispered it down in her soul, written his love on her heart! Joy overwhelmed her, completely, and she looked up at the ceiling with tears streaming and a smile on her face.

You see me and know my name! She was overwhelmed at the thought of God knowing her name and telling her He loved her. God loved her. It was almost too much. She couldn't wait to return to Nathan and Ian. She was going home! "Thank you, Jesus! Thank you!"

FORTY TWO

Nathan was in the barn, repairing a harness when he heard horse hooves in the distance. Grabbing his rag and wiping the grime from his hands he gave a heavy sigh. He wasn't in the mood for company. He hadn't been in the mood for company for many weeks. He preferred to be here alone, keeping all his wounds guarded against the outside. He had poured himself into his work these past months. He had quickly regained his physical build, if not more than before he had been purged. He pushed himself physically, always wishing it would relieve the ache on the inside. Nothing helped, though. He was exhausted, physically and emotionally. He prayed a lot for Abigail, and for peace in his own soul. He had no idea how he was going to move on with his life after Abigail, but he was trying to lean on Jesus, even in his confusion and heartbreak.

Papa was down at the mill today, so he left the barn and went around the corner of the cabin, cleaning his hands as he walked. He looked down the road, shielding his eyes from the afternoon sun and squinted, trying to make out who it was. Then, his eyes widened, and his rag fell to the ground. *Abigail.*

His heart forgot to beat for a moment. All he could do was stare.

She stopped the horse a little way off and climbed down. He saw Grace strapped to her back, her little head peeking out over Abigail's shoulder. *Why is she here, Lord?* His heart couldn't handle an encounter with her only to watch her walk away from him. He watched as she shielded her eyes from the sun and looked in his direction. *Lord...*

Go to her.

That was all the confirmation he needed. He cried out and his feet took flight. He ran towards her, and when Abigail saw him she began running as fast as she could with Grace strapped to her back. They ran towards each other, not stopping until they came together.

"Abigail!" He rushed up to her and took her in his arms. He pulled her close, holding her head against his chest, gripping her tight as if he didn't believe she was standing here.

"Oh, Nathan," she wept against him, clutching his shirt in her fists. He pulled back after some time and cupped her face in his hands.

"I've come home," she rasped out in a broken voice.

He saw something in her eyes that he hadn't seen before and it made his heart skip. "Abigail..."

"I found Jesus, Nathan." Tears continued to stream down her face. "Or rather, He found me," she laughed through her tears, looking at his chest and wiping at the wet spot she had left. He grabbed her hand, kissed her palm and brought it to his cheek.

"You are radiant," he whispered, overwhelmed by the joy he saw in her countenance.

"Everything you said about Jesus is true. His grace is enough to cover all the stains of my past. I am new because of Him." Nathan watched the passion fill her eyes, as she spoke of Jesus and what she had discovered.

"He loved me first before I knew I needed His love." Tears continued to fall as she spoke of all Lizzy had told her, and the dream she had.

"His grace and mercy are never ending, love." He pushed the wisps of hair back from her face. "His love is as constant as the river. He will never leave you...never." He brought his forehead down to hers and whispered what was burning in his heart. "I love you."

She nodded through her tears. "I know...you were Jesus to me when I didn't know what to look for." She brought a hand to his cheek and then said the words that filled him with so much joy that it wiped away every bit of the ache and exhaustion he had felt these past three months.

"I love you, Nathan."

Tears slipped down his cheeks, and he didn't try to stop them. "And you are the beat of my heart, Abigail." He kissed her temple, the corner of her eye, her cheeks that were wet with tears. "I love you," he whispered again, their tears mingling together as they stood close, clinging to each other.

Grace began to fuss, and Abigail pulled the wrap loose that held her in place, letting Nathan take her from inside the little cocoon she was nestled in. She kicked and cooed, so excited to see Nathan again. He brought her close and kissed her cheek.

"Hello, little one! I sure did miss you!" Nathan's heart overflowed when she gave him that little grin with only a few teeth in it. This little girl owned his heart, too. He kissed her neck, eliciting a baby giggle.

The sound of horse hooves drew their attention back to the cabin. Nathan saw Papa dismounting his horse, and he turned to Abigail. "Papa will be overjoyed to see you!"

She smiled at him and grabbed the reins of the horse to lead him towards the cabin. With one arm around Abigail's shoulder and Grace in his other arm, Nathan led them back towards Papa, back towards home. When papa saw them coming he beamed. He came down from the porch and hurried towards them. Abigail stepped away from Nathan, dropped the reins and ran to meet him. Papa enveloped her in a hug that swallowed her tiny frame. Nathan stopped and watched two of the three people he loved more than his own life embrace each other. Papa pulled back finally and placed a kiss to Abigail's forehead. Her cries came soft and gentle.

"Oh, dearest. We've missed you so very much," Papa whispered, his eyes wet with tears.

"I-I've come home, Ian…home to Nathan…and you…if you'll have me."

Papa's eyes filled with tears. "You've found Jesus." He whispered it, searching her eyes. "Oh, child. You bring me such joy!" Papa looked at Nathan as he spoke, and Nathan nodded his agreement. He walked up to them and placed his arm around Abigail's shoulder. He wanted to be close to her, to stay close to her, forever.

Papa laughed with joy when he saw Grace. "My little one!" Grace kicked and giggled, and Nathan released her to Papa, who held her up into the sunlight, laughing and twirling, eliciting squeals of laughter from her belly.

Abigail leaned into Nathan, laying her head on his chest. Papa stepped up in front of them both and wrapped an arm around Abigail, with Grace nestled in the middle of them all. They stood there a moment, and Nathan felt peace settle in their midst.

Papa looked up at the sky and said, "Those who live in the shelter of the Most High will find rest in the shadow of the Almighty." He looked at Abigail. "He is your shelter, Abigail. You will always be safe under His shadow." He tenderly ran a hand over Abigail's head. "Do you know the meaning of your name?"

"No." She said, tilting her head in curiosity.

He cupped her cheek with his roughened, work worn hand. "Abigail means, your Father rejoices."

She stared at him a moment, then smiled the most radiant smile, as if she had just unearthed the most wondrous treasure.

"My Father rejoices," she said, reverently.

Papa smiled and nodded. "Always remember that He sees you, He knows your name, and He calls you daughter."

Abigail beamed up at Nathan, who kissed the top of her head

"Come!" Papa backed up and twirled around once with Grace, bringing forth more squeals. "You are just in time to sit and eat with us!" He laughed and kissed Grace's cheek.

Nathan drew Abigail close and they both followed Papa up the steps into the cabin.

Nathan's heart had come home, today. She had come home! *Lord, you are good! You've given me more than I could have ever imagined!* He had doubted, had even been angry with God for letting his heart be broken, and yet, this had been his plan all along. He looked down at Abigail in awe of what God had done. She had chosen to come back to him. *Lord, make me worthy of her. Help me to be the man she deserves.* With his heart overflowing, he led his love into the cabin, where they sat down together and ate.

FORTY THREE

"Abigail, do you understand the meaning of baptism?" Ian asked as they all sat around the table, bellies full from the meal they had shared. Grace sat in her little chair at the table, working hard to pick up the leftover pieces of potato on her plate.

"I only know that God commands it, but I don't really know why," Abigail said. In her village, everyone was baptized as a baby. Ian went and grabbed his Bible then came back to the table.

"Jesus was baptized before he began his ministry on this Earth," Ian said, opening his Bible to the passage and reading about it.

"Why did the Son of God need to be baptized?" Abigail asked, curious.

"Everything Jesus did was for us. He was baptized to signify that he was stepping into what the Father was calling him to do." Ian said, leaning back and crossing his arms over his chest. "He doesn't demand anything of us, but he asks us to do the same, once we've received him as our Savior, to declare to the world that he has washed away the old and made us new."

Abigail understood that. Nothing felt the same ever since Lizzy had prayed with her to receive Jesus into her life. That decision had changed everything, and she really did feel like her past was washed clean because of Jesus. Should she be baptized?

The River, Love.

Abigail sat up straight, eyes wide at the sound of that voice, again. Yes! She wanted to be baptized, she needed to be baptized! What better place than the river she had known her whole life? She wanted to declare to the world that Jesus had made her new. She turned to Nathan.

"I-I want to be baptized…in the river." She grabbed his hand, breathless with excitement. "Can you…will you do it?" She hesitated a moment, then, "I want it to be you…because you are the one who showed me the way," she whispered.

Nathan took her hand in his and kissed her fingers, eyes glistening. "It would be my honor." He said, voice full of emotion.

Now?" She asked, eyes bright and expectant.

Nathan laughed and stood, pulling her up to stand with him and kissing her temple. "Now!"

Ian stood and hoisted Grace into his arms. They all left the cabin and made their way to the river, Abigail's hand in Nathan's and Grace nestled in Ian's side.

~~~

Abigail looked back to where Ian stood, holding Grace. Her heart overflowed at the sight of them. God had sent her Ian to reveal the love of a Papa, and He had provided shelter for her when she had been alone. Her little Grace was just that; a daily reminder that God's mercy and love are forever, that his grace is never ending. She looked up at Nathan, her Nathan, and tears came, anew.

"Thank you for being so faithful to me, even in my brokenness and wandering." Her voice broke on the tears that trailed her cheeks. Nathan reached up with his thumb and caught one of her tears, bringing it to his lips. He always treated her tears as if they were drops of gold that he treasured.

"You will never walk alone, love. Jesus will be with you until your last breath…and he will meet you on the other side when your time on this Earth is done."

Abigail nodded. "I'm ready."

Nathan led her into the water until they were almost waist deep. She closed her eyes and faced the sun, remembering the last time she had waded into this river, and how hopeless she had been. Now she waded into these waters brimming with hope and life. She couldn't stop the tears. *Thank you, Jesus.*

Nathan put a hand on her back and turned her out towards the river, then leaned close to her ear as he spoke. "Do you confess Jesus as your Savior, Abigail?" he asked.

"I do," she responded, with strength and conviction, even as the tears continued to come.

"Do you commit to following him all the days of your life, no matter the cost?" Nathan's voice was gentle but filled with authority.

"I do." She closed her eyes as she answered.

"Then, I now baptize you in the name of the Father, the Son, and the Holy Spirit."

He gently laid her back into the water, and she felt it rush over her whole body. Just as the blood of Jesus had washed away her shame and sorrow, this water represented the newness of her life. She was clean and free of shame! Nathan pulled her back up and set her on her feet. He pulled her into an embrace, laughing a deep, rich laugh. Abigail laughed with him, even as she continued to cry, feeling as though her heart could not hold all the joy she felt. She stepped back from his embrace and cupped his cheek with a hand. He covered it with his own.

"I love you, Abigail." His eyes were on fire as he stared into hers. "Can I show you something?"

Abigail nodded, and Nathan began unbuttoning his shirt. He pulled it from his breeches and slid it off his arms, tossing it towards the river's bank. Abigail's eyes roved the scars that had formed from his wounds; the wounds he had taken for her.

"I want you to see these wounds Abigail, and know that I treasure every single one." His eyes blazed with a fiery passion that took her breath away.

Abigail hesitantly reached out and ran a finger over the puckered flesh running right over his heart. She began to cry again, and Nathan wrapped his arms around her. She laid her head right against the scar running across his heart. They stood there a moment, Nathan's scarred body wrapped around Abigail's small, freshly baptized body, and she wept.

"You are worth every one of these scars." His voice was filled with emotion and Abigail looked up to see tears running down his face.

"I love you, Nathan." Water trailed her face, droplets hanging from her nose and chin. Nathan cupped her cheek and then, he kissed her. He pulled her close, with an arm around her waist. She wrapped her arms around his neck and kissed him back, all the passion she had for him tumbling out. Nathan's kiss made her feel cherished, priceless and loved; all new sensations to her. She felt as if her heart might beat right out of her chest with love for him. He pulled her up into his arms out of the water and twirled her around, laughing. She stretched her arms out as if she were flying, laughing with him. Nathan lowered her down into the water, cupped her face and kissed her again. Then, he brought his forehead to hers.

"I am yours Abigail. For as long as I live, I'm yours. Will you have me? Will you be my wife? Will you let me be a father to Grace?"

"Yes. With all my heart, yes!" She laid her head against his chest. "You saved me, Nathan. Over and over you saved me. Then, you showed me the one who could save my soul forever. You led me to Jesus, and he led me back to you." She stepped back then, and cupped his cheek. "I am yours, Nathan. For as long as I live, I'm yours."

He kissed her again, with a passion that left her breathless and wanting more. Then, he scooped her up into his arms and walked out of the river. She looked ahead at Ian and Grace and felt her Father in Heaven rejoicing over her with song and dance. He had filled every broken piece of her heart with his infinite grace and mercy. She would give herself to Nathan whole and complete, because of Jesus. She looked up at the sun streaming through the trees onto her face as the love of her life carried her towards their new life together. She smiled at the thought that filled her heart…

Jesus has made me new.

She knew it was true because she felt the very presence of His grace filling her soul. He knew all of her pain and had redeemed every single sorrow. She smiled as peace flooded her, and she was sure she heard the voice of her Savior, whisper to her heart on the wind…

I make all things new…

EPILOGUE

Abigail wasn't aware of how tightly she gripped Nathan's hand. She was so relieved to have him here with her. She felt safe, knew she could do this because she wasn't alone. Jesus was with her, and Nathan. She stopped at the entrance to the village. She turned towards Nathan, letting him fill her vision. He smiled that warm, inviting smile of his, and she felt peace settle in her heart.

"Are you ready, love?" He asked, gently.

She nodded, definitively. "I am. It's time."

"I'm with you, until the end," he said, rubbing a finger gently along her jaw.

"I know. I believe you." She reached up and grabbed his hand, holding it to her heart. To think that this man was her husband! *Thank you, Jesus! Thank you!* She turned and walked through the gate of the village. She hadn't been here since the day Nathan carried her out. It overwhelmed her, coming to this place. How different life was for her now. How different she was now. She was thankful that Nathan was with her. She looked around as she made her way towards the village center. Everything looked the same, just older and worn down. It had been eight years. She didn't bring Grace. Grace would never experience the horrors of this place. She was a beautiful little girl, full of joy and life. That thought buoyed Abigail's spirit and gave her more courage. The cycle was broken. Her daughter would walk in freedom, never in shame.

She saw some faces she recognized, and some recognized her, stopping to stare, clearly shocked to see her in the village. She didn't waver on her mission though. She kept walking, Nathan right beside her, holding tight to her hand. She walked through the town center and came to the purging post. She stopped a moment, staring at it, remembering. It didn't look like it had been used in a long, long time.

Nathan stepped closer, put an arm around her shoulder and leaned in to whisper. "Redeemed, love. You are chosen and redeemed."

Tears welled in her eyes, not from the memory of sorrow and pain, but at the overwhelming presence of God's spirit that filled her. Here she stood in the very place that had been meant to break her, to shame her…and she felt freedom. *I am free!*

"I am free." She turned her face to Nathan as she spoke. He kissed her forehead, then wrapped his arms around her.

"Indeed. She whom the Son sets free…"

"Is free indeed." She whispered, burying her face in his shoulder.

"Free indeed." He whispered back.

They made their way then to her old house and stopped at the door. "He is dying, Nathan. What if I go in there and it is too much?"

"Grace, Abigail." He looked up at the sky then back at her. "He gives us grace for each moment. He will not fail you…and I won't leave your side."

With that, she pushed the door open and stepped into the house. The darkness seemed to lay heavy on the place. Dust covered most surfaces and no fire burned. She walked to the middle of the room and ran a hand over the worn table that had been such a place of hurt and confusion. She felt no hatred, not even anger. She did feel a twinge of sadness, thinking of what had never been, of what she had lost. She saw her father's door open slightly and she walked over to it, feeling Nathan's presence right behind her. Pushing the door open, she saw him there in the bed. Nathan had heard her father was dying on one of his trips to Boston. He had seen a man from the village, and the man had remembered Nathan taking Abigail away so long ago. He had told Nathan that Abigail's father laid in his bed, dying a slow death. No one seemed to know what the sickness was, there weren't any visible signs. It was as if something ate away at him, inside.

Abigail went over to the side of the bed and hesitated only a moment before sitting down beside him. He stirred at the movement of the bed and opened his eyes. It took him a moment to register who she was, and when he did, his eyes went wide.

"A-abigail," his voice was scratchy from sickness. "Is it you?"

"Hello, father." She responded. "I've come to see you."

Nathan stood behind her, a quiet but protective presence. She saw in her father's eyes that he remembered Nathan.

He looked away from them both. "W-why are you here?" His voice was shaky, not the strong booming one she remembered.

"I've come to see you...to tell you that I... love you." The lump formed in her throat, causing her voice to falter. She picked up his pale, thin hand with both of hers. "I forgive you father, and I want to share the God I've found since leaving you." She spoke through tears. "I've found Jesus, and He set me free. "She paused a moment. "This is Nathan." She held a hand out to him, and he took it, stepping closer. "Nathan is my husband. He is the one who saved me from…" her voice trailed off.

Her father was staring at her as if he still hadn't registered that she sat there beside him. Then, with a shuddering sigh, he began to cry. His frail, thin body shook beneath the sheet with sobs. He reached up a shaky hand and touched her cheek. Her tears fell over his cold hand and for a while, they simply wept together.

"Oh, Abigail…please, please forgive me." He wept harder as if a place inside of him long closed up broke open, and he could not stop the wave of weeping. Abigail felt Nathan's hand on her shoulder, and she knew she could do this. She knew that she had the power inside of her to release her father from all the debt he owed. In that moment, she saw through all of his actions, to his heart. He had acted all those years out of a place of deep hurt and grief. She leaned over and scooped his frail, thin body into her arms. She held him as she did Grace when she hurt. He wrapped his thin arms around her, clutching her as if she would disappear at any moment. He wept on her shoulder, and she cried on his.

"Abigail, oh, my sweet Abigail. Forgive me. Please, forgive me."

After a while, Abigail laid him gently back onto his pillow and took hold of his hands. "I do, Father. I did a long time ago."

He laughed through his tears, a sound that seemed to release the burden he had carried for so very long.

"Can I tell you my story, Father? Can I tell you what Jesus has done in me?" She asked softly.

He nodded, tears continuing to fall down his withered cheeks.

Abigail told him her story. She left nothing out, as she poured it out to him. She told him the parts that hurt, was honest about the pain he had caused, the pain being in this place had caused…but she also told him of the hope she had found. Her face glowed with the words that came forth. Nathan came at one point with a cup of water for her and her father. He was there the whole time, quietly watching over both of them as they talked.

Her father asked questions along the way, hanging on her every word. When at last she finished, her father turned his eyes to Nathan.

"You have been for her everything I was not." He reached a shaky hand out.

Nathan came and knelt down by the bed, taking the offered hand. "She has my heart, sir. I will love her until the day I die." He spoke softly, looking into her father's eyes.

A cloud passed over father's face. "What, Father? What is it?"

"Samuel." Just the mention of his name brought tears to both his eyes and hers.

"I know, Father. I know." She wiped her tears on her skirt. "We must trust Jesus will find him, as he found me."

"It is my fault. I love the boy, but I never showed him. I never once showed him." Abigail could see he was going to get himself worked up again, and she was concerned.

"Father, rest now. We will stay. We will be here when you awaken." She rubbed his coarse gray hair back from his forehead. "Rest."

He closed his eyes on a whisper. "Abigail...my sweet Abigail..." and with that, he fell into a deep sleep.

Abigail and Nathan stayed until the end. They both sensed that now that she had come, he felt free to leave and would go soon. They shared Jesus with him over the course of the days they were with him. They told him stories of Jesus' grace and compassion. He clung to their words as if they were a medicine for his soul, which they were. They shared stories of Grace, and how beautiful and sweet she was. He delighted in the stories of her and asked once, very humbly, if they would take his Bible to give her, as a gift from him. They discovered as they were in the village, that everything looked the same, but nothing was the same. Many of the children had grown up and left, stirred by the cause of freedom. Abigail found out that Mary had run away from the village not long after Nathan had rescued Abigail. Thomas had disappeared too, after Nathan's purging. The village had been declining ever since as if the power that held it together had dissipated. What had once been a place of fear and dominance for Abigail was now nothing but a desolate village of withering people. Nathan visited the different homes in the village while they were there, sharing Jesus with those who still lived there. Many received his message of grace.

When at last Abigail's father was coming to his end, Abigail and Nathan sat on either side of him. "Papa," Abigail whispered, never having used that word to describe him. She leaned close, so he could reach his hand out to her cheek. "Give Mama a hug and kiss for me," she said, softly, through her tears.

He smiled at her and then he spoke words that were like a healing oil to her soul. "I love you, my Abigail. I love you." She cried harder, laying her head on his chest. "I love you, Papa." He put his hand gently on her head.

He turned to Nathan and reached out a hand. Nathan took it. "Thank you for saving her from me...and this place." His voice was weak, fading.

Nathan's cheeks were wet with tears. "I will never leave her. You have my word."
Moments later, with both Abigail and Nathan beside him, her Papa released his last breath and left this world, with a soft smile on his face.

Abigail looked up at Nathan, tears streaming her face. Neither spoke, for they both felt God's spirit, so very present with them. They felt the very presence of grace in the room, and there were no words to describe it. All that had been lost, God had restored to Abigail. All that had been dust and ash had been turned into gold.

She and Nathan left the village, and some left with them, so in awe of this message of grace they had discovered. Some went west, some went north, some south. Nathan and Abigail built a beautiful life together, filled with the joy of knowing Jesus. Abigail's heart stayed steady and her soul wrapped in the truth. God was faithful. His love was everlasting. He had never forsaken her, and she knew, He never would.

Dear Reader,

When the Holy Spirit gave me Abigail's story, I was in a season of deep brokenness. I shed many tears in the secret place, where only Jesus could see me. I was at a loss for words during that time, not even knowing what to pray except "Jesus, help me." Oh, did He.

One morning, in the midst of that season I woke up with this vivid scene in my mind. It was the scene where Nathan comes into the village and rescues Abigail from her purging. I didn't know who these people were, didn't even know their names, but I had an overwhelming sense that I needed to write it down. So, I did. The moment in that scene were Nathan leans over and says to Abigail, "I'm going to carry you out of this place. Will you trust me?" was the moment that I knew Jesus was close to me, and that I was going to be okay. I then spent six months writing Abigail's story and I can say with no amount of exaggeration that I cried many tears as I wrote of her pain, and then of Nathan's gentle love for her.

Jesus healed my heart in the process of writing Abigail's story, and I knew when I finished that she would be a beacon of light for other hurting hearts, needing to know exactly how Jesus comes to us in our pain.

He has not abandoned you in your suffering, friend. Sometimes, it is easy to think He has because the pain is so real and so overwhelming, but He has not and He will not. He finds us in our brokenness and He speaks words of life to us, healing those wounds that only He can heal.

I pray you have found hope in Abigail's story. If reading of her has opened up some wounds in your own life, or if it's made you yearn to know the Jesus that Nathan represents, then I have a beautiful idea for you which you can read more about on the next page.

Jesus loves you, friend. He wants to come to you in your pain, as Nathan did for Abigail, and redeem every part of your story. There is so much hope in Him to be made whole.

Thank you for taking the journey with me through Abigail's story. I don't take for granted that Jesus entrusted me with such a message and that you received that message through this story. May the God of all hope come to you and fill you with peace, and reveal His tender love for you.

With Hope,
Shannon

In 2017 God birthed this little idea inside of me of an online community where women would have a safe place to share their stories, especially the most painful parts, and find healing. I had no idea what exactly would come of my little Facebook post where I invited women who might be suffering from wounds of the soul to come into my private group and find encouragement for healing. What happened was truly miraculous. One by one women joined, and kept joining, until it finally occurred to me that Jesus was truly up to something much bigger than I imagined.

Table Talk is an online gathering of women who need a safe place to share the painful parts of their story and find restoration through Jesus. Each group, or "table", is kept small so that relationship and intimacy can develop through weekly discussion. If you are interested in finding out more, you can visit: shannonkeys.com.

We would love to have you gather with us at the table and share in the feast Jesus has prepared!

Made in the USA
San Bernardino, CA
18 August 2018